THE GOODBYE LOOK . . .

Lew Archer had seen it many times. It was an odd look —one that settled on men's faces when they knew they were going to die . . . and wanted to.

Archer first saw it during the war, and too many times since. Now it was all around him again. And he was in the middle of a mystery that had its roots in a trio of ghosts and a handful of carefully guarded secrets. If he didn't solve it, he'd see the goodbye look again . . . on the face of the next murder victim!

Bantam books by Ross Macdonald
Ask your bookseller for the books you have missed

THE GOODBYE LOOK

by Ross Macdonald

A NATIONAL GENERAL COMPANY

To HENRI COULETTE

*This low-priced Bantam Book
has been completely reset in a type face
designed for easy reading, and was printed
from new plates. It contains the complete
text of the original hard-cover edition.*
NOT ONE WORD HAS BEEN OMITTED.

THE GOODBYE LOOK

*A Bantam Book / published by arrangement with
Alfred A. Knopf, Inc.*

PRINTING HISTORY

*Knopf edition published May 1969
8 printings through 1969
Mystery Guild edition published July 1969
Bantam edition published June 1970*

Published simultaneously in the United States and Canada

*Bantam Books are published by Bantam Books, Inc., a National
General company. Its trade-mark, consisting of the words "Bantam
Books" and the portrayal of a bantam, is registered in the United
States Patent Office and in other countries. Marca Registrada.
Bantam Books, Inc., 666 Fifth Avenue, New York, N.Y. 10019.*

PRINTED IN THE UNITED STATES OF AMERICA

I

The lawyer, whose name was John Truttwell, kept me waiting in the outer room of his offices. It gave the room a chance to work me over gently. The armchair I was sitting in was covered in soft green leather. Oil paintings of the region, landscapes and seascapes, hung on the walls around me like subtle advertisements.

The young pink-haired receptionist turned from the switchboard. The heavy dark lines accenting her eyes made her look like a prisoner peering out through bars.

"I'm sorry Mr. Truttwell's running so late. It's that daughter of his," the girl said rather obscurely. "He should let her go ahead and make her own mistakes. The way I have."

"Oh?"

"I'm really a model. I'm just filling in at this job because my second husband ran out on me. Are you really a detective?"

I said I was.

"My husband is a photographer. I'd give a good deal to know who—where he's living."

"Forget it. It wouldn't be worth it."

"You could be right. He's a lousy photographer. Some very good judges told me that his pictures never did me justice."

It was mercy she needed, I thought.

A tall man in his late fifties appeared in the open doorway. High-shouldered and elegantly dressed, he was handsome and seemed to know it. His thick white hair was carefully arranged on his head, as carefully arranged as his expression.

"Mr. Archer? I'm John Truttwell." He shook my hand with restrained enthusiasm and moved me along the corridor to his office. "I have to thank you for coming down from Los Angeles so promptly, and I apologize for keeping you waiting. Here I'm supposed to be semi-retired but I've never had so many things on my mind."

Truttwell wasn't as disorganized as he sounded. Through

1

the flow of language his rather sad cold eyes were looking me over carefully. He ushered me into his office and placed me in a brown-leather chair facing him across his desk.

A little sunlight filtered through the heavily draped windows, but the room was lit by artificial light. In its diffused whiteness Truttwell himself looked rather artificial, like a carefully made wax image wired for sound. On a wall shelf above his right shoulder was a framed picture of a clear-eyed blonde girl who I supposed was his daughter.

"On the phone you mentioned a Mr. and Mrs. Lawrence Chalmers."

"So I did."

"What's their problem?"

"I'll get to that in a minute or two," Truttwell said. "I want to make it clear at the beginning that Larry and Irene Chalmers are friends of mine. We live across from each other on Pacific Street. I've known Larry all my life, and so did our parents before us. I learned a good deal of my law from Larry's father, the judge. And my late wife was very close to Larry's mother."

Truttwell seemed proud of the connection in a slightly unreal way. His left hand drifted softly over his side hair, as if he was fingering an heirloom. His eyes and voice were faintly drowsy with the past.

"The point I'm making," he said, "is that the Chalmerses are valuable people—personally valuable to me. I want you to handle them with great care."

The atmosphere of the office was teeming with social pressures. I tried to dispel one or two of them. "Like antiques?"

"Somewhat, but they're not old. I think of the two of them as objects of art, the point of which is that they don't have to be useful." Truttwell paused, and then went on as if struck by a new thought. "The fact is Larry hasn't accomplished much since the war. Of course he's made a great deal of money, but even that was handed to him on a silver platter. His mother left him a substantial nest egg, and the bull market blew it up into millions."

There was an undertone of envy in Truttwell's voice, suggesting that his feelings about the Chalmers couple were complicated and not entirely worshipful. I let myself react to the nagging undertone:

"Am I supposed to be impressed?"

2

Truttwell gave me a startled look, as if I'd made an obscene noise, or allowed myself to hear one. "I can see I haven't succeeded in making my point. Larry Chalmers's grandfather fought in the Civil War, then came to California and married a Spanish land-grant heiress. Larry was a war hero himself, but he doesn't talk about it. In our instant society that makes him the closest thing we have to an aristocrat." He listened to the sound of the sentence as though he had used it before.

"What about Mrs. Chalmers?"

"Nobody would describe Irene as an aristocrat. But," he added with unexpected zest, "she's a hell of a good-looking woman. Which is all a woman really has to be."

"You still haven't mentioned what their problem is."

"That's partly because it's not entirely clear to me." Truttwell picked up a sheet of yellow foolscap from his desk and frowned over the scrawling on it. "I'm hoping they'll speak more freely to a stranger. As Irene laid out the situation to me, they had a burglary at their house while they were away on a long weekend in Palm Springs. It was a rather peculiar burglary. According to her, only one thing of value was taken—an old gold box that was kept in the study safe. I've seen that safe—Judge Chalmers had it put in back in the twenties—and it would be hard to crack."

"Have Mr. and Mrs. Chalmers notified the police?"

"No, and they don't plan to."

"Do they have servants?"

"They have a Spanish houseman who lives out. But they've had the same man for over twenty years. Besides, he drove them to Palm Springs." He paused, and shook his white head. "Still it does have the feel of an inside job, doesn't it?"

"Do you suspect the servant, Mr. Truttwell?"

"I'd rather not tell you whom or what I suspect. You'll work better without too many preconceptions. Well as I know Irene and Larry, they're very private people, and I don't pretend to understand their lives."

"Have they any children?"

"One son, Nicholas," he said in a neutral tone.

"How old is he?"

"Twenty-three or -four. He's due to graduate from the university this month."

"In January?"

"That's right. Nick missed a semester in his freshman year. He left school without telling anyone, and dropped out of sight completely for several months."

"Are his parents having trouble with him now?"

"I wouldn't put it that strongly."

"Could he have done this burglary?"

Truttwell was slow in replying. Judging by the changes in his eyes, he was trying out various answers mentally: they ranged from prosecution to defense.

"Nick could have done it," he said finally. "But he'd have no reason to steal a gold box from his mother."

"I can think of several possible reasons. Is he interested in women?"

Truttwell said rather stiffly: "Yes, he is. He happens to be engaged to my daughter Betty."

"Sorry."

"Not at all. You could hardly be expected to know that. But do be careful what you say to the Chalmerses. They're accustomed to leading a very quiet life, and I'm afraid this business has really upset them. The way they feel about their precious house, it's as if a temple had been violated."

He crumpled the yellow foolscap in his hands and threw it into a wastebasket. The impatient gesture gave the impression that he would be glad to be rid of Mr. and Mrs. Chalmers and their problems, including their son.

II

Pacific Street rose like a slope in purgatory from the poor lower town to a hilltop section of fine old homes. The Chalmerses' California Spanish mansion must have been fifty or sixty years old, but its white walls were immaculate in the late-morning sun.

I crossed the walled courtyard and knocked on the iron-bound front door. A dark-suited servant with a face that belonged in a Spanish monastery opened the door and took my name and left me standing in the reception hall. It was an enormous two-storied room that made me feel small and then, in reaction, large and self-assertive.

I could see into the great white cave of the living room. Its

4

walls were brilliant with modern paintings. Its doorway was equipped with black wrought-iron gates, shoulder high, which gave the place a museum atmosphere.

This was partly dispelled by the dark-haired woman who came in from the garden to greet me. She was carrying a pair of clippers and a clear red Olé rose. She laid the clippers down on a hall table but kept the rose, which exactly matched the color of her mouth.

Her smile was bright and anxious. "Somehow I expected you to be older."

"I'm older than I look."

"But I asked John Truttwell to get me the head of the agency."

"I'm a one-man agency. I co-opt other detectives when I need them."

She frowned. "It sounds like a shoestring operation to me. Not like the Pinkertons."

"I'm not big business, if that's what you want."

"It isn't. But I want somebody good, really good. Are you experienced in dealing with—well—" Her free hand indicated first herself and then her surroundings—"people like me?"

"I don't know you well enough to answer that."

"But you're the one we're talking about."

"I assume Mr. Truttwell recommended me, and told you I was experienced."

"I have a right to ask my own questions, don't I?"

Her tone was both assertive and lacking in self-assurance. It was the tone of a handsome woman who had married money and social standing and never could forget that she might just as easily lose these things.

"Go ahead and ask questions, Mrs. Chalmers."

She caught my gaze and held it, as if she were trying to read my mind. Her eyes were black and intense and impervious.

"All I really want to know is this. If you find the Florentine box—I assume John Truttwell told you about the gold box?"

"He said that one was missing."

She nodded. "Assuming you find it, and find out who took it, is that as far as it goes? I mean, you won't march off to the authorities and tell them all about it?"

"No. Unless they're already involved?"

"They aren't, and they're not going to be," she said. "I

want this whole thing kept quiet. I wasn't even going to tell John Truttwell about the box, but he wormed it out of me. However, him I trust. I think."

"And me you think you don't?"

I smiled, and she decided to respond. She tapped me on the cheek with her red rose, then dropped it on the tile floor as if it had served its purpose. "Come into the study. We can talk privately there."

She led me up a short flight of steps to a richly carved oak door. Before she closed it behind us I could see the servant in the reception hall picking up after her, first the clippers, then the rose.

The study was an austere room with dark beams supporting the slanting white ceiling. The single small window, barred on the outside, made it resemble a prison cell. As if the prisoner had been looking for a way out, there were shelves of old law books against one wall.

On the facing wall hung a large picture which appeared to be an oil painting of Pacific Point in the old days, done in primitive perspective. A seventeenth-century sailing vessel lay in the harbor inside the curve of the point; beside it naked brown Indians lounged on the beach; over their heads Spanish soldiers marched like an army in the sky.

Mrs. Chalmers seated me in an old calf-covered swivel chair in front of a closed roll-top desk.

"These pieces don't go with the rest of the furniture," she said as if it mattered. "But this was my father-in-law's desk, and that chair you're sitting in was the one he used in court. He was a judge."

"So Mr. Truttwell told me."

"Yes, John Truttwell knew him. I never did. He died a long time ago, when Lawrence was just a small boy. But my husband still worships the ground his father walked on."

"I'm looking forward to meeting your husband. Is he at home?"

"I'm afraid not. He went to see the doctor. This burglary business has him all upset." She added: "I wouldn't want you to talk to him, anyway."

"Does he know I'm here?"

She moved away from me, leaning over a black oak refectory table. She fumbled a cigarette from a silver box and lit it with a matching table lighter. The cigarette, which she puffed on furiously, laid down a blue smokescreen between us.

"Lawrence didn't think it was a good idea to use a private detective. I decided to go ahead with you anyway."

"Why did he object?"

"My husband likes his privacy. And this box that was stolen—well, it was a gift to his mother from an admirer of hers. I'm not supposed to know that, but I do." Her smile was crooked. "In addition to which, his mother used it to keep his letters in."

"The admirer's letters?"

"My husband's letters. Larry wrote her a lot of letters during the war, and she kept them in the box. The letters are missing, too—not that they're of any great value, except maybe to Larry."

"Is the box valuable?"

"I think it is. It's covered with gold, and very carefully made. It was made in Florence during the Renaissance." She stumbled on the word, but got it out. "It has a picture on the lid, of two lovers."

"Insured?"

She shook her head, and crossed her legs. "It hardly seemed necessary. We never took it out of the safe. It never occurred to us that the safe could be broken into."

I asked to be allowed to see the safe. Mrs. Chalmers took down the primitive painting of the Indians and the Spanish soldiers. Where it had hung a large cylindrical safe was set deep in the wall. She turned the dial several times and opened it. Looking over her shoulder, I could see that the safe was about the diameter of a sixteen-inch gun and just as empty.

"Where's your jewelry, Mrs. Chalmers?"

"I don't have much, it never has interested me. What I do have, I keep in a case in my room. I took the case along with me to Palm Springs. We were there when the gold box was taken."

"How long has it been missing?"

"Let me see now, this is Tuesday. I put it in the safe Thursday night. Next morning we went to the desert. It must have been stolen after we left, so that makes four days, or less. I looked in the safe last night when we got home, and it was gone."

"What made you look in the safe last night?"

"I don't know. I really don't," she added, making it sound like a lie.

"Did you have some idea that it might be stolen?"

"No. Certainly not."

"What about the servant?"

"Emilio didn't take it. I can vouch for him, absolutely."

"Was anything taken besides the box?"

She considered the question. "I don't think so. Except the letters, of course, the famous letters."

"Were they important?"

"They were important to my husband, as I said. And of course to his mother. But she's been dead a long time, since the end of the war. I never met her myself." She sounded a little worried, as if she'd been denied a maternal blessing, and still felt defrauded.

"Why would a burglar take them?"

"Don't ask me. Probably because they were in the box." She made a face. "If you do find them, don't bother to bring them back. I've already heard them, or most of them."

"Heard them?"

"My husband used to read them aloud to Nick."

"Where is your son?"

"Why?"

"I'd like to talk to him."

"You can't." She was frowning again. Behind her beautiful mask there was a spoiled girl, I thought, like a faker huddled in the statue of a god. "I wish John Truttwell had sent me someone else. Anyone else."

"What did I do wrong?"

"You ask too many questions. You're prying into our family affairs, and I've already told you more than I should."

"You can trust me." Immediately I regretted saying it.

"Can I really?"

"Other people have." I could hear an unfortunate selling note in my voice. I wanted to stay with the woman and her peculiar little case: she had the kind of beauty that made you want to explore its history. "And I'm sure Mr. Truttwell would advise you not to hold back with me. When a lawyer hires me I have the same privilege of silence as he does."

"Exactly what does that mean?"

"It means I can't be forced to talk about what I find out. Not even a Grand Jury with contempt powers can make me."

"I see." She had caught me off base, trying to sell myself, and now in a certain sense she could buy me; not with money, necessarily. "If you promise to be absolutely close-

8

mouthed, even with John Truttwell, I'll tell you something. This may not be an ordinary burglary."

"Do you suspect it was an inside job? There's no sign that the safe was forced."

"Lawrence pointed that out. It's why he didn't want you brought into the case. He didn't even want me to tell John Truttwell."

"Who does he think stole the box?"

"He hasn't said. I'm afraid he suspects Nick, though."

"Has Nick been in trouble before?"

"Not this kind of trouble." The woman's voice had dropped almost out of hearing. Her whole body had slumped, as if the thought of her son was a palpable weight inside of her.

"What kind of trouble has he had?"

"Emotional problems so called. He turned against Lawrence and me for no good reason. He ran away when he was nineteen. It took the Pinkertons months to find him. It cost us thousands of dollars."

"Where was he?"

"Working his way around the country. Actually, his psychiatrist said it did him some good. He's settled down to his studies since. He's even got himself a girl." She spoke with some pride, or hope, but her eyes were somber.

"And you don't think he stole your box?"

"No, I don't." She tilted up her chin. "You wouldn't be here if I thought so."

"Can he open the safe?"

"I doubt it. We've never given him the combination."

"I noticed you've got it memorized. Do you have it written down anywhere?"

"Yes."

She opened the bottom right-hand drawer of the desk, pulled it all the way out and turned it over, dumping the yellow bank statements it contained. Taped to the bottom of the drawer was a slip of paper bearing a series of typewritten numbers. The tape was yellow and cracked with age, and the paper was so worn that the figures on it were barely decipherable.

"That's easy enough to find," I said. "Is your son in need of money?"

"I can't imagine what for. We give him six or seven hundred a month, more if he needs it."

"You mentioned a girl."

"He's engaged to Betty Truttwell, who is not exactly a gold digger."

"No other girls or women in his life?"

"No." But her answer was slow and dubious.

"How does he feel about the box?"

"Nick?" Her clear forehead wrinkled, as if my question had taken her by surprise. "As a matter of fact, he used to be interested in it when he was little. I used to let him and Betty play with it. We used—they used to pretend that it was Pandora's box. Magic, you know?"

She laughed a little. Her whole body was dreaming of the past. Then her eyes changed again. Her mind came up to their surface, hard and scared. She said in a thinner voice:

"Maybe I shouldn't have built it up so much. But I still can't believe he took it. Nick has usually been honest with us."

"Have you asked him if he took it?"

"No. We haven't seen him since we got back from the desert. He has his own apartment near the university, and he's taking his final exams."

"I'd like to talk to him, at least get a yes or no. Since he is under suspicion—"

"Just don't tell him his father suspects him. They've been getting along so well these last couple of years, I'd hate to see it spoiled."

I promised her to be tactful. Without any further persuasion she gave me Nick Chalmers's phone number and his address in the university community. She wrote them on a slip of paper in a childish unformed hand. Then she glanced at her watch.

"This has taken longer than I thought. My husband will be coming home for lunch."

She was flushed and brilliant-eyed, as if she was terminating an assignation. She hurried me out to the reception hall, where the dark-suited servant was standing with a blank respectful face. He opened the front door, and Mrs. Chalmers practically pushed me out.

A middle-aged man in a fine tweed suit got out of a black Rolls Royce in front of the house. He crossed the courtyard with a kind of military precision, as if each step he took, each movement of his arms, was separately controlled by orders sent down from on high. The eyes in his lean brown face had a kind of bright blue innocence. The lower part of

10

his face was conventionalized by a square-cut, clipped brown mustache.

His pale gaze drifted past me. "What's going on here, Irene?"

"Nothing. I mean—" She drew in her breath. "This is the insurance man. He came about the burglary."

"You sent for him?"

"Yes." She gave me a shame-faced look. She was lying openly and asking me to go along with it.

"That was rather a silly thing to do," her husband said. "The Florentine box wasn't insured, at least not to my knowledge." He looked at me in polite inquiry.

"No," I said in a wooden voice.

I was angry with the woman. She had wrecked my rapport with her, and any possible rapport with her husband.

"Then we won't keep you further," he said to me. "I apologize for Mrs. Chalmers's blunder. I'm sorry your time has been wasted."

Chalmers moved toward me smiling patiently under his mustache. I stepped to one side. He edged past me in the deep doorway, taking care not to brush against me. I was a commoner, and it might be catching.

III

I stopped at a gas station on the way to the university, and called Nick's apartment from an outdoor pay phone. A girl's voice answered:

"Nicholas Chalmers's residence."

"Is Mr. Chalmers there?"

"No he is not." She spoke with a professional lilt. "This is his answering service."

"How can I get in touch with him? It's important."

"I don't know *where* he is." An unprofessional note of anxiety had entered her voice. "Is this connected with his missing his exams?"

"It may very well be," I said in an open-ended way. "Are you a friend of Nick's?"

"Yes I am. Actually I'm not his answering service. I'm his fiancée."

"Miss Truttwell?"

"Do I know you?"

"Not yet. Are you in Nick's apartment?"

"Yes. Are you a counselor?"

"Roughly speaking, yes. My name is Archer. Will you wait there in the apartment for me, Miss Truttwell? And if Nick turns up, will you ask him to wait for me, too?"

She said she would. "I'll do anything that will help Nick." The implication seemed to be that he needed all the help he could get.

The university stood on a mesa a few miles out of town, beyond the airport. From a distance its incomplete oval of new buildings looked ancient and mysterious as Stonehenge. It was the third week in January, and I gathered that the midyear exams were in progress. The students I saw as I circled the campus had a driven preoccupied air.

I'd been there before, but not for several years. The student body had multiplied in the meantime, and the community attached to the campus had turned into a city of apartment buildings. It was strange, after Los Angeles, to drive through a city where everyone was young.

Nick lived in a five-storied building which called itself the Cambridge Arms. I rode the self-service elevator to the fifth floor and found the door of his apartment, which was number 51.

The girl opened the door before I knocked. Her eyes flickered when she saw it was only me. She had clean straight yellow hair that brushed the shoulders of her dark slacks suit. She looked about twenty.

"No Nick?" I said.

"I'm afraid not. You're Mr. Archer?"

"Yes."

She gave me a quick probing look, and I realized she was older than I'd thought. "Are you really a counselor, Mr. Archer?"

"I said roughly speaking. I've done a lot of counseling in an amateur sort of way."

"What do you do in a professional sort of way?"

Her voice wasn't unfriendly. But her eyes were honest and sensitive, ready to be affronted. I didn't want that to happen. She was the nicest thing I'd come across in some time.

"I'm afraid if I tell you, Miss Truttwell, you won't talk to me."

"You're a policeman, aren't you?"

12

"I used to be. I'm a private investigator."

"Then you're perfectly right. I don't want to talk to you."

She was showing signs of alarm. Her eyes and nostrils were dilated. Her face had a kind of sheen or glare on it. She said:

"Did Nick's parents send you here to talk to me?"

"How could they have? You're not supposed to be here. Since we are talking, by the way, we might as well do it inside."

After some hesitation, she stepped back and let me in. The living room was furnished in expensive but dull good taste. It looked like the kind of furniture the Chalmerses might have bought for their son without consulting him.

The whole room gave the impression that Nick had kept himself hidden from it. There were no pictures on the walls. The only personal things of any kind were the books in the modular bookcase, and most of these were textbooks, in politics, law, psychology, and psychiatry.

I turned to the girl. "Nick doesn't leave much evidence of himself lying around."

"No. He's a very secret boy—man."

"Boy or man?"

"He may be trying to make up his mind about that."

"Just how old is he, Miss Truttwell?"

"He just turned twenty-three last month—December 14. He's graduating half a year late because he missed a semester a few years ago. That is, he'll graduate if they let him make up his exams. He's missed three out of four now."

"Why?"

"It's not a school problem. Nick's quite brilliant," she said as though I'd denied it. "He's a whizz in poli sci, which is his major, and he's planning to study law next year." Her voice was a little unreal, like that of a girl reciting a dream or trying to recall a hope.

"What kind of a problem is it, Miss Truttwell?"

"A life problem, as they call it." She took a step toward me and stood with her hands hanging loose, palms facing me. "All of a sudden he quit caring."

"About you?"

"If that was all, I could stand it. But he cut loose from everything. His whole life has changed in the last few days."

"Drugs?"

"No. I don't think so. Nick knows how dangerous they are."

"Sometimes that's an attraction."

"I know, I know what you mean."

"Has he discussed it with you?"

She seemed confused for a second. "Discussed what?"

"The change in his life in the last few days."

"Not really. You see, there's another woman involved. An older woman." The girl was wan with jealousy.

"He must be out of his mind," I said by way of complimenting her.

She took it literally. "I know. He's been doing things he couldn't do if he were completely sane."

"Tell me about the things he's been doing."

She gave me a look, the longest one so far. "I *can't* tell you. I don't even know you."

"Your father does."

"Really?"

"Call him up if you don't believe me."

Her gaze wandered to the telephone, which stood on an end table by the chesterfield, then came back to my face. "That means you are working for the Chalmerses. They're Dad's clients."

I didn't answer her.

"What did Nick's parents hire you to do?"

"No comment. We're wasting time. You and I both want to see Nick get back inside his skin. We need each other's help."

"How can I help?"

I felt I was reaching her. "You obviously want to talk to someone. Tell me what Nick's been up to."

I was still standing like an unwanted guest. I sat down on the chesterfield. The girl approached it carefully, perching on one arm beyond my reach.

"If I do, you won't repeat it to his parents?"

"No. What have you got against his parents?"

"Nothing, really. They're nice people, I've known them all my life as friends and neighbors. But Mr. Chalmers is pretty hard on Nick; they're such different types, you know. Nick is very critical of the war, for example, and Mr. Chalmers considers that unpatriotic. He served with distinction in the last war, and it's made him kind of rigid in his thinking."

"What did he do in the war?"

14

"He was a naval pilot when he was younger than Nick is now. He thinks Nick is a terrible rebel." She paused. "He isn't really. I admit he was pretty wild-eyed at one time. That was several years ago, before Nick settled down to study. He was doing so well until last week. Then everything went smash."

I waited. Tentative as a bird, she slid off the arm of the chesterfield and plopped down beside me. She made a sour face and shut her eyes tight, holding back tears. In a minute she went on:

"I think that woman is at the bottom of it. I know what that makes me. But how can I help being jealous? He dropped me like a hotcake and took up with a woman old enough to be his mother. She's even married."

"How do you know that?"

"He introduced her to me as Mrs. Trask. I'm pretty sure she's from out of town—there are no Trasks in the phone book."

"He introduced you?"

"I forced him to. I saw them together in the Lido Restaurant. I went to their table and stayed there until Nick introduced me to her and the other man. His name was Sidney Harrow. He's a bill collector from San Diego."

"Did he tell you that?"

"Not exactly. I found out."

"You're quite a finder-outer."

"Yes," she said, "I am. Ordinarily I don't believe in snooping." She gave me a half-smile. "But there are times when snooping is called for. So when Mr. Harrow wasn't looking I picked up his parking ticket, which was lying on the table beside his plate. I took it out to the Lido parking lot and got the attendant to show me which was his car. It was a junky old convertible, with the back window torn out. The rest was easy. I got his name and address from the car registration in the front and put in a call to his place in San Diego, which turned out to be a collection agency. They said he was on his vacation. Some vacation."

"How do you know he isn't?"

"I haven't finished." For the first time she was impatient, carried along by her story. "It was Thursday noon when I met them in the restaurant. I saw the old convertible again on Friday night. It was parked in front of the Chalmerses' house. We live diagonally across the street and I can see their

15

house from the window of my workroom. Just to make sure that it was Mr. Harrow's car, I went over there to check on the registration. This was about nine o'clock Friday night.

"It was his, all right. He must have heard me close the car door. He came rushing out of the Chalmerses' house and asked me what I was doing there. I asked him what he was doing. Then he slapped my face and started to twist my arm. I must have let out some kind of a noise, because Nick came out of the house and knocked Mr. Harrow down. Mr. Harrow got a revolver out of his car and I thought for a minute he was going to shoot Nick. They had a funny look on both their faces, as if they were both going to die. As if they really *wanted* to kill each other and be killed."

I knew that goodbye look. I had seen it in the war, and too many times since the war.

"But the woman," the girl said, "came out of the house and stopped them. She told Mr. Harrow to get into his car. Then she got in and they drove away. Nick said that he was sorry, but he couldn't talk to me right then. He went into the house and closed the door and locked it."

"How do you know he locked it?"

"I tried to get in. His parents were away, in Palm Springs, and he was terribly upset. Don't ask me why. I don't understand it at all, except that that woman is after him."

"Do you know that?"

"She's that kind of woman. She's a phony blonde with a big red sloppy mouth and poisonous eyes. I can't understand why he would flip over her."

"What makes you think he has?"

"The way she talked to him, as if she owned him." She spoke with her face and the front of her body averted.

"Have you told your father about this woman?"

She shook her head. "He knows I'm having trouble with Nick. But I can't tell him what it is. It makes Nick look so bad."

"And you want to marry Nick."

"I've waited for a long time." She turned and faced me. I could feel the pressure of her cool insistence, like water against a dam. "I intend to marry him, whether my father wants me to or not. I'd naturally prefer to have his approval."

"But he's opposed to Nick?"

Her face thinned. "He'd be opposed to any man whom I wanted to marry. My mother was killed in 1945. She was

16

younger then than I am now," she added in faint surprise. "Father never remarried, for my sake. I wish for my sake he had."

She spoke with the measured emphasis of a young woman who had suffered.

"How old are you, Betty?"

"Twenty-five."

"How long is it since you've seen Nick?"

"Not since Friday night, at his house."

"And you've been waiting for him here since then?"

"Part of the time. Dad would worry himself sick if I didn't come home at night. Incidentally, Nick hasn't slept in his own bed since I started waiting for him here."

"When was that?"

"Saturday afternoon." She added with a seasick look: "If he wants to sleep with her, let him."

At this point the telephone rang. She rose quickly and answered it. After listening for a moment she spoke rather grimly into the receiver:

"This is Mr. Chalmers' answering service ... No, I don't know where he is ... Mr. Chalmers does not provide me with that information."

She listened again. From where I sat I could hear a woman's emotional voice on the line, but I couldn't make out her words. Betty repeated them: " 'Mr. Chalmers is to stay away from the Montevista Inn.' I see. Your husband has followed you there. Shall I tell him that? ... All right."

She put the receiver down, very gently, as if it was packed with high explosives. The blood mounted from her neck and suffused her face in a flush of pure emotion.

"That was Mrs. Trask."

"I was wondering. I gather she's at the Montevista Inn."

"Yes. So is her husband."

"I may pay them a visit."

She rose abruptly. "I'm going home. I'm not going to wait here any longer. It's humiliating."

We went down together in the elevator. In its automatic intimacy she said:

"I've spilled all my secrets. How do you make people do it?"

"I don't. People like to talk about what's hurting them. It takes the edge off the pain sometimes."

"Yes, I believe it does."

"May I ask you one more painful question?"

17

"This seems to be the day for them."

"How was your mother killed?"

"By a car, right in front of our house on Pacific Street."

"Who was driving?"

"Nobody knows, least of all me. I was just a small baby."

"Hit-run?"

She nodded. The doors slid open at the ground floor, terminating our intimacy. We went out together to the parking lot. I watched her drive off in a red two-seater, burning rubber as she turned into the street.

IV

Montevista lay on the sea just south of Pacific Point. It was a rustic residential community for woodland types who could afford to live anywhere.

I left the freeway and drove up an oak-grown hill to the Montevista Inn. From its parking lot the rooftops below seemed to be floating in a flood of greenery. I asked the young man in the office for Mrs. Trask. He directed me to Cottage Seven, on the far side of the pool.

A bronze dolphin spouted water at one end of the big old-fashioned pool. Beyond it a flagstone path meandered through live oaks toward a white stucco cottage. A red-shafted flicker took off from one of the trees and crossed a span of sky, wings opening and closing like a fan lined with vivid red.

It was a nice place to be, except for the sound of the voices from the cottage. The woman's voice was mocking. The man's was sad and monotonous. He was saying:

"It isn't so funny, Jean. You can wreck your life just so many times. And my life, it's my life, too. Finally you reach a point where you can't put it back together. You should learn a lesson from what happened to your father."

"Leave my father out of this."

"How can I? I called your mother in Pasadena last night, and she says you're still looking for him. It's a wild-goose chase, Jean. He's probably been dead for years."

18

"No! Daddy's alive. And this time I'm going to find him."

"So he can ditch you again?"

"He never ditched me."

"That's the way I heard it from your mother. He ditched you both and took off with a piece of skirt."

"He did not." Her voice was rising. "You mustn't say such things about my father."

"I can say them if they're true."

"I won't listen!" she cried. "Get out of here. Leave me alone."

"I will not. You're coming home to San Diego with me and put up a decent front. You owe me that much after twenty years."

The woman was silent for a moment. The sounds of the place lapped in like gentle waves: a towhee foraging in the underbrush, a kinglet rattling. Her voice, when she spoke again, was calmer and more serious:

"I'm sorry, George, I truly am, but you might as well give up. I've heard everything you're saying so often, it just goes by like wind."

"You always came back before," he said with a note of hopefulness in his voice.

"This time I'm not."

"You have to, Jean."

His voice had thinned. Its hopefulness had twisted into a kind of threat. I began to move around the side of the cottage.

"Don't you dare touch me," she said.

"I have a legal right to. You're my wife."

He was saying and doing all the wrong things. I knew, because I'd said and done them in my time. The woman let out a small scream, which sounded as if she was tuning up for a bigger one.

I looked around the corner of the cottage, where the flagstone path ran into a patio. The man had pinned the woman in his arms and was kissing the side of her blond head. She had turned her face away, in my direction. Her eyes were chilly, as if her husband's kisses were freezing cold.

"Let go of me, George. We have company."

He released her and backed away, red-faced and wet-eyed. He was a large middle-aged man who moved awkwardly, as if he was the intruder instead of me.

19

"This is my wife," he said, more in self-excuse than introduction.

"What was she yelling about?"

"It's all right," the woman said. "He wasn't hurting me. But you better leave now, George, before something does happen."

"I have to talk to you some more." He reached out a thick red hand toward her. The gesture was both menacing and touching, like something done by Frankenstein's innocent monster.

"You'd only get stirred up again."

"But I've got a right to plead my case. You can't cut me off without a hearing. I'm not a criminal like your father was. But even a criminal gets his day in court. You've got to give me a hearing."

He was getting very excited, and it was the kind of spinning excitement that could change to violence if it came up tails.

"You better go, Mr. Trask."

His wild wet gaze roved to me. I showed him an old Special Deputy badge I carried. He examined it closely, as if it was a curio.

"Very well, I'll go." He turned and walked away, pausing at the corner of the building to call back: "I'm not going very far."

The woman turned to me, sighing. Her hair had been disarranged, and she was fixing it with nervous fingers. It was done in a fluffy doll-like fashion that didn't go with her forty years or so. But in spite of Betty's description of her, she wasn't a bad-looking woman. She had a good figure under her blouse, and a handsome, heavy face.

She also had a quality that bothered me, a certain doubt and dimness about the eyes, as if she had lost her way a long time ago.

"That was good timing," she said to me. "You never know what George is going to do."

"Or anybody else."

"Are you the security man around here?"

"I'm filling in."

She looked me up and down, like a woman practicing to be a divorcee. "I owe you a drink. Do you like Scotch?"

"On the rocks, please."

"I have some ice. My name is Jean Trask, by the way."

I told her my name. She took me into the living room of

20

the cottage and left me there while she went into the kitchen. Around the walls of the room a series of English hunting prints followed some red-coated hunters and their hounds over hills and through valleys to the death of the fox.

Ostensibly studying the prints, I circled the room to the open door of the bedroom and looked in. On the nearest of the two beds a woman's blue weekend case lay open, and the gold box was in it. On its painted lid a man and a woman in skimpy antique clothes disported themselves.

I was tempted to walk in and take the box, but John Truttwell wouldn't have liked that. Even without him, I'd probably have let the thing lie. I was beginning to sense that the theft of the box was just a physical accident of the case. Any magic it possessed, black or white or gold, was soaked up from the people who handled it.

But I took two steps into the bedroom and lifted the heavy lid of the box. It was empty. I heard Mrs. Trask crossing the living room, and I retreated in her direction. She slammed the bedroom door.

"We won't be using that room."

"What a pity."

She gave me a startled look, as if she was unaware of her own rough candor. Then she shoved a lowball glass at me. "Here."

She went into the kitchen and returned with a dark-brown drink for herself. As soon as she had taken a swallow or two, her eyes turned moist and bright and her color rose. She was a drinker, I thought, and I was there essentially because she didn't want to drink alone.

She knocked her drink back in a hurry and made herself another, while I nursed mine. She sat down in an armchair facing me across a coffee table. I was almost enjoying myself. The room was large and tranquil, and through the open front door I could hear quail muttering and puttering.

I had to spoil it. "I was admiring your gold box. Is it Florentine?"

"I suppose it is," she said, offhandedly.

"Don't you know? It looks quite valuable."

"Really? Are you an expert?"

"No. I was thinking in terms of security. I wouldn't leave it lying around like that."

"Thanks for your advice," she said unthankfully. She was quiet for a minute, sipping her drink. "I didn't mean to be rude just now; I have things on my mind." She leaned toward

21

me in a show of interest. "Have you been in the security business long?"

"Over twenty years, counting my time with the police."

"You used to be a policeman?"

"That's right."

"Perhaps you can help me. I'm involved in a kind of nasty situation. I don't feel up to explaining it all right now, but I hired a man named Sidney Harrow to come here with me. He claimed to be a private detective but it turned out his main experience is repossessing cars. He's a fast man with a tow bar. Also he's dangerous." She finished her drink, and shivered.

"How do you know he's dangerous?"

"He almost killed my boyfriend. He's a fast man with a gun, too."

"You also have a boyfriend?"

"I call him my boyfriend," she said with a half-smile. "Actually we're more like brother and sister, or father and daughter—I mean mother and son." Her smile turned to a simper.

"What's his name?"

"That has no bearing on what I'm telling you. The point is that Sidney Harrow nearly shot him the other night."

"Where did this happen?"

"Right out in front of my boyfriend's house. I realized then that Sidney was a wild man, and he's been no use to me since. He has the picture and stuff but he's not doing anything with them. I'm afraid to go and ask for it back."

"And you want me to?"

"Maybe. I'm not committing myself yet." She spoke with the foolish wisdom of a woman who had no feeling for men and would always make the wrong decisions about them.

"What would Sidney be doing with the picture and stuff?"

"Finding out facts," she said carefully. "That's what I hired him to do. But I made the mistake of giving him some money and all he does is sit in his motel room and drink. I haven't even heard from him in two days."

"Which motel?"

"The Sunset, on the beach."

"How did you get involved with Sidney Harrow?"

"I'm not *involved* with him. A man I know brought him to the house last week and he seemed so lively and alert, just the man I was looking for." As if to renew the promise of

22

that occasion, she raised her glass and drained the last few drops, coaxing them with her tongue. "He reminded me of my father when he was a young man."

For a moment she seemed at ease in the double memory. But her feelings were very shifty, and she couldn't hold this one long. I could see her quick-remembered happiness dying in her eyes.

She rose and started for the kitchen, then stopped abruptly, as if she'd come up against invisible glass. "I'm drinking too much," she said. "And I'm talking too much."

She left her glass in the kitchen and came back and stood over me. Her unhappy eyes regarded me suspiciously, as if I was the source of the unhappiness.

"Please get out of here, will you? Forget what I said to you, eh?"

I thanked her for the drink and drove downhill to the Ocean Boulevard and along it to the Sunset Motor Hotel.

V

It was one of the older buildings on the Pacific Point waterfront, two-storied and solidly constructed of red brick. In the harbor across the boulevard, sailboats lay in their slips like birds with their wings folded. A few Capris and Seashells were scudding down the channel before the January wind.

I parked in front of the motor hotel and went into the office. The gray-haired woman behind the desk gave me a bland experienced glance that took in my age and weight, my probable income and credit rating, and whether I was married.

She said she was Mrs. Delong. When I asked for Sidney Harrow, I could see my credit rating slip in the ledger of her eyes.

"Mr. Harrow has left us."

"When?"

"Last night. In the course of the night."

"Without paying his bill?"

Her look sharpened. "You know Mr. Harrow, do you?"

"Just by reputation."

"Do you know where I can get in touch with him? He

23

gave us a San Diego business address. But he only worked part-time for them, they said, and they wouldn't assume any responsibility or give me his home address—if he has a home." She paused for breath. "If I knew where he lived I could get the police after him."

"I may be able to help you."

"How is that?" she said with some suspicion.

"I'm a private detective, and I'm looking for Harrow, too. Has his room been cleaned?"

"Not yet. He left his Do Not Disturb card out, which he did most of the time anyway. It was just a little while ago I noticed his car was gone and used my master key. You want to look over the room?"

"It might be a good idea. While we think of it, Mrs. Delong, what's his car license number?"

She looked it up in her file. "KIT 994. It's an old convertible, tan-colored, with the back window torn out. What's Harrow wanted for?"

"I don't know yet."

"Are you sure you're a detective?"

I showed her my photostat, and it satisfied her. She made a careful note of my name and address, and handed me the key to Harrow's room. "It's number twenty-one on the second floor at the back."

I climbed the outside stairs and went along the alley toward the rear. The windows of number twenty-one were closely draped. I unlocked the door and opened it. The room was dim, and sour with old smoke. I opened the drapes and let the light sluice in.

The bed had apparently not been slept in. The spread was rumpled, though, and several pillows were squashed against the headboard. A half-empty fifth of rye stood on the bedside table on top of a girlie magazine. I was a little surprised that Harrow had left behind a bottle with whisky in it.

He had also left, in the bathroom cabinet, a toothbrush and a tube of toothpaste, a three-dollar razor, a jar of hair grease, and a spray can of a spicy scent called Swingeroo. It looked as if Harrow had planned to come back, or had left in a great hurry.

The second possibility seemed more likely when I found an unmatched shoe in the darkest corner of the closet. It was a new pointed black Italian shoe for the left foot. Along with the shoe for the right foot it would have been worth at least twenty-five dollars. But I couldn't find the right shoe anywhere in the room.

In the course of looking for it I did find, on the high shelf of the closet under spare blankets, a brown envelope containing a small-size graduation picture. The smiling young man in the picture resembled Irene Chalmers and was probably, I decided, her son Nick.

My guess was pretty well confirmed when I found the Chalmerses' address, 2124 Pacific Street, penciled on the back of the envelope. I slid the picture back into the envelope and put it in my inside pocket and took it away with me.

After reporting the general situation to Mrs. Delong, I crossed the street to the harbor. The boats caught in the maze of floating docks rocked and smacked the water. I felt like getting into one of them and sailing out to sea.

My brief dip into Sidney Harrow's life had left a stain on my nerves. Perhaps it reminded me too strongly of my own life. Depression threatened me like a sour smoke drifting in behind my eyes.

The ocean wind blew it away, as it nearly always could. I walked the length of the harbor and crossed the asphalt desert of the parking lots toward the beach. The waves were collapsing like walls there, and I felt like a man escaping from his life.

You can't, of course. An old tan Ford convertible with a torn-out rear window was waiting for me at the end of my short walk. It was parked by itself in a drift of sand at the far edge of the asphalt. I looked in through the rear window and saw the dead man huddled on the back seat with dark blood masking his face.

I could smell whisky and the spicy odor of Swingeroo. The doors of the convertible weren't locked, and I could see the keys in the ignition. I was tempted to use them to open the trunk.

Instead I did the right thing, for prudential reasons. I was outside of Los Angeles County, and the local police had a very strong sense of territory. I found the nearest telephone, in a bait and tackle shop at the foot of the breakwater, and called the police. Then I went back to the convertible to wait for them.

The wind spat sand in my face and the sea had a shaggy green theatening look. High above it, gulls and terns were wheeling like a complex mobile suspended from the sky. A city police car crossed the parking lot and skidded to a stop beside me.

Two uniformed officers got out. They looked at me, at the dead man in the car, at me again. They were young men, with few discernible differences except that one was dark, one fair. Both had heavy shoulders and jaws, unmoved eyes, conspicuous guns in their holsters, and hands ready.

"Who is he?" said the blue-eyed one.

"I don't know."

"Who are you?"

I told them my name, and handed over my identification.

"You're a private detective?"

"That's right."

"But you don't know who this is in the car?"

I hesitated. If I told them it was Sidney Harrow, as I guessed, I'd have to explain how I found that out and would probably end up telling them everything I knew.

"No," I said.

"How did you happen to find him?"

"I was passing by."

"Passing by to where?"

"The beach. I was going to take a walk on the beach."

"That's a funny place to take a walk on a day like this," said the fair one.

I was ready to agree. The place had changed. The dead man had bled it of life and color. The men in uniform had changed its meaning. It was a dreary official kind of place with a cold draft blowing.

"Where you from?" the dark one asked me.

"Los Angeles. My address is on my photostat. I want it back, by the way."

"You'll get it back when we're finished with you. You got a car, or you come to town by public carrier?"

"Car."

"Where is your car?"

It hit me then, in a reaction that had been delayed by the shock of finding Harrow, if that's who he was. My car was parked in front of the Sunset Motor Hotel. Whether I told them about it or not, the police would find it there. They'd talk to Mrs. Delong and learn that I'd been on Harrow's trail.

That was what happened. I told them where my car was, and before long I was in an interrogation room in police headquarters being questioned by two sergeants. I asked several times for a lawyer, specifically the lawyer who had brought me to town.

They got up and left me alone in the room. It was an airless cubicle whose dirty gray plaster walls had been scribbled with names. I passed the time reading the inscriptions. Duke the Dude from Dallas had been there on a bum rap. Joe Hespeler had been there, and Handy Andy Oliphant, and Fast Phil Larrabee.

The sergeants came back and regretted to say that they hadn't been able to get in touch with Truttwell. But they wouldn't let me try to phone him myself. In a way this breach of my rights encouraged me: it meant that I wasn't a serious suspect.

They were on a fishing expedition, hoping I'd done their work for them. I sat and let them do some of mine. The dead man was Sidney Harrow, without much question: his thumbprint matched the thumbprint on his driver's license. He'd been shot in the head, once, and been dead for at least twelve hours. That placed the time of death no later than last midnight, when I had been at home in my apartment in West Los Angeles.

I explained this to the sergeants. They weren't interested. They wanted to know what I was doing in their county, and what my interest in Harrow was. They wheedled and begged and coaxed and pleaded and threatened me and made jokes. It gave me a queer feeling, which I didn't mention to them, that I had indeed inherited Sidney Harrow's life.

VI

A man in plain dark clothes came quietly into the room. Both the sergeants stood up, and he dismissed them. He had clipped gray hair, eyes that were hard and sober on either side of a scarred and broken nose. His mouth was chewed and ravaged by lifelong doubt and suspicion, and it kept working now. He sat down facing me across the table.

"I'm Lackland, Captain of Detectives. I hear you been giving our boys a bad time."

"I thought it was the other way around."

His eyes searched my face. "I don't see any marks on you."

"I have a right to a lawyer."

"We have a right to your cooperation. Try bucking us and you could end up flat on your rear end without a license."

"That reminds me, I want my photostat back."

Instead, he took a manila envelope out of his inside pocket and opened it. Among other things it contained a snapshot, or a piece of snapshot, which Lackland pushed across the table to me.

It was a picture of a man in his forties. He had fair thinning hair, bold eyes, a wry mouth. He looked like a poet who had missed his calling and had had to settle for grosser satisfactions.

His picture had been cut from a larger picture which had included other people. I could see girls' dresses on either side of him, but not the girls. The thing looked like a blown-up snapshot at least twenty years old.

"Know him?" Captain Lackland said.

"No."

He thrust his scarred face toward me like a warning of what my face might become. "You're sure about that, are you?"

"I'm sure." There was no use mentioning my unsupported guess that this was a picture Jean Trask had given Harrow, and that it was a picture of her father.

He leaned toward me again. "Come on now, Mr. Archer, help us out. Why was Sidney Harrow carrying this?" His forefinger jabbed at the blown-up snapshot.

"I don't know."

"You must have some idea. Why were *you* interested in Harrow?"

"I have to talk to John Truttwell. After that I may be able to say something."

Lackland got up and left the room. In about ten minutes he came back accompanied by Truttwell. The lawyer looked at me with concern.

"I understand you've been here for some time, Archer. You should have got in touch with me before." He turned to Lackland. "I'll talk to Mr. Archer in private. He's employed by me in a confidential capacity."

Lackland retreated slowly. Truttwell sat down across from me. "Why are they holding you, anyway?"

"A part-time bill collector named Sidney Harrow was shot last night. Lackland knows I was following Harrow. He doesn't know that Harrow was one of several people involved in the theft of the gold box."

Truttwell was startled. "You've found that out already?"

"It wasn't hard. This is the sloppiest burglary in history. The woman who has the box now keeps it lying around in plain view."

"Who is she?"

"Her married name is Jean Trask. Who she really is is another question. Apparently Nick stole the box and gave it to her. Which is why I can't talk freely, to Lackland or anyone else."

"I should certainly say you can't. Are you sure about all this?"

"Unless I've been having delusions." I stood up. "Can't we finish this outside?"

"Of course. Wait here for a minute."

Truttwell went out, closing the door behind him. He came back smiling and handed me the photostat of my license. "You're sprung. Oliver Lackland's a fairly reasonable man."

In the narrow corridor that led to the parking lot, I ran the gauntlet of Lackland and his sergeants. They nodded at me, too many times for comfort.

I told Truttwell what had happened as we drove across town in his Cadillac. He turned up Pacific Street.

"Where are we going?"

"To my house. You made quite an impression on Betty. She wants to ask your advice."

"What about?"

"It's probably something to do with Nick. He's all she thinks about." Truttwell added after a long pause: "Betty seems to believe I'm prejudiced against him. That's really not the case. But I don't want her to make any unnecessary mistakes. She's the only daughter I have."

"She told me she's twenty-five."

"Betty's very young for her age, though. Very young and vulnerable."

"Superficially, maybe. She struck me as a resourceful woman."

Truttwell gave me a look of pleased surprise. "I'm glad

you think so. I brought her up by myself, and it's been quite a responsibility." After another pause he added: "My wife died when Betty was only a few months old."

"She told me her mother was killed by a hit-run driver."

"Yes, that's true." Truttwell's voice was almost inaudible.

"Was the driver ever caught?"

"I'm afraid not. The Highway Patrol found the car, near San Diego, but it was a stolen car. Strangely enough, whoever it was had made an attempt to burglarize the Chalmerses' house. My wife apparently saw them enter the house and scared them out of there. They ran her down when they made their getaway."

He gave me a bleak look which resisted further questions. We drove in silence the rest of the way to his house, which was diagonally across the street from the Chalmerses' Spanish mansion. He dropped me at the curb, said he had a client waiting, and drove away.

The architecture on upper Pacific Street was traditional but eclectic. Truttwell's house was a white colonial one, with green shutters upstairs and down.

I knocked on the green front door. It was answered by a gray little woman in a housekeeper's dim quasi-uniform. The formal lines which bracketed her mouth softened when I told her who I was.

"Yes. Miss Truttwell is expecting you." She led me up a curving stair to the door of a front room. "Mr. Archer is here to see you."

"Thanks, Mrs. Glover."

"Can I get you anything, dear?"

"No thanks."

Betty delayed her appearance till Mrs. Glover had gone. I could see why. Her eyes were swollen and her color was bad. She held her body tensely, like a kicked animal expecting to be kicked again.

She stood back to let me enter the room, and closed the door behind me. It was a young woman's study, bright with chintz and Chagall, its shelves loaded with books. She faced me standing up, with her back to the windows overlooking the street.

"I've heard from Nicholas." She indicated the orange telephone on the worktable. "You won't tell Father, will you?"

"He already suspects it, Betty."

"But you won't tell him anything more?"

"Don't you trust your father?"

"About anything else, yes. But you mustn't tell him what I'm going to tell you."

"I'll do my best, that's all I can promise. Is Nick in trouble?"

"Yes." She hung her head, and her bright hair curtained her face. "I think he intends to kill himself. I don't want to live, either, if he does."

"Did he say why?"

"He's done something terrible, he says."

"Like kill a man?"

She flung her hair back and looked at me with blazing dislike. "How can you say such a thing?"

"Sidney Harrow was shot on the waterfront last night. Did Nick mention him?"

"Of course not."

"What *did* he say?"

She was quiet for a minute, remembering. Then she recited slowly: "That he didn't deserve to live. That he'd let me down, and let his parents down, and he couldn't face any of us again. Then he said goodbye to me—a final goodbye." A hiccup of grief shook her.

"How long ago did he make the call?"

She looked at the orange phone, and then at her watch. "About an hour. It seems like forever, though."

She moved vaguely past me to the other side of the room and took a framed photograph down from a wall bracket. I moved up behind her and looked at it over her shoulder. It was a larger copy of the photograph in my pocket, which I had found in the closet of Harrow's motel room. I noticed now that in spite of his smiling mouth, the young man in the picture had somber eyes.

"I take it that's Nick," I said.

"Yes. It's his graduation picture."

She replaced it on its bracket, with a faintly ritual air, and went to the front windows. I followed her. She was looking out across the street toward the closed white front of the Chalmers house.

"I don't know what to do."

"We've got to find him," I said. "Did he say where he was calling from?"

"No, he didn't."

"Or anything else at all?"

"I don't remember anything else."

"Did he say what suicide method he had in mind?"

She hid her face behind her hair again and answered in a hushed voice: "He didn't say, this time."

"You mean he's gone through this routine before?"

"Not really. And you mustn't speak of it in that way. He's terribly serious."

"So am I." But I was angry at the boy for what he had done and was doing to the girl. "What did he do or say the other times?"

"He often talked about suicide when he got depressed. I don't mean that he threatened to do it. But he talked about ways and means. He never held anything back from me."

"Maybe it's time he started."

"You sound like Father. You're both prejudiced against him."

"Suicide is a cruel business, Betty."

"Not if you love the person. A depressed person can't help the way he feels."

I didn't argue any further. "You were going to tell me how he planned to do it."

"It wasn't a *plan*. He was simply talking. He said a gun was too messy, and pills were uncertain. The cleanest way would be to swim out to sea. But the thing that really haunted him, he said, was the thought of the rope."

"Hanging?"

"He told me he'd thought of hanging himself ever since he was a child."

"Where did he get that idea?"

"I don't know. But his grandfather was a Superior Court judge, and some people in town considered him a hanging judge—one who liked to sentence people to death. It may have influenced Nick, in a negative way. I've read of stranger things in history."

"Did Nick ever mention the hanging judge in the family?"

She nodded.

"And suicide?"

"Many times."

"That's quite a courtship he's been treating you to."

"I'm not complaining. I love Nick, and I want to be of some use to him."

I was beginning to understand the girl, and the more I

understood the better I liked her. She had a serviceability that I had noticed before in widowers' daughters.

"Think back to his telephone call," I said. "Did he give any indication of where he was?"

"I don't remember any."

"Give it some time. Go and sit by the telephone."

She sat in a chair beside the table, with one hand on the instrument as if to keep it quiet.

"I could hear noises in the background."

"What kind of noises?"

"Wait a minute." She raised her hand for silence, and sat listening. "Children's voices, and splashing. Pool noises. I think he must have called me from the public booth at the Tennis Club."

VII

Though I'd visited the Tennis Club before, the woman at the front desk was strange to me. But she knew Betty Truttwell, and greeted her warmly.

"We never see you any more, Miss Truttwell."

"I've been terribly busy. Has Nick been here today?"

The woman answered with some reluctance: "As a matter of fact, he has been. He came in an hour or so ago, and went into the bar for a while. He wasn't looking too well when he came out."

"Do you mean that he was drunk?"

"I'm afraid he was, Miss Truttwell, since you asked me. The woman with him, the blonde, was under the weather, too. After they left I gave Marco a piece of my mind. But he said he only served them two drinks each. He said the woman was tight when they arrived, and Mr. Chalmers can't handle liquor."

"He never could," Betty agreed. "Who was the woman?"

"I forget her name—he's brought her in once before." She consulted the guest register which lay on the desk in front of her. " 'Jean Swain.' "

"Not Jean Trask?" I said.

"It looks like 'Swain' to me."

She pushed the register toward me, indicating with her red

fingertips where Nick had signed the woman's name and his own. It looked like 'Swain' to me, too. Her home address was given as San Diego. "Is she a fairly large blonde with a good figure, fortyish?"

"That's her. A good figure," she added, "if you like the fleshy type." She herself was very thin.

Betty and I walked toward the bar along the gallery that overlooked the pool. The children were still making pool noises. A few adults were stretched out on long chairs in corners, catching the thin warmth of the January sun.

The bar was empty except for a couple of men prolonging their lunch. The bartender and I exchanged nods of recognition. Marco was a short, quick, dark man in a red waistcoat. He admitted gloomily that Nick had been there.

"Matter of fact, I asked him to leave."

"Did he have a lot to drink?"

"Not here he didn't. I served him two single shots of bourbon, you can't make a federal case out of that. What happened, did he wreck his car?"

"I hope not. I'm trying to catch up with him before he wrecks anything. Do you know where he went?"

"No, but I'll tell you one thing, he was in a hell of a mood. When I wouldn't give him a third drink, he wanted to put up a fight. I had to show him my pool cue." Marco reached under the bar and showed it to us: the sawed-off butt of a heavy cue about two feet long. "I hated to pull it on a member, you know, but he was carrying a gun and I wanted him out of here, fast. Anyone else, I would have called the sheriff."

"He had a gun?" Betty said in a small, high voice.

"Yeah, it was in the pocket of his jacket. He kept it out of sight but you can't hide a big heavy gun like that." He leaned across the bar and peered into Betty's eyes. "What's the matter with him, anyway, Miss Truttwell? He never acted like this before."

"He's in trouble," she said.

"Does the dame have anything to do with his trouble? The blonde dame? She drinks like she's got a hollow leg. She shouldn't be making him drink."

"Do you know who she is, Marco?"

"No. But she looks like trouble to me. I don't know what he thinks he's doing with *her*."

Betty started for the door, then turned back to Marco again. "Why didn't you take the gun away from him?"

"I don't fool around with guns, Miss. That isn't my department."

We went out to Betty's two-seater in the parking lot. The club was on a cove of the Pacific, and I caught a whiff of the sea. It was a raw and rueful smell, conjuring up the place where I had found Sidney Harrow.

Betty and I were both silent and thoughtful as she drove up the long hill to the Montevista Inn. The young man in the office remembered me.

"You're just in time if you want to see Mrs. Trask. She's getting ready to leave."

"Did she say why?"

"I think she's had bad news. It must be serious, because she didn't even put up an argument when I had to charge her for an extra day. They usually put up an argument."

I made my way through the oak grove and tapped on the screen door of the stucco cottage.

The inner door was open, and Jean Trask answered from the bedroom: "My bags are ready, if you want to carry them out."

I crossed the living room and entered the bedroom. The woman was sitting at the dressing table, shakily applying lipstick.

Our eyes met in the mirror. Her hand wandered, describing a red clown mouth around her real one. She turned and got up clumsily, upsetting her stool.

"They sent you for my bags?"

"No. But I'll be glad to carry them." I picked up her matched blue bags. They were light enough.

"Put them down," she said. "Who are you anyway?"

She was ready to be afraid of anyone for any reason—so full of fear that some of it slopped over into me. Her huge red mouth alarmed me. Chilly laughter convulsed my stomach.

"I asked about you at the office," she said. "They told me they don't have a security guard. So what are you doing here?"

"At the moment I'm looking for Nick Chalmers. We don't have to beat around the bush. You must know he's in serious emotional trouble."

She answered as if she was glad to have someone to talk to: "He certainly is. He's talking about suicide. I thought a couple of drinks would do him good. They only made him worse."

"Where is he now?"

"I made him promise to go home and sleep it off. He said he would."

"Home to his apartment?"

"I guess so."

"You're pretty vague, Mrs. Trask."

"I try to keep myself that way. It's less painful," she added wryly.

"How did you get so interested in Nick?"

"It's none of your business. And I'm not taking any static from you."

Her voice rose as she gained confidence in her own anger. But a steady trill of fear ran through it.

"What are you so afraid of, Mrs. Trask?"

"Sidney Harrow got himself zapped last night." Her voice was rough with self-concern. "You must know that."

"How do *you* happen to know it?"

"Nick told me. I'm sorry I ever opened this can of worms."

"Did he kill Sidney?"

"I don't think he knows—that's how far off base he is. And I'm not waiting around to find out."

"Where are you going?"

She refused to tell me.

I went back to Betty and told her what I had learned, or part of it. We decided to go out to the university community in separate cars. My car was where it was supposed to be, in front of the Sunset Motor Motel. There was a parking ticket under the windshield wiper.

I tried to follow Betty's red two-seater, but she drove too fast for me, close to ninety on the straightaway. She was waiting for me when I reached the parking lot of the Cambridge Arms.

She ran toward me. "He's here. At least that's his car."

She pointed at a blue sports car standing beside her red one. I went and touched the hood. The engine was hot. The key was in the ignition.

"You stay down here," I said.

"No. If he makes trouble—I mean he won't if I'm there."

"That's a thought."

We went up together in the elevator. Betty knocked on Nick's door and called his name. "This is Betty."

36

There was a long waiting silence. Betty knocked again. Abruptly the door was pulled open. She took an involuntary step into the room, and ended up with her face against Nick's chest. He held her with one hand and with the other he pointed a heavy revolver at my stomach.

I couldn't see his eyes, which were hidden by dark wrap-around glasses. In contrast, his face was very pale. His hair was uncombed and hung down over his forehead. His white shirt was dirty. My mind recorded these things as if they might add up to my last sight of the world. I felt resentment more than fear. I hated the idea of dying for no good reason at the hands of a mixed-up overgrown boy I didn't even know.

"Drop it," I said routinely.

"I don't take orders from you."

"Come on now, Nick," Betty said.

She moved closer to him, trying to use her body to distract him. Her right arm slid around his waist, and she pressed one thigh forward between his legs. She raised her left arm as if she was going to loop it around his neck. Instead she brought it sharply down on his gun arm.

The revolver was pointing at the floor now. I dove for it and wrenched it out of his hand.

"Damn you!" he said. "Damn you both!"

A boy with a high voice or a girl with a low one came out of the apartment across the hall. "What's going on?"

"Initiation," I said.

Nick tore himself loose from Betty and swung at my face. I shifted and let his fist go by. I lowered my head and bulled him backward into his living room. Betty shut the door and leaned on it. Her color was high. She was breathing through her mouth.

Nick came at me again. I went under his fists and hit him solidly in the solar plexus. He lay down gasping for breath.

I spun the cylinder of his revolver. One shell had been fired. It was a Colt .45. I got out my black notebook and made a record of its number.

Betty moved between us. "You didn't have to hurt him."

"Yes I did. But he'll get over it."

She kneeled beside him and touched his face with her hand. He rolled away from her. The sounds he made fighting for breath gradually subsided. He sat up with his back against the chesterfield.

I sat on my heels facing him, and showed him his revolver. "Where did you get this, Nick?"

"I don't have to answer that. You can't make me incriminate myself."

His voice had a queer inhuman tone, as if it was being played back on tape. I couldn't tell what the tone meant. His eyes were effectively masked by the wrap-around glasses.

"I'm not a policeman, Nick, if that's what you think."

"I don't care what you are."

I tried again. "I'm a private detective working on your side. But I'm not quite clear what your side is. Do you want to talk about it?"

He shook his head like a child in a tantrum, whipping it rapidly from side to side until his hair blurred out. Betty said in a pained voice:

"Please don't do that, Nicholas. You'll hurt your neck."

She smoothed his hair with her fingers. He sat perfectly still.

"Let me look at you," she said.

She took off his dark glasses. He grabbed for them, but she held them out of his reach. His eyes were black and glistening like asphalt squeezed from a crevice. They seemed to be leading a strange life of their own, with an inward look and an outward look alternating anxiety and aggression. I could understand why he wore the glasses to hide his sad changing eyes.

He covered his eyes with his hands and peered between his fingers.

"Please don't do that, Nick." The girl was kneeling beside him again. "What happened? Please tell me what happened."

"No. You wouldn't love me any more."

"Nothing could stop me loving you."

"Even if I killed somebody?" he said between his hands.

"Did you kill somebody?" I said.

He nodded slowly, once, keeping his head down and his face hidden.

"With this revolver?"

His head jerked downward in the affirmative.

Betty said: "He's in no condition to talk. You mustn't force him."

"I think he wants to get it off his chest. Why do you suppose he phoned you from the club?"

38

"To say goodbye."

"This is better than saying goodbye. Isn't it?"

She answered soberly: "I don't know. I don't know how much I can stand."

I turned to Nick again. "Where did you get the revolver?"

"It was in his car."

"Sidney Harrow's car?"

He dropped his hands from his face. His eyes were puzzled and fearful. "Yes. It was in his car."

"Did you shoot him in his car?"

His whole face clenched like a frightened baby's getting ready to cry. "I don't remember." He struck himself on the forehead with his fist. Then he struck himself in the mouth, hard.

"You're tormenting him," the girl said. "Can't you see he's sick?"

"Stop mothering him. He already has a mother."

His head came up in a startled movement. "You mustn't tell my mother. Or my father. Dad will kill me."

I made no promises. His parents would have to be told. "You were going to tell me where the shooting occurred, Nick."

"Yes. I remember now. We went to the hobo jungle back of Ocean Boulevard. Someone had left a fire burning and we sat by the coals. He wanted me to do a bad thing." His voice was naïve, like a child's. "I took his gun and shot him."

He made another scowling baby-face, so tight that it hid his eyes. He began to sob and moan, but no tears came. It was hard to watch his dry crying.

Betty put her arms around him. I said across the rhythms of his noise:

"He's had breakdowns before, hasn't he?"

"Not like this."

"Did he stay at home, or was he hospitalized?"

"Home." She spoke to Nick. "Will you come home with me?"

He said something that might have been yes. I called the Chalmerses' number and got the servant, Emilio. He brought Irene Chalmers to the phone.

"This is Archer. I'm with your son in his apartment. He's not in a good way, and I'm bringing him home."

"Is he hurt?"

"He's mentally hurt, and talking about suicide."

"I'll get in touch with his psychiatrist," she said. "Dr. Smitheram."

"Is your husband there?"

"He's in the garden. Do you want to talk to him?"

"It isn't necessary. But you'd better prepare him for this."

"Can you handle Nick?"

"I think so. I have Betty Truttwell with me."

Before we left the apartment I called the Bureau of Criminal Investigation in Sacramento. I gave the number of the revolver to a man I knew named Roy Snyder. He said he'd try to check the name of the original owner. When we went down to my car I put the revolver in the trunk, locked in an evidence case.

VIII

We rode in my car, with Betty driving and Nick on the front seat between us. He didn't speak or move until we stopped in front of his parents' house. Then he begged me not to make him go in.

I had to use a little force to get him out of the car. With one hand on his arm, and Betty walking on his far side, I marched him across the courtyard. He moved with deep reluctance, as if we planned to stand him up against the white wall and execute him.

His mother came out before we reached the front door. "Nick? Are you all right?"

"I'm okay," he said in his tape-recorder tone.

As we moved into the reception hall she said to me: "Do you *have* to talk to my husband?"

"Yes I do. I asked you to prepare him."

"I just couldn't do it," she said. "You'll have to tell him yourself. He's in the garden."

"What about the psychiatrist?"

"Dr. Smitheram had a patient with him, but he'll be here in a little while."

"You'd better call John Truttwell, too," I said. "This thing has legal angles."

I left Nick with the two women in the living room. Betty was solemn and quiet, as if Irene Chalmers's dark beauty cast a shadow over her.

Chalmers was in the walled garden, working among the plants. In clean, sun-faded Levis he looked thin, almost fragile. He was digging vigorously with a spade around some bushes which had been cut back for the winter and looked like dead thorny stumps.

He glanced up sharply at me, then slowly straightened, striking his spade upright in the earth. Greek and Roman statues stood around like nudists pitted by years of inclement weather.

Chalmers said rather severely: "I thought it was understood that the Florentine box was not insured."

"I wouldn't know about that, Mr. Chalmers. I'm not in the insurance business."

He got a little pale and tense. "I understood you to say you were."

"It was your wife's idea. I'm a private detective. John Truttwell called me in on your wife's behalf."

"Then he can damn well call you off again." Chalmers did a mental double take. "You mean my wife went to Truttwell behind my back?"

"It wasn't such a bad idea. I know you're concerned about your son, and I just brought him home. He's been running around with a gun, talking very loosely about suicide and murder."

I filled Chalmers in on what had been said and done. He was appalled. "Nick must be out of his mind."

"He is to a certain extent," I said. "But I don't think he was lying."

"You believe he committed a murder?"

"A man named Sidney Harrow is dead. There was bad blood between him and Nick. And Nick has admitted shooting him."

Chalmers swayed slightly and leaned on his spade, head down. There was a bald spot on the crown of his head, with a little hair brushed over it as if to mask his vulnerability. The moral beatings that people took from their children, I was thinking, were the hardest to endure and the hardest to escape.

But Chalmers wasn't thinking of himself. "Poor Nick. He was doing so well. What's happened to him?"

"Maybe Dr. Smitheram can tell you. It seems to have

started with the gold box. Apparently Nick took it from your safe and gave it to a woman named Jean Trask."

"I never heard of her. What would she want with my mother's gold box?"

"I don't know. It seems important to her."

"Have you talked to this Trask woman?"

"Yes, I have." .

"What did she do with my letters to my mother?"

"I don't know. I looked in the box, but it was empty."

"Why didn't you ask her?"

"She's a difficult woman to deal with. And more important things kept coming up."

Chalmers bit his mustache in chagrin. "Such as?"

"I learned that she hired Sidney Harrow to come to Pacific Point. Apparently they were searching for her father."

Chalmers gave me a puzzled look which wandered across the garden and over the wall to the sky. "What has all this got to do with us?"

"It isn't clear, I'm afraid. I have a suggestion, subject to John Truttwell's approval. And yours, of course. It might be a good idea to turn the gun over to the police and let them make ballistics tests."

"You mean give up without a fight?"

"Let's take this a step at a time, Mr. Chalmers. If it turns out that Nick's gun didn't kill Harrow, his confession is probably fantasy. If it did kill Harrow, we can decide then what to do next."

"We'll take it up with John Truttwell. I don't seem to be thinking too clearly." Chalmers put his fingers to his forehead.

"It still wouldn't be hopeless," I said, "even if Nick did kill him. I believe there may have been mitigating circumstances."

"How so?"

"Harrow had been throwing his weight around. He threatened Nick with a gun, possibly the same gun. This happened in front of your house the other night, when the box was stolen."

Chalmers gave me a doubtful look. "I don't see how you can possibly know that."

"I have an eyewitness." But I didn't name her.

"Do you have the gun with you?"

"It's in the trunk of my car. I'll show it to you."

We went through a screened lanai into the house and down

a corridor to the reception hall. Nick and his mother and Betty were sitting in a stiff little group on a sofa in the living room, like people at a party that had died some time ago. Nick had put on his dark glasses again, like a black bandage over his eyes.

Chalmers went into the living room and stood in front of him looking down as if from a great height. "Is it true that you shot a man?"

Nick nodded dully. "I'm sorry. I didn't want to come home. I meant to kill myself."

"That's cowardly talk," Chalmers said. "You've got to act like a man."

"Yes, Dad," he said without hope.

"We'll do everything we can for you. Don't despair. Promise me that, Nick."

"I promise, Dad. I'm sorry."

Chalmers turned with a kind of military abruptness and came back to me. His face was stoical. Both he and Nick must have been aware that no real communication had taken place.

We went out the front door. On the sidewalk Chalmers looked down at his gardening clothes self-consciously.

"I hate to appear like this in public," he said, as if the neighbors might be watching him.

I opened the trunk of my car and showed him the revolver without removing it from the evidence case. "Have you ever seen it before?"

"No. As a matter of fact Nick never owned a gun. He's always detested the whole business of guns."

"Why?"

"I suppose he got it by osmosis from me. My father taught me to hunt when I was a boy. But the war destroyed my pleasure in hunting."

"I hear you had quite a lot of war experience."

"Who told you that?"

"John Truttwell."

"I wish John would keep his own counsel. And mine. I prefer not to talk about my part in the war." He looked down at the revolver with a kind of sad contempt, as if it symbolized all the forms of violence. "Do you really think we should entrust this gun to John?"

"What do you suggest?"

"I know what I'd *like* to do. Bury it ten feet deep and forget about it."

"We'd only have to dig it up again."

"I suppose you're right," he said.

Truttwell's Cadillac came into view, far down Pacific Street. He parked it in front of his own house and came across the street at a half-trot. He absorbed the bad news about Nick as if his mind had been tuned in to receive it.

"And this is the gun. It's loaded." I handed him the case with the key in the lock. "You better take charge of it until we decide what to do. I have a query in on its original ownership."

"Good." He turned to Chalmers. "Where's Nick?"

"In the house. We're expecting Dr. Smitheram."

Truttwell laid his hand on Chalmers's bony shoulder. "Too bad you and Irene have to go through it again."

"Please. We won't discuss it." Chalmers pulled away from Truttwell's hand. He turned abruptly and marched in his stoical way toward the front door.

I followed Truttwell across the street to his house. In his study, he locked the evidence case in a fireproof steel cabinet. I said:

"I'm glad to get that off my hands. I didn't want Lackland to catch me with it."

"Do you think I should turn it over to him today?"

"Let's see what Sacramento says about ownership. What did you mean, by the way, about Chalmers going through it all again? Has Nick been in this kind of trouble before?"

Truttwell took his time about answering. "It depends on what you mean by this kind of trouble. He's never been mixed up in a homicide before, at least not to my knowledge. But he's had one or two episodes—isn't that what the psychiatrists call them? A few years ago he ran away, and it took a nationwide search to bring him home."

"Was he on the hippie kick?"

"Not really. Actually he was trying to support himself. When the Pinkertons finally tracked him down on the east coast, he was working as a busboy in a restaurant. We managed to persuade him that he should come home and finish his education."

"How does he feel about his parents?"

"He's very close to his mother," Truttwell said dryly, "if that's desirable. I think he idolizes his father, but feels he can't measure up. Which is exactly how Larry Chalmers felt about his own father, the Judge. I suppose these patterns have to go on repeating themselves."

44

"You mentioned more than one episode," I prompted him.

"So I did." He sat down facing me. "It goes much further back, fourteen or fifteen years, and it may be the root of Nick's trouble. Dr. Smitheram seems to think so. But beyond a certain point he won't discuss it with me."

"What happened?"

"That's what Smitheram won't discuss. I think Nick was picked up by some sort of sexual psychopath. His family got him back in a hurry, but not before Nick was frightened out of his wits. He was only eight years old at the time. You can understand why nobody likes to talk about it."

I wanted to ask Truttwell some more questions, but the housekeeper tapped on the study door and opened it. "I heard you come in, Mr. Truttwell. Is there anything I can get you?"

"No thanks, Mrs. Glover. I'm going right out again. Where's Betty, by the way?"

"I don't know, sir." But the woman looked at me, rather accusingly.

"She's at the Chalmers house," I said.

Truttwell got to his feet, his entire body making an angry gesture. "I don't like that at all."

"It couldn't be helped. She was with me when I took Nick. She handled herself very well. And handled him."

Truttwell struck his thigh with his fist. "I didn't bring her up to be nurse to a psycho."

The housekeeper had a terrified expression. She withdrew and closed the door without any sound.

"I'm going over there and bring her home," Truttwell said. "She's wasted her entire girlhood on that weakling."

"She doesn't seem to think it was all waste."

"So you're on *his* side?" He sounded like a rival.

"No. I'm on Betty's side, and probably yours. This is a hell of a time to force a decision on her."

Truttwell got the message after a moment's thought. "You're right, of course."

IX

Before he left the house, Truttwell filled a pipe and lit it with a kitchen match. I stayed behind in his study to make a phone call to Roy Snyder in Sacramento. It was five minutes to five by my watch, and I was just in time to catch Snyder before he quit for the night.

"Archer again. Do you have any information on the ownership of the Colt?"

"Yes, I do. It was bought new by a Pasadena man named Rawlinson. Samuel Rawlinson." Snyder spelled out the surname. "He made the purchase in September of 1941, and at the same time he got a permit to carry it from the Pasadena police. The permit was allowed to lapse in 1945. That's all I have."

"What reason did Rawlinson give for carrying a gun?"

"Business protection. He was the president of a bank," Snyder added dryly. "The Pasadena Occidental Bank."

I thanked him and dialed Pasadena Information. The Pasadena Occidental Bank was not listed, but Samuel Rawlinson was.

I put in a person-to-person call to Rawlinson. A woman answered. Her voice was rough and warm.

"I'm sorry," she explained to the operator. "It's hard for Mr. Rawlinson to come to the phone. Arthritis."

"I'll talk to her," I said.

"Go ahead, sir," the operator said.

"This is Lew Archer. Who am I talking to?"

"Mrs. Shepherd. I look after Mr. Rawlinson."

"Is he ill?"

"He's old," she said. "We all get old."

"You're so right, Mrs. Shepherd. I'm trying to trace possession of a gun which Mr. Rawlinson bought in 1941. A .45 Colt revolver. Will you ask him what he did with it?"

"I'll ask him."

She left the phone for a minute or two. It was a noisy line, and I could hear distant babblings, scraps of conversation fading just before I could grasp their meaning.

"He wants to know who you are," Mrs. Shepherd said.

46

"And what right you have to ask him about any gun." She added apologetically: "I'm only quoting what Mr. Rawlinson said. He's a stickler."

"So am I. Tell him I'm a detective. The gun may or may not have been used last night to commit a crime."

"Where?"

"In Pacific Point."

"He used to spend his summers there," she said. "I'll ask him again." She went away and came back. "I'm sorry, Mr. Archer, he won't talk. But he says if you want to come here and explain what it's all about, he'll discuss it with you."

"When?"

"This evening if you want. He never goes out evenings. The number is 245 on Locust Street."

I said I'd be there as soon as I could make it.

I was in my car, ready to go, when I realized I couldn't leave just yet. A black Cadillac convertible with a medical caduceus was parked just ahead of me. I wanted to have a word with Dr. Smitheram.

The front door of the Chalmers house was standing open, as if its security had been breached. I walked into the reception hall. Truttwell stood with his back to me, arguing with a large balding man who had to be the psychiatrist. Lawrence and Irene Chalmers were on the fringes of the argument.

"The hospital is contraindicated," Truttwell was saying. "We can't be sure what the boy will say, and hospitals are always full of leaks."

"My clinic isn't," the large man said.

"Possibly, just possibly, it isn't. Even so, if you or one of your employees were asked a question in court, you'd have to answer it. Unlike the legal profession—"

The doctor interrupted Truttwell: "Has Nick committed a crime of some sort?"

"I'm not going to answer that question."

"How can I look after a patient without information?"

"You have plenty of information, more than I have." Truttwell's voice seemed to buzz with an old resentment. "You've sat on that information for fifteen years."

"At least you recognize," Smitheram said, "that I haven't gone running to the police with it."

"Would the police be interested, doctor?"

"I'm not going to answer that question."

The two men faced each other in a quiet fury. Lawrence

47

Chalmers tried to say something to them but they paid no attention.

His wife moved toward me, and drew me to one side. Her eyes were dull and unsurprised, as if she'd been hit by something that she'd seen coming from a long way off.

"Dr. Smitheram wants to take Nick to his clinic. What do you think we should do?"

"I agree with Mr. Truttwell. Your son needs legal security as well as medical."

"Why?" she said bluntly.

"He killed a man last night, he says, and he's been talking about it quite freely."

I paused to let the fact sink in. She handled it almost as if she'd been expecting it. "Who is the man?"

"Sidney Harrow is his name. He was involved in the theft of your Florentine box. So was Nick, apparently."

"Nick was?"

"I'm afraid so. With all these things on his mind, I don't think you should put him in any kind of clinic or hospital. Hospitals are always full of leaks, as Truttwell says. Couldn't you keep him at home?"

"Who would watch him?"

"You and your husband."

She glanced at her husband, appraisingly. "Maybe. I don't know if Larry is up to it. It doesn't show but he's terribly emotional, especially where Nick is concerned." She moved closer, letting me feel the influence of her body. "Would you, Mr. Archer?"

"Would I what?"

"Stand watch over Nick tonight?"

"No." The word came out hard and definite.

"We're paying your salary, you know."

"And I've been earning it. But I'm not a psychiatric nurse."

"I'm sorry I asked you."

There was a sting in her words. She turned her back on me and moved away. I decided I'd better get out of town before she had me fired. I went and told John Truttwell where I was going and why.

Truttwell's argument with the doctor had cooled down. He introduced me to Smitheram, who gave me a soft handclasp and a hard look. There was a troubled intelligence in his eyes.

48

I said: "I'd like to ask you some questions about Nick."

"This isn't the time or the place."

"I realize that, doctor. I'll see you at your office tomorrow."

"If you insist. Now if you'll excuse me, I have a patient to attend to."

I followed him as far as the living-room gates, and glanced in. Betty and Nick were sitting on a rug, not together but near each other. Her body was turned toward him, supported by one straight arm. Nick's face was pressed against his own raised knees.

Neither of them seemed to move, even to breathe. They looked like people lost in space, frozen forever in their separate poses, his of despair, hers of caring.

Dr. Smitheram went and sat down near them on the floor.

X

I drove inland by way of Anaheim. It was a bad time of day, and in places the traffic crawled like a wounded snake. It took me ninety minutes to get from Chalmers's house to Rawlinson's house in Pasadena.

I parked in front of the place and sat for a minute, letting the freeway tensions drip off my nerve ends. It was one of a block of three-storied frame houses. They were ancient, as time went in California, ornamented with turn-of-the-century gables and cupolas.

Half a block further on, Locust Street came to an end at a black-and-white-striped barricade. Beyond it a deep wooded ravine opened. Twilight was overflowing the ravine, flooding the yards, soaking up into the thick yellow sky.

A light showed in Rawlinson's house as the front door opened and closed. A woman crossed the veranda and came down the steps skipping a broken one.

I saw as she approached my car that she must have been close to sixty. She moved with the confidence of a much younger woman. Her eyes were bright black behind her glasses. Her skin was dark, perhaps with a tincture of Indian or

Negro blood. She wore a staid gray dress and a multi-colored Mexican apron.

"Are you the gentleman who wants to see Mr. Rawlinson?"

"Yes. I'm Archer."

"I'm Mrs. Shepherd. He's just sitting down to dinner and he won't mind if you join him. He likes to have some company with his food. I only prepared enough for the two of us, but I'll be glad to pour you a cup of tea."

"I could use a cup of tea, Mrs. Shepherd."

I followed her into the house. The entrance hall was impressive if you didn't look too closely. But the parquetry floor was buckling and loose underfoot, and the walls were dark with mold.

The dining room was more cheerful. Under a yellowing crystal chandelier with one live bulb, a table had been set for one person, with polished silver on a clean white cloth. An old white-headed man in a rusty dinner coat was finishing off what looked like a bowl of beef stew.

The woman introduced me to him. He put his spoon down and struggled to his feet, offering me a gnarled hand. "Take it easy with my arthritis, please. Sit down. Mrs. Shepherd will get you a cup of coffee."

"Tea," she corrected him. "We're out of coffee." But she lingered in the room, waiting to hear what was said.

Rawlinson's eyes had a mica glint. He spoke with impatient directness. "This revolver you telephoned about—I gather it's been used for some illegal purpose?"

"Possibly. I don't know that it has."

"But if it hasn't you've come a long way for nothing."

"In my job everything has to be checked out."

"I understand you're a private detective," he said.

"That's correct."

"Employed by whom?"

"A lawyer named Truttwell in Pacific Point."

"John Truttwell?"

"Yes. Do you know him?"

"I met John two or three times through one of his clients. That was a long time ago, when he was young and I was middle-aged. It must be close to thirty years—Estelle's been dead for nearly twenty-four."

"Estelle?"

"Estelle Chalmers—Judge Chalmers's widow. She was a

50

hell of a woman." The old man smacked his lips like a wine-taster.

The woman still lingering by the door was showing signs of distress. "All that is ancient history, Mr. Rawlinson. The gentleman isn't interested in ancient history."

Rawlinson laughed. "It's the only kind of history I know. Where's that tea you were so freely offering, Mrs. Shepherd?" She went out, closing the door with emphasis. He turned to me. "She thinks she owns me. She doesn't, though. If I don't have a right to my memories, there isn't a great deal left at my time of life."

"I'm interested in your memories," I said, "specifically in the Colt revolver you bought in September 1941. It was probably used to shoot a man last night."

"What man?"

"Sidney Harrow was his name."

"I never heard of him," Rawlinson said, as if this cast some doubt on Harrow's reality. "Is he dead?"

"Yes."

"And you're trying to connect my gun with his death?"

"Not exactly. It either is connected or it isn't. I want to know which."

"Wouldn't ballistics show?"

"Possibly. The tests haven't been made yet."

"Then I think I should wait, don't you?"

"You certainly should if you're guilty, Mr. Rawlinson."

He laughed so hard his upper teeth slipped. He pushed them back into place with thumb and forefinger. Mrs. Shepherd appeared in the doorway with a tea tray.

"What's so funny?" she asked him.

"You wouldn't consider it funny, Mrs. Shepherd. Your sense of humor is deficient."

"Your sense of fittingness is. For an eighty-year-old man who used to be the president of a bank—" She set the tea tray down with a slight clash that completed her thought. "Milk or lemon, Mr. Archer?"

"I'll take it black."

She poured our tea in two bone china cups that didn't match. The rundown elegance of the household made me wonder if Rawlinson was a poor man or a miser; and what in hell had happened to his bank.

"Mr. Archer suspects me of committing a murder," he said to the woman in a slightly bragging tone.

She didn't think it was funny at all. Her dark face got darker, grim around the mouth and in the eyes. She turned on Rawlinson fiercely.

"Why don't you tell him the truth then? You know you gave that revolver to your daughter, and you know the exact date."

"Be quiet."

"I will not. You're playing tricks with yourself and I won't let you. You're a smart man but you don't have enough to occupy your mind."

Rawlinson showed no anger. He seemed to be pleased by her almost wifely concern. And his holding back about the gun had been just a game, apparently.

Mrs. Shepherd was the worried one. "Who got shot?"

"A part-time detective named Sidney Harrow."

She shook her head. "I don't know who that would be. Drink up your tea while it's hot. Can I get you a piece of fruitcake, Mr. Archer? There's some left over from Christmas."

"No thanks."

"I'll have some," Rawlinson said. "With a scoop of ice cream."

"We're out of ice cream."

"We seem to be out of everything."

"No, there's enough to eat. But money only stretches so far."

She left the room again. With her warmth and energy subtracted, the room changed. Rawlinson looked around it a little uneasily, as if he was feeling the cold weight of his bones.

"I'm sorry she saw fit to sic you onto my daughter. And I hope you won't go dashing off in her direction now. There'd be no point in it."

"Why?"

"It's true I gave Louise the gun in 1945. But it was stolen from her house some years later, in 1954, to be exact." He recited the dates as if he was proud of his memory. "This is not an *ad hoc* story."

"Who stole the gun?"

"How should we know? My daughter's house was burglarized."

"Why did you give her the gun in the first place?"

"It's an old story and a sad one," he said. "My daughter's husband abandoned her and left her stranded with Jean."

52

"Jean?"

"My granddaughter Jean. The two helpless females were left alone in the house. Louise wanted the gun for protection." He grinned suddenly. "I think Louise may have been hoping that he would come back."

"That who would come back?"

"Her husband. My egregious son-in-law Eldon Swain. If Eldon had come back, I have no doubt she'd have shot him. With my blessing."

"What did you have against your son-in-law?"

He laughed abruptly. "That's an excellent question. But with your permission I don't think I'll answer it."

Mrs. Shepherd brought us two narrow wedges of cake. She noticed that I wolfed mine.

"You're hungry. I'll make you a sandwich."

"Don't bother. I'm on my way to dinner."

"It wouldn't be any bother."

Her divided attention made Rawlinson uncomfortable. He said with the air of a comedian: "Mr. Archer wants to know what Eldon Swain did to me. Shall I tell him?"

"No. You're talking too much, Mr. Rawlinson."

"Eldon's defalcations are common knowledge."

"Not any more they're not. I say let it lie. We could all be a lot worse off than we are. I told Shepherd the same thing. When you talk about old trouble sometimes you can talk it back to life."

He reacted with jealous irritation. "I thought your husband was living in San Diego."

"Randy Shepherd isn't my husband. He's my ex."

"Have you been seeing him?"

She shrugged. "I can't help it when he comes back for a visit. I do my best to discourage him."

"So that's where the ice cream and coffee have been going!"

"It isn't so. I never give Shepherd a morsel of your food or a cent of your money."

"You're a liar."

"Don't call me that, Mr. Rawlinson. There are things I won't put up with, even from you."

Rawlinson looked quite happy again. He had the woman's attention, and all her heat, focused on him.

I stood up. "I've got to be going."

Neither of them offered any argument. Mrs. Shepherd accompanied me to the front door.

"I hope you got what you came for."

"Part of it, anyway. Do you know where his daughter lives?"

"Yessir." She gave me another address in Pasadena. "Just don't tell her I told you. Mrs. Eldon Swain doesn't approve of me."

"You seem to be bearing up under it," I said. "Is Jean Trask Mrs. Swain's daughter?"

"Yes. Don't tell me Jean's mixed up in all this."

"I'm afraid so."

"That's too bad. I can remember when Jean was an innocent little angel. Jean and my own little girl were best friends for years. Then everything went sour." She heard herself, and sucked her lips inward. "I'm talking too much myself, bringing the past back to life."

XI

Louise Swain lived on a poor street off Fair Oaks, between Old Town and the ghetto. A few children of various shades were playing under the light at the corner, islanded in the surrounding darkness.

There was a smaller light on the front porch of Mrs. Swain's stucco cottage, and a Ford sedan standing at the curb in front of it. The Ford was locked. I shone my flashlight into it. It was registered to George Trask, 4545 Bayview Avenue, San Diego.

I made a note of the address, got out my contact mike, and went around to the side of the stucco cottage, following two strips of concrete which made an exigent driveway. An old black Volkswagen with a crumpled fender stood under a rusty carport. I moved into its shadow and leaned on the wall beside a blinded window.

I didn't need my microphone. Inside the house, Jean's voice was raised in anger: "I'm not going back to George—"

An older woman spoke in a more controlled voice: "You better take my advice and go back to him. George still cares about you and he was asking for you early this morning—but it won't last forever."

"Who cares?"

"You ought to care. If you lose him you won't have anybody, and you don't know how that feels until you've tried it. Don't think you're coming back to live with me."

"I wouldn't stay if you begged me on your knees."

"That won't happen," the older woman said dryly. "I've got just enough room and enough money and enough energy left for myself."

"You're a cold woman, Mother."

"Am I? I wasn't always. You and your father made me that way."

"You're jealous!" Jean's voice had changed. A hiss of pleasure underlay her anger and distress. "Jealous of your own daughter and your own husband. It all comes clear. No wonder you gave him Rita Shepherd."

"I didn't give him Rita. She threw herself at his head."

"With a good strong assist from you, Mother. You probably planned the whole thing."

The older woman said: "I suggest you leave here before you say any more. You're nearly forty years old and you're not my responsibility. You're lucky to have a husband willing and able to look after you."

"I can't stand him," Jean said. "Let me stay here with you. I'm scared."

"So am I," her mother said. "I'm afraid for you. You've been drinking again, haven't you?"

"I did a little celebrating."

"What have *you* got to celebrate?"

"Wouldn't you like to know, Mother?" Jean paused. "I'll tell you if you ask me pretty please."

"If you have something to tell me, then tell me. Don't fool around."

"Now I'm not going to tell you." Jean sounded like a child playing a teasing game. "You can find out for yourself."

"There's nothing to find out," her mother said.

"Is that a fact? What would you say if I told you that Daddy's alive?"

"Really alive?"

"You bet he is," Jean said.

"Have you seen him?"

"I soon will. I've picked up his trail."

"Where?"

"That's my little secret, Mother."

"Augh, you've been imagining things again. I'd be crazy to believe you."

Jean made no answer that I could hear. I suspected the two women had exhausted the conversation and each other. I moved from the shadow of the carport into the dim street.

Jean came out onto the lighted porch. The door was slammed behind her. The light went out. I waited for her beside her car.

She backed away from me, stumbling on the broken sidewalk. "What do you want?"

"Give me the gold box, Jean. It isn't yours."

"Yes it is. It's an old family heirloom."

"Come off it."

"It's true," she said. "The box belonged to my Grandmother Rawlinson. She said it would come down to me. And now it has."

I half believed her. "Could we talk a little in your car?"

"That never does any good. The more you talk the more it hurts."

Her face was mournful and her body dragged. She gave off a peculiar feeling, that she was a ghost or cloudy emanation of the actual Jean Trask; her sense of herself was a vacuum, a cold emptiness.

"What's hurting, Jean?"

"My whole life." She spread both hands on her breasts as if the pain was overflowing her fingers. "Daddy ran off to Mexico with Rita. He didn't even send me a birthday card."

"How old were you?"

"Sixteen. I never had any fun after that."

"Is your father alive?"

"I think he is. Nick Chalmers said he saw him in Pacific Point."

"Where in Pacific Point?"

"Down by the railroad yards. That was a long time ago, when Nick was just a child. But he identified Daddy by his picture."

"How did Nick get into this?"

"He's my witness that Daddy is alive." Her voice rose in pitch and amplitude, as if she was speaking to the woman in the house instead of me: "Why shouldn't he be alive? He'd only be—let's see, I'm thirty-nine and Daddy was twenty-four when I was born. That makes him sixty-three, doesn't it?"

"Thirty-nine and twenty-four makes sixty-three."

"And sixty-three isn't old, especially not nowadays. He was always very youthful for his age. He could dive and dance

56

and spin like a top," she said. "He bounced me on his knee."

It sounded like something repeated from her childhood. Her mind was being carried down the stream of memory, swept willy-nilly through subterranean passages toward roaring falls.

"I'm going to find my Daddy," she said. "I'll find him dead or alive. If he's alive I'll cook and keep house for him. And I'll be happier than I ever was in my born days. If he's dead I'll find his grave and do you know what I'll do then? I'll crawl in with him and go to sleep."

She unlocked her car and drove away, turning south onto the boulevard. Perhaps I should have followed her, but I didn't.

XII

I knocked on the front door of the stucco cottage. After an interval, the porch light came on over my head. Then the door was opened about four inches on a chain.

A woman with fading blond hair peered at me through the opening. Her face was set grimly, as if she'd expected to see her daughter again. The atmosphere around her was still charged.

"What is it?"

"I've just been talking to your father," I said. "About a Colt revolver he bought in 1941."

"I don't know anything about a revolver."

"Aren't you Mrs. Eldon Swain?"

"Louise Rawlinson Swain," she corrected me. But then she asked: "Has something come up about my husband?"

"Possibly. Could we talk inside? I'm a private detective."

I handed her my photostat through the crack. She looked it over carefully, and did everything but bite it. Finally she handed it back.

"Who are you working for, Mr. Archer?"

"A lawyer in Pacific Point named John Truttwell. I'm looking into a couple of related crimes—a theft and a murder." I didn't bother adding that her daughter was connected with one of the crimes, possibly both.

She let me in. Her front room was poor and small. As in Rawlinson's house, there were relics of better days. On the mantel over the gas fire a Dresden shepherd and shepherdess exchanged adoring glances.

A small Oriental rug lay not on the floor, which was covered with worn matting, but over the back of the chesterfield. Facing the chesterfield was a television set with an electric clock on top of it, and beside it a telephone table with a drawer. Everything was clean and well-dusted, but the room had a musty taint, as if neither it nor the woman in it had been fully used.

Mrs. Swain didn't invite me to sit down. She stood facing me, a large woman like her daughter, with the same kind of heavy good looks.

"Who was murdered?"

"I'll come to that, Mrs. Swain. I wanted to ask you first about a box that was stolen. It's a Florentine gold box with classical figures on the lid, a man and a woman."

"My mother had a box like that," she said. "She used it as a jewel case. I never did know where it disappeared to after Mother died." But her eyes were alive with roving speculation. "What is this all about? Has Eldon been heard from?"

"I don't know."

"You said 'possibly.'"

"I didn't want to rule anything out. I really came here to talk about the revolver your father gave you. But we'll talk about anything you like."

"There's nothing I want to discuss." But after a moment she asked me: "What did Father say?"

"Simply that he gave you the Colt for protection, after your husband left you. The year he mentioned was 1945."

"All that is perfectly true," she said carefully. "Did he mention the circumstances in which Eldon left?"

I threw her a slow curve. "Mrs. Shepherd wouldn't let him."

It jarred her. "Was Mrs. Shepherd present at the conversation?"

"She was in and out of the dining room."

"She would be. What else did my father say in front of her?"

"I don't remember if this was said in front of Mrs. Shepherd. But he told me that your house was burglarized in 1954 and the Colt was taken."

58

"I see." She looked around the room as if to see how the story fitted into it.

"Did it happen in this house?" I asked her.

She nodded.

"Was the burglar ever caught?"

"I don't know. I don't believe so."

"Did you report the burglary to the police?"

"I don't remember." She wasn't a good liar, and she screwed up her mouth in a kind of self-disgust. "Why is it important?"

"I'm trying to trace possession of the revolver. If you have any idea who the burglar was, Mrs. Swain—" I left the sentence unfinished, and glanced at the electric clock. It was half past eight. "About twenty hours ago, that revolver may have been used to kill a man. A man named Sidney Harrow."

She knew the name. Her whole face caught and held it. The delicate skin around her eyes puckered in distress. After a moment she spoke.

"Jean didn't tell me. No wonder she was frightened." Mrs. Swain wrung her hands and walked away from me as far as the room would let her. "Do you suspect Eldon of killing Sidney Harrow?"

"Possibly. Was it your husband who took the gun in 1954?"

"Yes, it was." She spoke with her head down and her face averted, like a woman in a storm. "I didn't want to tell Father that Eldon had come back, or that I had seen him. So I made up a lie about a burglary."

"Why did you have to tell your father anything?"

"Because he asked me for the gun the very next morning. I believe he'd heard that Eldon had been in town, and he intended to shoot him with the gun. But Eldon already had it. That's quite an irony, isn't it?"

It wasn't the kind I could live on, but I agreed. "How did Eldon get hold of the revolver? You didn't give it to him?"

"No. I wouldn't do that. I kept it at the back of the telephone drawer." Her eyes moved past me to the telephone table. "I got it out when Eldon tapped on the door. I suspected it was Eldon, his knock was so distinctive. Shave and a haircut, two-bits, you know? That was Eldon's speed. He was capable of coming back after spending nine years in Mexico with another girl. And all the other dreadful things

59

he did to me and my family. And expect to smile it all away and charm us as he used to in the old days."

She looked at the door. "I didn't have the chain on the door at that time—I had it put on the following day. The door wasn't locked, and Eldon came in smiling, calling my name. I wanted to shoot him, but I couldn't pull the trigger of the gun. He walked right up and took it away from me."

Mrs. Swain sat down as if her strength had been taken away. She leaned back against the Oriental rug. I sat down beside her tentatively.

"What happened then?"

"Just what you'd expect of Eldon. He denied everything. He hadn't taken the money. He hadn't gone to Mexico with the girl. He ran away because he'd been falsely accused, and had been living in strictest celibacy. He even argued that my family owed him something, because Father publicly called him an embezzler and blackened his reputation."

"What was your husband supposed to have done?"

"There's no supposition about it. He was the cashier of my father's bank, and he embezzled over half a million dollars. You mean Father didn't tell you?"

"No, he didn't. When did all this happen?"

"July the first, 1945—the blackest day of my life. He ruined my father's bank and sold me into slavery."

"I don't quite follow, Mrs. Swain."

"Don't you?" She tapped her knee with her fist like a judge gaveling for order. "In the spring of 1945 I lived in a big house in San Marino. Before the summer was over, I had to move in here. Jean and I could have gone to live with Father on Locust Street, but I wouldn't live in the same house with Mrs. Shepherd. That meant I had to get out and find a job. The only thing I ever learned to do well is sew. For over twenty years now I've been demonstrating sewing machines. That's what I mean by slavery." Her fist clenched on her knee. "Eldon robbed me of all the good things of life, and then tried to deny it to my face."

"I'm sorry."

"So am I. I'm sorry I didn't shoot him. If I had another chance—" She took a deep breath and let it out in a sigh.

"It wouldn't do any good, Mrs. Swain. And there are worse places than this. One of them is the women's prison at Corona."

"I know that. I was just talking." But she leaned toward

me intently. "Tell me, has Eldon been seen in Pacific Point?"

"I don't know."

"The reason I ask, Jean claims she found some trace of him. It's why she employed that Harrow person."

"Did you know Harrow?"

"Jean brought him here last week. I didn't think much of him. But Jean was always impulsive about men. Now you tell me that he's dead."

"Yes."

"Shot with the revolver that Eldon took from me," she said dramatically. "Eldon would kill if he had to, you know. He'd kill anyone who tried to drag him back here and put him in jail."

"That wasn't what Jean planned to do, though."

"I know that. She idolized his memory, foolishly. But Sidney Harrow may have had other ideas. Harrow looked like a bum to me. And don't forget Eldon has stacks of money—over half-a-million."

"Provided he hung on to it."

She smiled fiercely. "You don't know Eldon. He wouldn't throw money away. Money was all he ever wanted in life. He went about getting it coldly and methodically. The bank examiners said that he'd been preparing his theft for well over a year. And when he got to Mexico he probably invested the whole thing at ten per cent."

I listened to her, without entirely believing her. According to her own story, she hadn't seen her husband since 1954. Her account of him had the swooping certainty of a mind tracking on fantasy. A woman could do a lot of dreaming in twenty years of demonstrating sewing machines.

"Are you still married to him, Mrs. Swain?"

"Yes, I am. He may have gotten a Mexican divorce but if he did I never heard of it. He's still living in sin with that Shepherd girl. Which is the way I want it."

"You're talking about Mrs. Shepherd's daughter?"

"That's right. Like mother like daughter. I allowed Rita Shepherd into my home and treated her like my own daughter. So she stole my husband."

"Which theft came first?"

She was puzzled for a moment. Then her brow cleared. "I see what you mean. Yes, Eldon was carrying on with Rita before he stole the money. I caught on to them very early in the game. It was during a swimming party at our house—we had a forty-foot pool where we lived in San Marino." Her voice sank almost out of hearing. "I can't bear to think about it."

The woman had been punished severely in the past hour, and I was weary of my part in it. I rose to go, and thanked her. But she wouldn't let me leave.

She got up heavily. "Do detectives ever do things on a contingency basis?"

"What do you have in mind?"

"I don't have the money to pay you. But if I could get back some of the money Eldon took—" Her sentence dangled in the air, hopefully, hopelessly. "We'd all be rich again," she said in a hushed and prayerful voice. "And of course I'd pay you very generously."

"I'm sure you would." I edged toward the door. "I'll keep my eyes open for your husband."

"Do you know what he looks like?"

"No."

"Wait. I'll get a picture of him, if my daughter left me any."

She went into a back room where I could hear her lifting and shoving things around. When she came back she had a dusty photograph in her hand and a smear of grime on her cheek, like a miner. "Jean took all my good family pictures, all my San Marino albums," she complained. "She used to sit and study them the way other young women read movie magazines. George tells me—George is her husband—that she's still watching the home movies we took in San Marino."

I took the photograph from her: a man of thirty-five or so, fair-haired, bold-eyed. He looked like the man whose picture Captain Lackland had found on Sidney Harrow. But the photograph wasn't clear enough to be absolutely certain.

XIII

I had dinner in Pasadena and drove home to West Los Angeles. The air in my second-floor apartment was warm and stale. I opened a window and a bottle of beer, and sat down with the bottle in the near-darkness of my front room.

62

I lived in a quiet section, away from the main freeways. Still I could hear them humming, remote yet intimate, like the humming of my own blood in my veins.

Cars went by in the street from time to time, flinging brief lights across the ceiling. The case I was on seemed as hard to hold in the mind as the vanishing lights and the humming city were.

The shape and feeling of the case were changing. They always changed as you moved around in them. Eldon Swain had come into the center, pulling his whole family with him. If he was alive, he could give me some answers I needed. If he was dead, the people who knew his history would have to provide the answers.

I turned on the light and got out my black notebook and put down some notes about the people:

"The Colt .45 I took off Nick Chalmers was bought in September 1941 by Samuel Rawlinson, president of the Pasadena Occidental Bank. Around July 1, 1945, he gave it to his daughter Louise Swain. Her husband, Eldon, cashier of the bank, had just embezzled over half a million and ruined the bank. He ran off, reportedly to Mexico, with Rita Shepherd, daughter of Rawlinson's housekeeper (and onetime 'best friend' of his own daughter, Jean).

"Eldon Swain turned up at his wife's house in 1954 and took the Colt from her. How did it get from Swain to Nick Chalmers? Via Sidney Harrow, or through other people?

"N.B. San Diego: Harrow lived there, ditto Swain's daughter Jean and her husband, George Trask, ditto Mrs. Shepherd's ex-husband."

When I finished writing it was nearly midnight. I called John Truttwell's house in Pacific Point and at his request I read my notes to him, twice. I said it might be a good idea after all to turn the Colt revolver over to Lackland for testing. Truttwell said he already had. I went to bed.

At seven by my radio clock the phone jarred me awake. I picked up the receiver and pronounced my own name with a dry mouth.

"Captain Lackland here. I know it's early to call. But I've been up all night myself, supervising tests on the revolver you turned in to your lawyer."

"Mr. Truttwell isn't my lawyer."

"He's been doing your talking for you. But under present circumstances that isn't good enough."

63

"What are the circumstances?"

"I don't believe in discussing evidence over the phone. Can you be here in the station in an hour?"

"I can try."

I skipped breakfast and walked into Lackland's office at two minutes to eight by the electric clock on his wall. He nodded curtly. His eyes had sunk deeper into his head. Glinting gray beard had sprouted on his face, like wire growing out from a central steel core.

His desk was cluttered with photographs. The top one was a blown-up microphotograph of a pair of bullets. Lackland waved me into a hard chair opposite him.

"It's time you and I had a meeting of minds."

"You make it sound more like a clash of personalities, Captain."

Lackland didn't smile. "I'm in no mood for wisecracks. I want to know where you got hold of this gun." He pulled the revolver on me suddenly, producing a plywood board to which it had been attached with wire.

"I can't tell you that. The law says I don't have to."

"What do you know about the law?"

"I'm working under a good lawyer. I accept his interpretation."

"I don't."

"You make that clear, Captain. I'm willing to cooperate in any way I can. The fact that you have the gun is proof of that."

"The real proof would be for you to tell me where you got it."

"I can't do that."

"Would it change your mind if I told you we know?"

"I doubt it. Try me."

"Nick Chalmers was known to be carrying a gun yesterday. I have a witness. Another witness places him in the vicinity of the Sunset Motor Hotel at the approximate time of the Harrow killing."

Lackland's voice was dry and official, as if he was already testifying at Nick's trial. He was watching my eyes as he spoke. I tried to keep them unresponsive, as cold as his were.

"No comment," I said.

"You'll have to answer in court."

"That's doubtful. Also, we're not in court."

"We may be sooner than you think. Right now I probably

64

have enough for a Grand Jury indictment." He slapped the pile of photographs on his desk. "I have positive proof that this revolver killed Harrow. The bullets we test-fired from it match up with the slug recovered from his brain. You want to take a look?"

I studed the microphotographs. I was no ballistics expert, but I could see that the slugs matched. The evidence against Nick was piling up.

There was almost too much evidence. Beside it, Nick's confession that he had murdered Harrow in the hobo jungle seemed less and less real.

"You don't waste any time, Captain."

The compliment depressed Lackland. "I wish that that was true. I've been working on this case for fifteen years—nearly all of it wasted." He gave me a long appraising look. "I really could use your help, you know. I like to cooperate as well as the next man."

"So do I. I don't understand what you mean about fifteen years."

"I wish I understood it myself." He lifted his microphotographs out of the way and produced some other pictures from the manila envelope he'd shown me yesterday. "Look here."

The first picture was the cropped one I'd already seen. It was Eldon Swain, all right, flanked by girls' dresses, with the girls cut away.

"Know him?"

"I may."

"You do or you don't," Lackland said.

There was no reason not to tell him. Lackland would trace the Colt revolver to Samuel Rawlinson, if he hadn't already done so. From there it was only a step to Rawlinson's son-in-law. I said:

"His name is Eldon Swain. He used to live in Pasadena."

Lackland smiled and nodded, like a teacher whose backward pupil is making progress. He brought out another picture from his manila envelope. It was a flash picture which showed the weary face of a sleeping man. I blinked, and saw that the sleeping man was dead.

"How about *him?*" Lackland said.

The man's hair had faded almost white. There were smudges of dirt or ashes on his face, and it had been burned by harsh suns. His mouth showed broken teeth and around it the marks of broken hopes.

65

"It could be the same man, Captain."

"That's my opinion, too. It's why I dug him out of the files."

"Is he dead?"

"For a long time. Fifteen years." Lackland's voice had a certain rough tenderness, which he seemed to reserve for the dead. "He got himself knocked off down in the hobo jungle. That was in 1954—I was a sergeant at the time."

"Was he murdered?"

"Shot through the heart. With this gun." He lifted the revolver on the board. "The same gun that killed Harrow."

"How do you know that?"

"Ballistics again." From a drawer in his desk he got out a labelled box which was lined with cotton, and took out a slug. "This bullet matches the ones we test-fired last night, and it's the one that killed the man in the jungle. I thought of it," he said with careful pride, "because Harrow was carrying this other picture." He tapped the cropped photograph of Eldon Swain. "And I was struck by the resemblance to the dead man in the jungle."

"I think the dead man is Swain," I said. "The timing is right." I told Lackland what I had learned about the passage of the revolver from Rawlinson's hands, into his daughter's, and from her hands into her wandering husband's.

Lackland was deeply interested. "You say Swain had been in Mexico?"

"For eight or nine years, apparently."

"That tends to confirm the identification. The dead man was dressed like a wetback, in Mexican clothes. It's one reason we didn't follow it up like maybe we should have. I used to be a border guard during the war, and I know how hard it is to trace a Mex."

"No fingerprints?"

"That's right, no fingerprints. The body was left with its hands in a fire—the coals of a bonfire." He showed me a hideous picture of the charred hands. "I don't know if it was accidental or not. Some wild things happen in the hobo jungle."

"Did you have any suspects at the time?"

"We rounded up the transients, of course. One of them looked promising at first—an ex-con named Randy Shepherd. He was carrying too much money for a tramp, and he'd been seen with the decedent. But he claimed they'd just met casually on the road and shared a bottle. We couldn't prove otherwise."

He shifted to further questions about Eldon Swain and the revolver, which I answered. Finally he said: "We've covered everything except the essential point. How did you get hold of the gun yesterday?"

"Sorry, Captain. At least you're not trying to pin this old hobo-jungle killing on Nick Chalmers. He was hardly big enough for a cap pistol at the time."

Lackland was as implacable as a chess player: "Children have been known to fire a gun."

"You can't be serious."

Lackland gave me a chilly smile which seemed to say that he knew more than I did, and always would.

XIV

I stopped by Truttwell's office to report to him. His pink-haired receptionist seemed relieved to see me.

"I've been trying to get you. Mr. Truttwell says it's urgent."

"Is he here?"

"No. He's at Mr. Chalmers's house."

The Chalmerses' servant, Emilio, let me in. Truttwell was sitting with Chalmers and his wife in the living room. The scene looked like a wake with the corpse missing.

"Has something happened to Nick?"

"He ran away," Chalmers said. "I didn't get any sleep last night, and I'm afraid he caught me with my wits down. He locked himself in an upstairs bathroom. It never occurred to me that he could squeeze himself out the window. But he did."

"How long ago?"

"Hardly more than half an hour," Truttwell said.

"That's too damn bad."

"I know it is." Chalmers was taut and anxious. The slow grinding passage of the night had worn flesh from his face. "We were hoping you could help us get him back."

"We can't use the police, you see," his wife said.

"I understand that. How was he dressed, Mr. Chalmers?"

"In the same clothes as he was wearing yesterday—he wouldn't undress last night. He had on a gray suit, a white shirt, and a blue tie. Black shoes."

"Did he take anything else with him?"

Truttwell answered for them: "I'm afraid he did. He took all the sleeping pills in the medicine cabinet."

"At least they're missing," Chalmers said.

"Exactly what is missing?" I asked him.

"Some chloral hydrate capsules, and quite a few ¾-grain Nembutal."

"And a good deal of Nembu-Serpin," his wife added.

"Did he have money?"

"I presume he did," Chalmers said. "I didn't take his money away. I was trying to avoid anything that would upset him."

"Which way did he go?"

"I don't know. It took me a few minutes to realize he was gone. I'm not a very good jailer, I'm afraid."

Irene Chalmers made a clucking noise with her tongue. It was hardly audible, and she made it only once, but it conveyed the idea that she could think of other things he wasn't very good at.

I asked Chalmers to show me Nick's escape route. He took me up a short tile staircase and along a windowless corridor to the bathroom. The rifled medicine cabinet was standing open. The window, set deep in the far wall, was about two feet wide by three feet high. I opened it and leaned out.

In a flower bed about twelve feet below the window I could see deep footprints, toes pointed inward to the house. Nick must have climbed out feet first, I thought, hung from the sill and dropped. There was no other trace of him.

We went downstairs to the living room where Irene Chalmers was waiting with Truttwell. "You're wise," I said, "not to think in terms of the police. I wouldn't tell them, or anyone, that he's gone."

"We haven't, and we don't intend to," Chalmers said.

"What kind of emotional state was he in when he left?"

"Pretty fair, I thought. He didn't sleep much, but we did some quiet talking in the course of the night."

"Do you mind telling me what about?"

"I don't mind. I talked about our need to stick together, our willingness to support him."

"How did he react?"

"Hardly at all, I'm afraid. But at least he didn't get angry."

"Did he mention the shooting of Harrow?"

"No. Nor did I ask him."

"Or the shooting of another man fifteen years ago?"

Chalmers's face lengthened in surprise. "What on earth do you mean?"

"Skip it for now. You've got enough on your mind."

"I prefer not to skip it." Irene Chalmers rose and moved toward me. She had dark circles under her eyes; her skin was yellowish; her lips moved uncertainly. "Ycu can't be accusing my son of another shooting?"

"I simply asked a question."

"It was a terrible question."

"I agree." John Truttwell got to his feet and came over to me. "I think it's time we got out of here. These people have put in a hellish night."

I gave them a semiapologetic salute and followed Truttwell toward the front door. Emilio came running to let us out. But Irene Chalmers intercepted him and us.

"Where did this alleged shooting take place, Mr. Archer?"

"In the local hobo jungle. Apparently it was done with the same gun that killed Harrow."

Chalmers came up behind his wife. "How can you know that?" he said to me.

"The police have ballistic evidence."

"And they suspect Nick? Fifteen years ago he was only eight."

"I pointed that out to Captain Lackland."

Truttwell turned on me in surprise. "You've already discussed this with him?"

"Not in the sense that I answered his questions. He's the source for most of my information about that earlier killing."

"How did it come up between you?" Truttwell said.

"Lackland brought it up. I mentioned it just now because I thought I should."

"I see." Truttwell's manner to me was smooth and neutral. "If you don't mind, I'd like to discuss this in private with Mr. and Mrs. Chalmers."

I waited outside in my car. It was a bright January day, with enough wind to put an edge on its sparkle. But the weight of what had happened in the house, and what had been said, lay heavily on my mind. I was afraid the Chalmerses were going to fire me off the case. It wasn't an easy case, but after a day and a night with the people involved in it, I wanted to finish it.

Truttwell came out eventually and got into the front seat of my car. "They asked me to dismiss you. I talked them out of it."

"I don't know if I should thank you."

"Neither do I. They're not easy people to deal with. They had to be convinced you weren't playing footsie with Lackland."

He meant it as a question, which I answered: "I wasn't. I do have to cooperate with him, though. He's been on this case for fifteen years. I've been on it less than one day."

"Did he specifically accuse Nick of anything?"

"Not quite. He mentioned that a child could fire a gun."

Truttwell's eyes grew small and bright, like little pellets of ice. "Do you think that really happened?"

"Lackland seems to be playing with the idea. Unfortunately, he has a dead man to back him up."

"Do you know who the dead man was?"

"It isn't definitely established. It may have been a wanted man named Eldon Swain."

"Wanted for what?"

"Embezzlement. There's one other thing which I hate to mention but I have to." I paused. I really did hate to mention it. "Before I brought Nick in yesterday he made a sort of confession to a shooting. His confession fits the old shooting, the Swain shooting, better than the shooting of Harrow. Actually he may have been confessing both at once."

Truttwell rapped his fists together several times. "We have to get him back before he talks his life away."

"Is Betty at home?"

Her father glanced sharply at me. "You're not going to use her as a decoy, or a bird dog."

"Or a woman? She is one."

"Before everything else she's my daughter." It was one of Truttwell's more self-revealing statements. "She's not getting mixed up in a murder case."

I didn't bother reminding him that she already was. "Does Nick have any other friends I could talk to?"

"I doubt it. He's always been pretty much of a loner. Which was one of my objections—" Truttwell cut himself short. "Dr. Smitheram may be your best bet, if you can get him to talk. I've been trying to for fifteen years." He added dryly: "He and I suffer from professional incompatibility, I'm afraid."

"When you say fifteen years—?"

Truttwell answered my half-finished question: "I remember that something did happen involving Nick when he was in second or third grade. One day he didn't come home from school. His mother phoned me and asked me what to do. I gave her some standard advice. Whether or not she followed it I still don't know. But the boy was home the following day. And Smitheram's been treating him off and on ever since. Not too successfully, I might add."

"Did Mrs. Chalmers give you any idea of what happened?"

"Nick either ran away or was abducted. I think the latter. And I think—" Truttwell wrinkled his nose as if at a bad smell—"sex was involved."

"So you said yesterday. What kind of sex?"

"Abnormal," he said shortly.

"Did Mrs. Chalmers say so?"

"Not explicitly. It was everyone's deep silence on the subject." His voice trailed off.

"Murder makes for even deeper silence."

Truttwell sniffed. "An eight-year-old boy is incapable of murder, in any real sense."

"I know that. But eight-year-old boys don't know it, especially if the whole thing is hushed up around them."

Truttwell moved uncomfortably in the seat, as if he was being crowded by ugly images. "I'm afraid you're jumping to conclusions, Archer."

"These aren't conclusions. They're hypotheses."

"Aren't we getting rather far afield from your initial assignment?"

"We always expected to, didn't we? Incidentally, I wish you'd reconsider about Betty. She may know where Nick is."

"She doesn't," Truttwell said shortly. "I asked her myself."

XV

I dropped Truttwell off downtown. He told me how to get to Dr. Smitheram's clinic, which turned out to be a large new building on the fashionable borders of Montevista. "Smitheram Clinic, 1967" was cut in the stone facing over the main door.

A handsome woman with dark-brown hair came out into the windowless waiting room and asked me if I had an appointment.

I said I hadn't. "There's an emergency involving one of Dr. Smitheram's patients."

"Which one?"

Her blue eyes were concerned. There was a slash of grey in her brown hair, as if time had thrust a loving hand through it.

"I'd rather tell the doctor," I said.

"You can discuss it with me. I'm Mrs. Smitheram, and I work professionally with my husband." She gave me a smile which may have been professional but felt real. "Are you a relative?"

"No. My name is Archer—"

"Of course," she said. "The detective. Dr. Smitheram has been expecting you to call." She scanned my face, and frowned a little. "Has something else happened?"

"All hell has been breaking loose. I wish you'd let me talk to the doctor."

She looked at her watch. "I simply can't. He has a patient with him, with half an hour to go. I can't interrupt them except in a serious emergency."

"This is one. Nick's run away again. And I think the police are getting ready to make a move."

She reacted as if she was Nick's co-conspirator: "To arrest him?"

"Yes."

"That's foolish and unfair. He was just a small boy—" She cut the sentence in half, as if a censor had come awake in her head.

"Just a small boy when he did what, Mrs. Smitheram?"

72

She drew a deep angry breath and let it out in a faint droning sound of resignation. She went through an inner door and closed it behind her.

Eventually Smitheram came out, enormous in a white smock. He looked slightly remote, like a man coming out of a waking dream, and he shook hands with me impatiently.

"Where has Nick gone to, anyway?"

"I have no idea. He just took off."

"Who was looking after him?"

"His father."

"That's preposterous. I warned them that the boy needed security, but Truttwell vetoed that." His anger was running on, finding new objects, as if it was really anger with himself. "If they refuse to take my advice I'll wash my hands of the business."

"You can't do that and you know it," his wife said from the doorway. "The police are after Nick."

"Or soon will be," I said.

"What have they got on him?"

"Suspicion of two killings. You probably know more about the details than I do."

Dr. Smitheram's eyes met mine in a kind of confrontation. I could feel that I was up against a strong devious will.

"You're assuming a good deal."

"Look, doctor. Couldn't we put down the foils and talk like human beings? We both want to bring Nick home safe, keep him out of jail, get his sickness cured—whatever it is."

"That's a large order," he said with a cheerless smile. "And we don't seem to be making much progress, do we?"

"All right. Where would he go?"

"That's hard to say. Three years ago he was gone for several months. He wandered all over the country as far as the east coast."

"We don't have three months, or three days. He took along several batches of sleeping pills and tranquilizers—chloral hydrate, Nembutal, Nembu-Serpin."

Smitheram's eyes wavered and darkened. "That's bad. He's sometimes suicidal, as you undoubtedly know."

"Why is he suicidal?"

"He's had an unfortunate life. He blames himself, as if he was criminally responsible for his misfortunes."

"You mean he isn't?"

"I mean that no one is." He said it as if he believed it. "But you and I shouldn't be standing here talking. In any case, I'm not going to divulge my patient's secrets." He made a move toward the inner door.

"Wait a minute, doctor. Just one minute. Your patient's life may be in danger, you know that."

"Please," Mrs. Smitheram said. "Talk to the man, Ralph."

Dr. Smitheram turned back to me, bowing his head in a slightly exaggerated attitude of service. I didn't ask him the question I wanted to, about the dead man in the hobo jungle; it would only produce widening circles of silence.

"Did Nick talk to you at all last night?" I said.

"He did to some extent. His parents and his fiancée were present most of the time. They were an inhibiting influence, naturally."

"Did he mention any names, of people or places? I'm trying to get a line on where he might have gone."

The doctor nodded. "I'll get my notes."

He left the room and brought back a couple of sheets of paper, illegibly scrawled over. He put on reading glasses and scanned them rapidly.

"He mentioned a woman named Jean Trask whom he's been seeing."

"How did he feel about her?"

"Ambivalent. He seemed to blame her for his troubles—it wasn't clear why. At the same time he seemed rather interested in her."

"Sexually interested?"

"I wouldn't put it that way. His feeling was more fraternal. He also referred to a man named Randy Shepherd. In fact he wanted my help in finding Shepherd."

"Did he say why?"

"Apparently Shepherd was or may have been a witness to something that happened long ago."

Smitheram left me before I could ask any further questions. His wife and I exchanged the numbers of our respective telephone-answering services. But she wouldn't let me go just yet. Her eyes were slightly wilted, as if she'd disappointed herself in some way.

"I know it's exasperating," she said, "not to be given the facts. We operate this way because we have to. My husband's patients hold nothing back, you see. It's essential to treatment."

"I understand that."

"And please believe me when I say that we're very much in Nick's corner. Both Dr. Smitheram and I are very fond of him—of his whole family. They've had more than their share of misfortune, as he said."

Both the Smitherams were masters of the art of talking quite a lot without saying much. But Mrs. Smitheram seemed to be a lively woman who would have liked to talk freely. She followed me to the door, still dissatisfied with what she'd said or left unsaid.

"Believe me, Mr. Archer, there are things in my files you wouldn't want to know."

"And in mine. Someday we'll exchange histories."

"That will be a day," she said with a smile.

There was a public phone in the lobby of the Smitheram building. I called San Diego Information, got George Trask's number, and put in a call to his home. The phone rang many times before the receiver was lifted.

"Hello?" It was Jean Trask's voice, and it sounded scared and dim. "Is that you, George?"

"This is Archer. If Nick Chalmers shows up there—"

"He better not. I don't want anything more to do with him."

"If he does, though, keep him with you. He's carrying a pocketful of barbiturates, and I think he plans to take them."

"I suspected he was psycho," the woman said. "Did he kill Sidney Harrow?"

"I doubt it."

"He did, though, didn't he? Is he after me? Is that why you called?" The quick forced rhythms of fear had entered her voice.

"I have no reason to think so." I changed the subject: "Do you know a Randy Shepherd, Mrs. Trask?"

"It's funny you should ask me that. I was just—" Her voice stopped dead.

"You were just what?"

"Nothing. I was thinking of something else. I don't know anybody by that name."

She was lying. But you can't unravel lies on the telephone. San Diego was an easy trip, and I decided to go there, unannounced.

"Too bad," I said, and hung up.

I tried Information again. Randy Shepherd had no phone listed in the San Diego area. I called Rawlinson's house in Pasadena, and Mrs. Shepherd answered.

"Archer speaking. Remember me?"

"Naturally, I remember you. If it's Mr. Rawlinson you want, he's still in bed."

"It's you I want, Mrs. Shepherd. How can I get in touch with your former husband?"

"You can't through me. Has he done wrong again?"

"Not to my knowledge. A boy I know is carrying a lot of sleeping pills and planning suicide. Shepherd may be able to lead me to him."

"What boy are you talking about?" she said in a guarded tone.

"Nick Chalmers. You wouldn't know him."

"No, I wouldn't. And I can't give you Shepherd's address, I doubt he has one. He lives someplace in the Tijuana River Valley, down by the Mexican border."

XVI

I got to San Diego shortly before noon. The Trask house on Bayview Avenue stood near the base of Point Loma, overlooking North Island and the bay. It was a solid hillside ranchhouse with a nicely tended lawn and flowerbeds.

I knocked on the front door with an iron knocker shaped like a seahorse. No answer. I knocked and waited, and tried the knob. The door didn't open.

I walked around the outside of the house, peering into the windows, trying to act like a prospective purchaser. The windows were heavily draped. Apart from a glimpse of birch cupboard and a stainless-steel sink pagodaed with dirty dishes, I couldn't see anything. The attached garage was latched on the inside.

I went back to my car, which I'd parked diagonally across the street, and settled down to wait. The house was ordinary enough, but somehow it gripped my attention. The traffic of the harbor and the sky, ferries and fishing boats, planes and gulls, all seemed to move in relation to it.

The waiting minutes were long-drawn-out. Delivery vans

went by, and a few carsful of children chauffeured by mothers. The street wasn't much used by the people who lived on it, except for transportation. The people kept to their houses, as if to express a sense of property, and a sense of isolation.

An old car that didn't belong on the street came up the hill trailing oil smoke and preceded by the clatter of a fan belt that needed lubrication. A big rawboned man wearing a dirty gray windbreaker and a dirty gray beard got out and crossed the street, silent in worn sneakers. He was carrying a round Mexican basket under one arm. He knocked, as I had, on the Trask's front door. He tried the knob, as I had.

He looked up and down the street and at me, the movements of his head as quick and instinctive as an old animal's. I was reading a San Diego County road map. When I looked at the man again, he had opened the door and was closing it behind him.

I got out of my car and noted the registration of his: Randolph Shepherd, Conchita's Cabins, Imperial Beach. His keys were in the ignition. I put them in the same pocket as my keys.

A folded copy of the Los Angeles *Times* lay on the right side of the front seat, open at the third page. Under a two-column head there was an account of Sidney Harrow's death and a picture of his young swinger's face, which I had never really seen.

I was named as the discoverer of the body, nothing more. Nick Chalmers wasn't named. But Captain Lackland was quoted as saying that he expected to make an arrest within the next twenty-four hours.

My head was still in Shepherd's car when he opened the door of the Trask house. He came out furtively but rapidly, almost with abandon, as if he'd been pushed out by an explosion in the house. For a moment his eyes were perfectly round, like clouded marbles, and his mouth a round red hole in his beard.

He stopped short when he saw me. He looked up and down the open sunlit street as if he was in a cul-de-sac surrounded by high walls.

"Hello, Randy."

He showed his brown teeth in a grin of puzzlement. With enormous unwillingness, like a man wading into a cold deepening sea, he came across the road toward me. He let his grin become loose and foolish.

"I was just bringing Miss Jean some tomatoes. I used to tend the garden for Miss Jean's daddy. I got a real green thumb, see."

He raised his thumb. It was big and spatulate, grained with dirt, and armed with a jagged dirty nail.

"Do you always pick the lock when you make a delivery, Randy?"

"How come you know my name? Are you a cop?"

"Not exactly."

"How come you know my name?"

"You're famous. I've been wanting to meet you."

"Who are you? A cop?"

"A private cop."

He made a quick bad decision. He had been making them all his life: his scarred face bore the record of them. He jabbed at my eyes with his thumbnail. At the same time he tried to knee me.

I caught his jabbing hand and twisted it. For a moment we were perfectly poised and still. Shepherd's eyes were bright with rage. He couldn't sustain it, though. His face went through a series of transformations, like stop-time pictures of a man growing tired and old. His hand went limp, and I let go of it.

"Listen, boss, is it all right if I go now? I got a lot of other deliveries to make."

"What are you delivering? Trouble?"

"No sir. Not me." He glanced at the Trask house as if its presence on the street had caught him by surprise. "I got a quick temper but I wouldn't hurt nobody. I didn't hurt *you.* You were the one hurt me. I'm the one that's always getting hurt."

"But not the only one."

He winced as if I had made a cruel remark. "What are you getting at, mister?"

"There've been a couple of killings. That isn't news to you." I reached for the newspaper on the seat of his car and showed him Harrow's picture.

"I never saw him in my life," he said.

"You had the paper open at this story."

"Not me. I picked it up that way at the station. I always pick up my papers at the station." He leaned toward me, sweaty and jumpy. "Listen, I got to go now, okay? I got a serious call of nature."

"This is more important."

"Not to me it isn't."

"To you, too. You know a young man named Nick Chalmers?"

"He isn't—" He caught himself, and started over: "What did you say?"

"You heard me. I'm looking for Nick Chalmers. He may be looking for you."

"What for? I never touched him. When I found out that Swain was planning a snatch—" He caught himself again and covered his mouth with his hand, as if he could force the words back in or hide them like birds in his beard.

"Did Swain snatch the Chalmers boy?"

"Why ask me? I'm as clean as a whistle." But he peered up at the sky with narrowed eyes as if he could see a sky hook or a noose descending toward him. "I gotta get out of this sun. It gives me skin cancer."

"It's a nice slow death. Swain died a quicker one."

"You'll never pin it on me, 'bo. Even the cops at the Point turned me loose."

"They wouldn't have if they'd known what I do."

He moved closer to me, cringing on bent knees, making himself look smaller. "I'm clean, honest to God. *Please* let me go now, mister."

"We've barely started."

"But we can't just stand here."

"Why not?"

His head turned on his neck like an automatic mechanism, and he looked at the Trask house once again. My gaze followed his. I noticed that the front door was a few inches ajar.

"You left the front door open. We better go over and shut it."

"You shut it," he said. "I got a bad charley horse in my leg. I gotta sit down or I'll fall down."

He climbed in behind the wheel of his jalopy. He wouldn't get far without an ignition key, I thought, and I crossed the street. Looking through the crack between the door and the lintel, I could see red tomatoes scattered on the floor of the hallway. I went in, stepping carefully to avoid them.

There was a smell of burning from the kitchen. I found that a glass coffeemaker on an electric plate had boiled dry and cracked. Jean Trask was lying near it on the green vinyl floor.

I pulled the plug of the electric plate, and knelt down

beside Jean. She had stab wounds in her breast and one great gash in her throat. Her body was clothed in pajamas and a pink nylon robe, and it was still warm.

Even though Jean was dead, I could hear breathing somewhere. It sounded as if the house itself was breathing. An open door led through the back kitchen, past the washer and dryer, into the attached garage.

George Trask's Ford sedan was standing in the garage. Nick Chalmers was lying face up beside it on the concrete floor. I loosened his shirt collar. Then I looked at his eyes: they were turned up. I slapped him hard, once on each side of his face. No response. I heard myself groan.

Three empty drugstore tubes of varying sizes lay near him on the floor. I picked them up and put them in my pocket. There was no time for any further search. I had to get Nick to a stomach pump.

I raised the garage door, crossed the street for my car, and backed it into the driveway. I lifted Nick in my arms—he was a big man and it wasn't easy—and laid him on the back seat. I closed the garage. I pulled the front door of the house shut.

I noticed then that Randy Shepherd and his jalopy had gone. No doubt he was just as good at starting keyless cars as he was at opening locked doors. Under the circumstances, I could hardly blame him for leaving.

XVII

I drove down Rosecrans to Highway 80 and delivered Nick at the ambulance entrance of the hospital. There had been a recent auto accident, and everybody on the emergency ward was busy. Looking for a stretcher, I opened a door and saw a dead man and closed the door again.

I found a wheeled stretcher in another room, took it outside and heaved Nick onto it. I pushed him up to the emergency desk.

"This boy needs a stomach pump. He's full of barbiturates."

"Another one?" the nurse said.

She produced a paper form to be filled out. Then she

glanced at Nick's face and I think she was touched by his inert good looks. She dispensed with red tape for the present. She helped me to wheel Nick into a treatment room and called in a young doctor with an Armenian name.

The doctor checked Nick's pulse and respiration, and looked at the pupils of his eyes, which were contracted. He turned to me.

"What did he take, do you know?"

I showed him the drug containers I had picked up in the Trasks' garage. They had Lawrence Chalmers's name on them, and the names and amounts of the three drugs they had contained: chloral hydrate, Nembutal and Nembu-Serpin.

He looked at me inquiringly. "He hasn't taken all of these?"

"I don't know if the prescriptions were full. I don't think they were."

"Let's hope the chloral hydrate wasn't, anyway. Twenty of those capsules are enough to kill two men."

As he spoke, the doctor began to thread a flexible plastic tube into Nick's nostril. He told the nurse to cover him with a blanket, and prepare a glucose injection. Then he turned to me again.

"How long ago did he swallow the stuff?"

"I don't know exactly. Maybe two hours. What's Nembu-Serpin, by the way?"

"A combination of Nembutal and reserpine. It's a tranquil-izer used in treating hypertension, also in psychiatric treat-ment." His eyes met mine. "Is the boy emotionally dis-turbed?"

"Somewhat."

"I see. Are you a relative?"

"A friend," I said.

"The reason I ask, he'll have to be admitted. In suicide attempts like this the hospital requires round-the-clock nurs-es. That costs money."

"It shouldn't be any problem. His father's a millionaire."

"No kidding." He was unimpressed. "Also, his regular doctor should see him before he's admitted. Okay?"

"I'll do my best, doctor."

I found a telephone booth and called the Chalmerses' house in Pacific Point. Irene Chalmers answered.

"This is Archer. May I speak to your husband?"

"Lawrence isn't here. He's out looking for Nick."

"He can stop looking. I found him."

"Is he all right?"

"No. He took the drugs, and he's having his stomach pumped out. I'm calling from the San Diego Hospital. Have you got that?"

"The San Diego Hospital, yes. I know the place, I'll be there as soon as I can."

"Bring Dr. Smitheram with you, and John Truttwell."

"I'm not sure I can do that."

"Tell them it's a major emergency. It really is, Mrs. Chalmers."

"Is he dying?"

"He could die. Let's hope he doesn't. Incidentally you'd better bring a checkbook. He's going to need special nurses."

"Yes, of course. Thank you." Her voice was blank, and I couldn't tell if she had really heard me.

"You'll bring a checkbook, then, or some cash."

"Yes. Certainly. I was just thinking, life is so strange, it seems to go in circles. Nick was born in that same hospital, and now you say he may die there."

"I don't think he will, Mrs. Chalmers."

But she had begun to cry. I listened to her for a little while, until she hung up on me.

Because it wasn't good policy to leave a murder unreported, I called the San Diego Police Department and gave the sergeant on duty George Trask's address on Bayview Avenue. "There's been an accident."

"What kind of an accident?"

"A woman got cut."

The sergeant's voice became louder and more interested: "What is your name, please?"

I hung up and leaned on the wall. My head was empty. I think I almost fainted. Remembering that I'd missed my breakfast, I wandered through the hospital and found the cafeteria. I drank a couple of glasses of milk and had some toast with a soft-boiled egg, like an invalid. The morning's events had hit me in the stomach.

I went back to the emergency ward where Nick was still being worked on.

"How is he?"

"It's hard to tell," the doctor said. "If you'll fill out his form we'll admit him provisionally and put him in a private room. Okay?"

82

"That's fine. His mother and his psychiatrist should be here within an hour or so."

The doctor raised his eyebrows. "How sick is he?"

"You mean in the head? Sick enough."

"I was wondering." He reached under his white coat and produced a torn scrap of paper. "This fell out of his breast pocket."

He handed it to me. It was a penciled note:

"I am a murderer and deserve to die. Forgive me, Mother and Dad. I love you Betty."

"He isn't a murderer, is he?" the doctor said.

"No."

My denial sounded unconvincing to me, but the doctor accepted it. "Ordinarily the police would want to see that suicide note. But there's no use making further trouble for the guy."

I folded the note and put it in my wallet and got out of there before he changed his mind.

XVIII

I drove south to Imperial Beach. The cashier of a drive-in restaurant told me how to find Conchita's Cabins. "You wouldn't want to stay in them, though," she advised me.

I saw what she meant when I got there. It was a ruined place, as ancient-looking as an archeological digging. A sign on the office said: "One dollar per person. Children free." The cabins were small stucco cubes that had taken a beating from the weather. The largest building, with "Beer and Dancing" inscribed across its front, had long since been boarded up.

The place was redeemed by a soft green cottonwood tree and its soft gray shade. I stood under it for a minute, waiting for somebody to discover me.

A heavy-bodied woman came out of one of the cabins. She wore a sleeveless dress which showed her large brown arms, and a red cloth on her head.

"Conchita?"

"I'm Mrs. Florence Williams. Conchita's been dead for

thirty years. Williams and I kept on with her name when we bought the cabins." She looked around her as if she hadn't really seen the place for a long time. "You wouldn't think it, but these cabins were a real moneymaker during the war."

"There's a lot more competition now."

"You're telling me." She joined me in the shadow of the tree. "What can I do for you? If you're selling don't even bother to open your mouth. I just lost my second-to-last roomer." She made a farewell gesture toward the open door of the cabin.

"Randy Shepherd?"

She stepped away from me and looked me up and down. "You're after him, eh? I figured somebody was, the way he took off and left his things. The only trouble is, they're not worth much. They're not worth ten per cent of the money he owes me."

She was looking at me appraisingly, and I returned the look. "How much would that be, Mrs. Williams?"

"It adds up to hundreds of dollars, over the years. After my husband died, he talked me into investing money in his big treasure hunt. That was back around 1950, when he got out of the clink."

"Treasure hunt?"

"For buried money," she said. "Randy rented heavy equipment and dug up most of my place and half the county besides. This place has never been the same since, and neither have I. It was like a hurricane went through."

"I'd like to buy a piece of that treasure hunt."

She countered rapidly: "You can have my share for a hundred dollars, even."

"With Randy Shepherd thrown in?"

"I don't know about *that*." The talk of money had brightened her dusty eyes. "This wouldn't be blood money that we're talking about?"

"I'm not planning to kill him."

"Then what's he so a-scared of? I never saw him scared like this before. How do I know you won't kill him?"

I told her who I was and showed her my photostat. "Where has he gone, Mrs. Williams?"

"Let's see the hundred dollars."

I got two fifties out of my wallet and gave her one of them. "I'll give you the other after I talk to Shepherd. Where can I find him?"

She pointed south along the road. "He's on his way to the

border. He's on foot, and you can't miss him. He only left here about twenty minutes ago."

"What happened to his car?"

"He sold it to a parts dealer up the hike. That's what makes me think he's crossing over to Mexico. I know he's done it before, he's got friends to hide him."

I started for my car. She followed me, moving with surprising speed.

"Don't tell him I told you, will you? He'll come back some dark night and take it out of my hide."

"I won't tell him, Mrs. Williams."

With my road map on the seat beside me, I drove due south through farmland. I passed a field where Holstein cattle were grazing. Then the tomato fields began, spreading in every direction. The tomatoes had been harvested, but I could see a few hanging red and wrinkled on the withering vines.

When I had traveled about a mile and a half, the road took a jog and ran through low chaparral. I caught sight of Shepherd. He was tramping along quickly, almost loping, with a bedroll bouncing across his shoulders and a Mexican hat on his head. Not far ahead of him Tijuana sloped against the sky like a gorgeous junk heap.

Shepherd turned and saw my car. He began to run. He plunged off the road into the brush and reappeared in the dry channel of a river. He had lost his floppy Mexican hat but still had his bedroll.

I left my car and went after him. A rattlesnake buzzed at me from under an ocotillo, and focused my attention. When I looked for Shepherd again, he had disappeared.

Making as little noise as possible, and keeping my head down, I moved through the chaparral to the road which ran parallel with the border fence. The road map called it Monument Road. If Shepherd planned to cross the border, he would have to cross Monument Road first. I settled down in the ditch beside it, keeping an alternating watch in both directions.

I waited for nearly an hour. The birds in the brush got used to me, and the insects became familiar. The sun moved very slowly down the sky. I kept looking one way and then the other, like a spectator at a languid tennis match.

When Shepherd made his move, it was far from languid. He came out of the brush about two hundred yards west of me, scuttled across the road with his bedroll bouncing, and headed up the slope toward the high wire fence that marked the border.

The ground between the road and the fence had been cleared. I cut across it and caught Shepherd before he went over. He turned with his back to the fence and said between hard breaths:

"You stay away from me. I'll cut your gizzard."

A knife blade stuck out of his fist. On the hillside beyond the fence a group of small boys and girls appeared as if they had sprouted from the earth.

"Drop the knife," I said a little wearily. "We're attracting a lot of attention."

I pointed up the hill toward the children. Some of them pointed back at me. Some waved. Shepherd was tempted to look, and turned his head a little to one side.

I moved hard on his knife arm and put an armlock on it which forced him to drop the knife. I picked it up and closed it and tossed it over the fence into Mexico. One of the little boys came scrambling down the hill for it.

Further up the hill, where the houses began, an invisible musician began to play bullfight music on a trumpet. I felt as if Mexico was laughing at me. It wasn't a bad feeling.

Shepherd was almost crying. "I'm not going back to a bum murder rap. You put me behind the walls again, it'll kill me."

"I don't think you killed Jean Trask."

He gave me an astonished look, which quickly faded. "You're just saying that."

"No. Let's get out of here, Randy. You don't want the border patrol to pick you up. We'll go some place where we can talk."

"Talk about what?"

"I'm ready to make a deal with you."

"Not me. I allus get the short end of the deals."

He had the cynicism of a small-time thief. I was getting impatient with him.

"Move, con."

I took him by the arm and walked him down the slope toward the road. A child's voice nearly as high as a whistle called to us from Mexico above the sound of the trumpet:

"Adios."

XIX

Shepherd and I walked east along Monument Road to its intersection with the road that ran north and south. He hung back when he saw my car. It could take him so fast and so far, all the way back to the penitentiary.

"Get it through your head, Randy, I don't want you. I want your information."

"And what do *I* get out of it?"

"What do you want?"

He answered quickly and ardently, like a man who has been defrauded of his rights: "I want a fair shake for once in my life. And enough money to live on. How can a man help breaking the law if he don't have money to live on?"

It was a good question.

"If I had my rights," he went on, "I'd be a rich man. I wouldn't be living on tortillas and chili."

"Are we talking about Eldon Swain's money?"

"It ain't Swain's money. It belongs to anybody who finds it. The statute of limitations ran out years ago," he said in the legalese of a cell-block lawyer, "and the money's up for grabs."

"Where is it?"

"Someplace in this very area." He made a sweeping gesture which took in the dry riverbed and the empty fields beyond. "I been making a study of this place for twenty years, I know it like the back of my hand." He sounded like a prospector who had worn out his wits in the desert looking for gold. "All I need is to get real lucky and find me the coordinates. I'm Eldon Swain's legal heir."

"How so?"

"We made a deal. He was interested in a relative of mine." He probably meant his daughter. "And so we made a deal."

The thought of it lifted his spirits. He got into my car without argument, hoisting his bedroll into the back seat.

"Where do we go from here?" he said.

"We might as well stay where we are for the present."

"And then?"

"We go our separate ways."

He glanced quickly at my face, as if to catch me in a false expression. "You're conning me."

"Wait and see. Let's get one thing out of the way first. Why did you go to Jean Trask's house today?"

"Take her some tomatoes."

"Why did you pick the lock?"

"I thought maybe she was sleeping. Sometimes she sleeps real heavy, when she's been drinking. I didn't know she was dead, man. I wanted to talk to her."

"About Sidney Harrow?"

"That was part of it. I knew the cops would be asking her questions about him. The fact is, I was the one introduced her to Sidney, and I wanted Miss Jean not to mention my name to the cops."

"Because you were a suspect in Swain's death?"

"That was part of it. I knew they'd be opening up that old case. If my name came up and they traced my connection with Swain, I'd be right back on the hooks. Hell, my connection with Swain went back thirty years."

"Which is why you didn't identify his body."

"That's right."

"And you let Jean go on thinking her father was alive, and go on looking for him."

"It made her feel better," he said. "She never found out how he died."

"Who shot him?"

"I don't know. Honest to God. I only know I didn't."

"You mentioned a snatch."

"That's right. It's where him and I parted company. I admit I been a thief in my time, but strong-arm stuff was never for me. When he started to plan this snatch, I backed out on him." Shepherd added meditatively: "When Swain came back from Mexico in 1954, he wasn't the man he used to was. I think he went a little crazy down there."

"Did Swain kidnap Nick Chalmers?"

"That's the one he was talking about. I never saw the boy myself. I was long gone when it happened. And it never came out in the papers. I guess the parents hushed it up."

"Why would a man with half a million dollars attempt a kidnapping?"

"Ask me another. Swain kept changing his story. Sometimes he claimed he had the half million, sometimes he said he didn't. Sometimes he claimed he had it and lost it. He said once he was highjacked by a border guard. His wildest story was the one about Mr. Rawlinson. Mr. Rawlinson was the president of the bank that Eldon Swain worked for, and he claimed Mr. Rawlinson took the money and framed him for it."

"Could that have happened?"

"I don't see how. Mr. Rawlinson wouldn't ruin his own bank. And he's been on his uppers ever since. I know that for certain because I got a relative works for him."

"Your ex-wife."

"You get around," he said in some surprise. "Did you talk to her?"

"A little."

He leaned toward me, keenly interested. "What did she say about me?"

"We didn't discuss you."

Shepherd seemed disappointed, as if he had been robbed of a dimension. "I see her from time to time. I bear no grudges, even if she did divorce me when I was in the pen. I was kind of glad to make the break," he said dolefully. "She's got mixed blood, you probably noticed that. It kind of hurt my pride to be married to her."

"We were talking about the money," I reminded him. "You're pretty certain that Swain took it and kept it."

"I know he did. He had it with him at Conchita's place. This was right after he lifted it."

"You saw it?"

"I know somebody who did."

"Your daughter?"

"No." He added with a touch of belligerence: "Leave my daughter out of this. She's going straight."

"Where?"

"Mexico. She went to Mexico with him and never came back from there." His answer sounded a little glib, and I wondered if it was true.

"Why did Swain come back?"

"He always planned to, that's my theory. He left the money buried on this side of the border, he told me so himself more than once. He offered me a share of it if I would go partners with him and drive him around and grubstake him. Like I said, he wasn't in very good shape when he came back. Fact is, he needed a keeper."

"And you were his keeper?"

"That's right. I owed him something. He was a pretty good

man at one time, Eldon Swain was. When I hit the pavement the first time, on parole, he took me on as a gardener at his place in San Marino. It was a real showplace. I used to grow him roses as big as dahlias. It's a terrible thing when a man like that ends up dead of lead poisoning in a railroad yard."

"Did you drive Swain to Pacific Point in 1954?"

"I admit that much. But that was before he started to talk about snatching the boy. I wouldn't drive him on that caper. I got out of town in a hurry. I wanted no part—"

"You didn't shoot him before you left, by any chance?"

He gave me a shocked look. "No *sir*. You don't know much about me, mister. I'm not a man of violence. I specialize in staying out of trouble, out of jail. And I'm still working at it."

"What were you sent up for?"

"Car theft. Break and enter. But I never carried a gun."

"Maybe somebody else shot Swain and you burned off his fingerprints."

"That's crazy. Why would I do that?"

"So that you wouldn't be traced through him. Let's say you took the ransom money from Swain."

"What ransom money? I never saw any ransom money. I was back here on the border by the time he took the boy."

"Was Eldon Swain a child molester?"

Shepherd squinted at the sky. "Could be. He always liked 'em young, and the older he got the younger he liked 'em. Sex was always his downfall."

I didn't believe Shepherd. I didn't disbelieve him. The mind that looked at me through his eyes was like muddy water continually stirred by fears and fantasies and greeds. He was growing old in the desperate hope of money, and by now he was willing to become whatever the hope suggested.

"Where are you going now, Randy? To Mexico?"

He was quiet for a moment, peering out across the flatland toward the sun, which was halfway down the west. A Navy jet flew over like a swallow towing the noises of a freight train. Shepherd watched it out of sight, as if it represented his last disappearing luck.

"I better not tell you where I'm going, mister. If we need to get in touch again I'll get in touch with you. Just don't try to pull a fast one on me. So you saw me at Miss Jean's house. That puts you on the same spot."

90

"Not quite. But I won't turn you in unless I find some reason."

"You won't. I'm as clean as soap. And you're a white man," he added, sharing with me his one dubious distinction. "How about a little traveling money?"

I gave him fifty dollars and my name, and he seemed satisfied. He got out of the car with his bedroll and stood waiting by the roadside until I lost sight of him in my rear-view mirror.

I drove back to the cabins and found Mrs. Williams still working in the one that Shepherd had vacated. When I appeared in the doorway, she looked up from her sweeping with pleased surprise.

"I never thought you'd come back," she said. "I guess you didn't find him, eh?"

"I found him. We had a talk."

"Randy's a great talker."

She was stalling, unwilling to ask me outright for the second installment of her money. I gave her the other fifty. She held it daintily in her fingers, as if she had captured some rare specimen of moth or butterfly, then tucked it away in her bosom.

"I thank you kindly. I can use this money. I guess you know how it is."

"I guess I do. Are you willing to help me with more information, Mrs. Williams?"

She smiled. "I'll tell you anything but my age."

She sat down on the stripped mattress of the bed, which creaked and sank under her weight. I took the only chair in the room. A shaft of sunlight fell through the window, swarming with brilliant dust. It laid down a swatch of brightness between us on the worn linoleum floor.

"What do you want to know?"

"How long has Shepherd been staying here?"

"Off and on since the war. He comes and he goes. When he got really hungry he used to travel with the fruit pickers sometimes. Or he'd pick up a dollar or two weeding somebody's garden. He was a gardener at one time."

"He told me that. He worked for a Mr. Swain in San Marino. Did he ever mention Eldon Swain to you?"

The question made her unhappy. She looked down at her knee and began pleating her skirt. "You want me to tell it like it is, like the kids say?"

"Please do."

"It don't make me look good. The trouble is in this business you get so you'll do things for money that you wouldn't start out doing when you're young and fresh. There's nothing people won't do for money."

"I know that. What are you leading up to, Florence?"

She said in a hurried monotone, as if to reduce the size and duration of her guilt: "Eldon Swain stayed here with his girl friend. She was Randy Shepherd's daughter. That's what brought Randy here in the first place."

"When was this?"

"Let's see. It was just before the trouble with the money, when Mr. Swain took off for Mexico. I don't have a good head for dates, but it was sometime along toward the end of the war." She added after a thinking pause: "I remember the Battle of Okinawa was going on. Williams and I used to follow the battles, so many of our roomers were sailor boys, you know."

I brought her back to the subject: "What happened when Shepherd came here?"

"Nothing much. A lot of loud talk mainly. I couldn't help but overhear some of it. Randy wanted to be paid for the loan of his daughter. That was the way his mind worked."

"What kind of a girl was the daughter?"

"She was a beautiful child." Mrs. Williams's eyes grew misty with the quasi-maternal feelings of a procuress. "Dark and tender-looking. It's hard to understand a girl like that, going with a man more than twice her age." She readjusted her position on the bed, and its springs squeaked in tired rhythms. "I don't doubt she was after her share of the money."

"This was before the money, you said."

"Sure, but Swain was already planning to take it."

"How do you know that, Mrs. Williams?"

"The officers said so. This place was swarming with officers the week after he took off. They said that he'd been planning it for at least a year. He picked this place for his final jumping-off place to Mexico."

"How did he cross the border?"

"They never did find out. He may have gone over the border fence, or crossed in the regular way under another name. Some of the officers thought he left the money behind. That's probably where Randy got the idea."

"What happened to the girl?"

"Nobody knows."

"Not even her father?"

"That's right. Randy Shepherd isn't the kind of father a girl would keep in touch with if she had a choice. Randy's wife felt the same way about him. She divorced him while he was in the pen the last time, and when he got out he came back here. He's been here off and on ever since."

We sat in silence for a little while. The rectangle of sunlight on the linoleum was lengthening perceptibly, measuring out the afternoon and the movement of the earth. Finally she asked me:

"Will Randy be coming back here, do you think?"

"I don't know, Mrs. Williams."

"I sort of hope he does. He's got a lot against him. But over the years a woman gets used to seeing a man around. It doesn't even matter what kind of man he is."

"Besides," I said, "he was your second-to-last roomer."

"How do you know that?"

"You told me."

"So I did. I'd sell this place if I could find a buyer."

I got up and moved toward the door. "Who's your last roomer?"

"Nobody you would know."

"Try me."

"A young fellow named Sidney Harrow. And I haven't seen *him* for a week. He's off on one of Randy Shepherd's wild-goose chases."

I produced the copy of Nick's graduation picture. "Did Shepherd give this to Harrow, Mrs. Williams?"

"He may have. I remember Randy showed me that picture. He wanted to know if it reminded me of anybody."

"Did it?"

"Nope. I'm not much good at faces."

XX

I went back to San Diego and drove out Bayview Avenue to George Trask's house. The sun had just set and everything was reddish, as if the blood in the kitchen of the house had formed a weak solution with the light.

A car I had seen before but couldn't remember where—a black Volkswagen with a crumpled fender—stood in the driveway of the Trask house. A San Diego police car was at the curb. I drove on by, and made my way back to the hospital.

Nick was in Room 211 on the second floor, the woman at the information desk told me. "But he's not allowed to have visitors unless you're immediate family."

I went up anyway. In the visitors' lounge across from the elevator Mrs. Smitheram, the psychiatrist's wife, was reading a magazine. A coat folded with the lining turned out was draped across the back of her chair. For some reason I was very glad to see her. I crossed to the lounge and sat down near her.

She wasn't reading after all, just holding the magazine. She was looking right at me, but she didn't see me. Her blue eyes were turned inward on her thoughts, which lent her face a grave beauty. I watched the changes in her eyes as she gradually became aware of me, and finally recognized me.

"Mr. Archer!"

"I wasn't expecting to see you, either."

"I just came along for the ride," she said. "I lived in San Diego County for several years during the war. I haven't been back here since."

"That's a long time."

She inclined her head. "I was just thinking about that long time and how it grew. But you're not interested in my autobiography."

"I am, though. Were you married when you lived here before?"

"In a sense. My husband was overseas most of the time. He was a flight surgeon on an escort carrier." Her voice had a rueful pride which seemed to belong entirely to the past.

"You're older than you look."

"I married young. Too young."

I liked the woman, and it was a pleasure to talk for once about something that had no bearing on my case. But she brought the conversation back to it:

"The latest on Nick is that he's coming out of it. The only question is in what condition."

"What does your husband think?"

"It's too early for Ralph to commit himself. Right now he's in consultation with a neurologist and a brain surgeon."

"They don't do brain surgery for barbiturate poisoning, do they?"

"Unfortunately, that's not the only thing the matter with Nick. He has a concussion. He must have fallen and hit the back of his head."

"Or been hit?"

"That's possible, too. How did he get to San Diego, anyway?"

"I don't know."

"My husband said you brought him here to the hospital."

"That's true. But I didn't bring him to San Diego."

"Where did you find him?"

I didn't answer her.

"Don't you want to tell me?"

"That's right." I changed the subject, not very smoothly. "Are Nick's parents here?"

"His mother's sitting with him. His father is on his way. There's nothing either you or I can do."

I stood up. "We could have dinner."

"Where?"

"The hospital cafeteria if you like. The food is fair."

She made a face. "I've eaten too many hospital-cafeteria dinners."

"I thought you mightn't want to go too far." The phrase had a double meaning that we both heard.

She said: "Why not? Ralph will be tied up for hours. Why don't we go out to La Jolla?"

"Is that where you used to live during the war?"

"You're a good guesser."

I helped her on with her coat. It was silver-blue mink complementing the slash of gray in her hair. In the elevator, she said:

"This is on one condition. You mustn't ask me questions about Nick and his family constellation. I can't answer certain questions, just as you can't, so why spoil things."

"I won't spoil things, Mrs. Smitheram."

"My name is Moira."

She was born in Chicago, she told me at dinner, and trained as a psychiatric social worker in the University of Michigan Hospital. There she met and married Ralph Smitheram, who was completing his residency in psychiatry. When he joined the Navy and was assigned to the San Diego Naval Hospital, she came along to California.

"We lived in a little old hotel here in La Jolla. It was sort of rundown but I loved it. After we finish dinner I want to go and see if it's still there."

"We can do that."

"I'm taking a chance, coming back here. I mean, you can't imagine how beautiful it was. It was my first experience of the ocean. When we went down to the cove in the early morning, I felt like Eve in the garden. Everything was fresh and new and spare. Not like this at all."

With a movement of her hand she dismissed her present surroundings: the thick pseudo-Hawaiian decor, the uniformed black waiters, the piped-in music, all the things that went with the fifteen-dollar Chateaubriand for two.

"This part of the town has changed," I agreed.

"Do you remember La Jolla in the forties?"

"Also the thirties. I lived in Long Beach then. We used to come down for the surf here and at San Onofre."

"Does 'we' refer to you and your wife?"

"Me and my buddies," I said. "My wife wasn't interested in surf."

"Past tense?"

"Historical. She divorced me back in those same forties. I don't blame her. She wanted a settled life, and a husband she could count on to be there."

Moira received my ancient news in silence. After a while she spoke half to herself: "I wish I'd gotten a divorce then." Her eyes came up to mine. "What did *you* want, Archer?"

"This."

"Do you mean being here with me?" I thought she was overeager for a compliment, then realized she was kidding me a little. "I hardly justify a lifetime of effort."

"The life is its own reward," I countered. "I like to move into people's lives and then move out again. Living with one set of people in one place used to bore me."

"That isn't your real motivation. I know your type. You have a secret passion for justice. Why don't you admit it?"

"I have a secret passion for mercy," I said. "But justice is what keeps happening to people."

She leaned toward me with that female malice which carries some sexual heat. "You know what's going to happen to you? You'll grow old and run out of yourself. Will that be justice?"

"I'll die first. That will be mercy."

"You're terribly immature, do you know that?"

"Terribly."

"Don't I make you angry?"

"Real hostility does. But you're not being hostile. On the contrary. You're off on the usual nurse kick, telling me I better marry again before I get too old, or I won't have anybody to nurse me in my old age."

"You!" She spoke with angry force, which changed into laughter.

After dinner we left my car where it was in the restaurant parking lot, and walked down the main street toward the water. The surf was high and I could hear it roaring and retreating like a sea lion frightened by the sound of his own voice.

We turned right at the top of the last slope and walked past a brand-new multistoried office building, toward a motel which stood on the next corner. Moira stood still and looked it over.

"I thought this was the corner, but it isn't. I don't remember that motel at all." Then she realized what had happened. "This *is* the corner, isn't it? They tore down the old hotel and put up the motel in its place." Her voice was full of emotion, as if a part of her past had been demolished with the old building.

"Wasn't it called the Magnolia Hotel?"

"That's right. The Magnolia. Did you ever stay there?"

"No," I said. "But it seems to have meant quite a lot to you."

"It did and does. I lived on there for two years after Ralph shipped out. I think now it was the realest part of my life. I've never told anyone about it."

"Not even your husband?"

"Certainly not Ralph." Her voice was sharp. "When you try to tell Ralph something, he doesn't hear it. He hears your motive for saying it, or what he thinks is your motive. He hears some of the implications. But he doesn't really hear the obvious meaning. It's an occupational hazard of psychiatrists."

"You're angry with your husband."

"Now you're doing it!" But she went on: "I'm deeply angry with him, and with myself. It's been growing on me for quite a while."

She had begun to walk, drawing me across the lighted corner and away from it downhill toward the sea. Spray hung in luminous clouds around the scattered lights. The green common and the waterfront path were virtually deserted. She began to talk again as we walked along the path.

"At first I was angry with myself for doing what I did. I was only nineteen when it started, and full of normal adolescent guilt. Later I was angry with myself for not following through."

"You're not making yourself entirely clear."

She had raised the collar of her coat against the spray. Now she looked at me over it like a desperado wearing a partial face mask: "I don't intend to, either."

"I think you want to, though."

"What's the use? It's all gone—completely past and gone."

Her voice was desolate. She walked quickly away from me, and I followed her. She was in an uncertain mood, a middle-aging woman groping for a line of continuity in her life. The path was dark and narrow, and it would be easy by accident or design to fall among the rocks in the boiling surf.

I caught up with her at the cove, the physical center of the past she had been talking about. The broken white water streamed up the slope of the beach. She took her shoes off and led me down the steps. We stood just above the reach of the water.

"Come and get me," she said to it or me or someone else.

"Were you in love with a man who died in the war?"

"He wasn't a man. He was just a boy who worked in the post office."

"Was he the one who came down here with you, when you felt like Eve in the garden?"

"He was the one. I still feel guilty about it. I lived here on the beach with another boy while Ralph was overseas defending his country." Her voice flattened sardonically whenever she spoke of her husband. "Ralph used to write me long dutiful letters, but somehow they made no difference. I actually wanted to undercut him, he was so superconfident and know-it-all. Do you think I'm slightly crazy?"

"No."

"Sonny was, you know. More than slightly."

"Sonny?"

"The boy I lived with in the Magnolia. Actually he'd been one of Ralph's patients, which is how I got to know him in

98

the first place. Ralph suggested that I keep an eye on him. There's an irony for you."

"Stop it, Moira. I thnk you're reaching for trouble."

"Some reach for it," she said. "Others have it thrust upon them. If I could just go back to that time and change a few things—"

"What would you change?"

"I'm not quite sure." She sounded rather dreary. "Let's not talk about it any more now."

She walked away from me. Her naked feet left wasp-waisted impressions in the sand. I admired the grace of her departing movements, but she came back toward me clumsily. She was walking backward, trying to fit her feet again into the prints she had made and not succeeding.

She walked into me and turned, her furred breast against my arm. I put my arm around her and held her. There were tears on her face, or spray. Anyway, it tasted salt.

XXI

The main street was quiet and bright when we walked back to the car. The stars were all in order, and quite near. I don't remember seeing any other people until I went into the restaurant to phone George Trask.

He answered right away, in a moist, overused voice: "This is the Trask residence."

I said I was a detective and would like to talk to him about his wife.

"My wife is dead."

"I'm sorry. May I come over and ask you a few questions?"

"I guess so." He sounded like a man who had no use for time.

Moira was waiting for me in the car, like a silver-blue cat in a cave.

"Do you want to be dropped at the hospital? I have an errand to do."

"Take me along."

"It's a fairly unpleasant errand."

"I don't care."

"You would if you lost your marriage and ended up with me. I spend a lot of my nights doing this kind of thing."

Her hand pressed my knee. "I know that I could be hurt. I've already made myself vulnerable. But I'm sick of always doing the professional thing for prudential reasons."

I took her along to Bayview Avenue. The police car was gone. The black Volkswagen with the crumpled fender was still in George Trask's driveway. I remembered now where I had seen it before; under Mrs. Swain's rusty carport in Pasadena.

I knocked on the front door and George Trask let us in. His gangling body was carefully dressed in a dark suit and black tie. He had an air of having made himself the servant of the situation, like a mortician. His grief showed only in his reddened eyes, and in the fact that he didn't remember me.

"This is Mrs. Smitheram, Mr. Trask. She's a psychiatric social worker."

"It's nice of you to come," he said to her. "But I don't need that kind of help. Everything's under control. Come into the living room and sit down, won't you? I'd offer to make you some coffee but I'm not allowed to go into the kitchen. And anyway," he went on, as if his voice was being piped in from someplace beyond his control, "the coffeemaker got broken this morning when my wife was murdered."

"I'm sorry," Moira said.

We followed George Trask into the living room and sat down beside each other, facing him. The window drapes were partly open, and I could see the lights of the city wavering on the water. The beauty of the scene and the woman beside me made me more aware of the pain George Trask was suffering, like solitary confinement in the world.

"The company is being very understanding," he said conversationally. "They're giving me a leave of absence, openended, with full pay. That will give me a chance to get everything squared away, eh?"

"Do you know who murdered your wife?"

"We have a pretty good suspect—man with a criminal record as long as your arm—he's known Jean all her life. The police asked me not to mention his name."

It had to be Randy Shepherd. "Has he been picked up?"

"They expect to get him tonight. I hope they do, and *when* they do, put him in the gas chamber. You know and I know why crime and murder are rampant. The courts won't convict and when they do convict they won't mete out the death penalty. And even when they do the law is flouted right and left. Convicted murderers walk free, they don't gas anybody any more, no wonder we have a breakdown of law and order." His eyes were wide and staring, as if they were seeing a vision of chaos.

Moira rose and touched his head. "Don't talk so much, Mr. Trask. It makes you upset."

"I know. I've been talking all day."

He put his large hands on his glaring face. I could see his eyes bright as coins between his fingers. His voice went on unmuffled, as if it were independent of his will:

"The dirty old son deserves to be gassed, even if he didn't kill her he's directly responsible for her death. He got her started on this latest mania of looking for her father. He came here to the house last week with his schemes and stories, told her he knew where her father was and she could be with him again. And that's what happened," he added brokenly. "Her father's dead in his grave and Jean is with him."

Trask began to cry. Moira quieted him with small noises more than words.

I noticed after a while that Louise Swain was standing in the hall doorway looking like her daughter's ruined ghost. I got up and went to her:

"How are you, Mrs. Swain?"

"Not very well." She drew a hand across her forehead. "Poor Jean and I could never get along—she was her father's daughter—but we cared about each other. Now I have no one left." She shook her head slowly from side to side. "Jean should have listened to me. I knew she was getting into deep water again, and I tried to stop her."

"What kind of deep water do you mean?"

"All kinds. It wasn't good for her to go wandering off into the past, imagining that her father was alive. And it wasn't safe. Eldon was a criminal and he consorted with criminals. One of them killed her because she found out too much."

"Do you know this, Mrs. Swain?"

"I know it in my bones. There are hundreds of thousands of dollars at stake, remember. For that kind of money anyone would murder anyone else." Her eyes seemed to be squinting against a bright light. "A man would even murder his own daughter."

I maneuvered her into the hallway, out of hearing of the

living room. "Could your husband still be alive, in your opinion?"

"He could be. Jean thought so. There has to be a reason for everything that's happened. I've heard of men changing their faces with plastic surgery so they could come and go." Her narrowed gaze swung to my face and stayed on it, as if she was looking for surgical scars that would mark me as Eldon Swain.

And other men, I was thinking, had disappeared and left in their places dead men who resembled them. I said to the woman:

"About fifteen years ago, at the time your husband came back from Mexico, a man was shot dead in Pacific Point. He's been identified as your husband. But the identification has to be tentative: it's based on pictures which aren't the best in the world. One of them is the photograph you gave me last night."

She looked at me in bewilderment. "Was that only last night?"

"Yes. I know how you feel. You mentioned last night that your daughter had all your best family pictures. You also mentioned some home movies. They could be useful in this investigation."

"I see."

"Are they here in this house?"

"Some of them are, anyway. I've just been going through them." She spread her fingers. "It's how I got the dust on my fingers."

"May I have a look at the pictures, Mrs. Swain?"

"That depends."

"On what?"

"Money. Why should I give you anything free?"

"It may be evidence in your daughter's murder."

"I don't *care*," she cried. "Those pictures are the only things I have left—all I have to show for my life. Whoever gets them has to pay for them, the way I've had to pay for things. And you can go and tell Mr. Truttwell that."

"How did he get into this?"

"You're working for Truttwell, aren't you? I asked my father about him, and he says Truttwell can well afford to pay me!"

"How much are you asking?"

"Let him make a bid," she said. "Incidentally, I found the gold box you were inquiring about—my mother's Florentine box."

102

"Where was it?"

"That's none of your business. The point is that I have it and it's for sale as well."

"Was it really your mother's?"

"It certainly was. I've found out what happened to it after her death. My father gave it to another woman. He didn't want to admit it when I asked him about it last night. But I forced it out of him."

"Was the other woman Estelle Chalmers?"

"You know about his liaison with her, eh? I guess everyone knows. He had his gall giving her Mother's jewel box. It was supposed to go to Jean, you know."

"What makes it so important, Mrs. Swain?"

She thought for a moment. "I guess it stands for everything that has happened to my family. Our whole life went to pieces. Other people ended up with our money and our furniture and even our little objects of art." She added after another thinking moment: "I remember when Jean was just a small child, my mother used to let her play with the box. She told her the story of Pandora's box—you know?—and Jean and her friends pretended that was what it was. When you lifted the lid you released all the troubles of the world." The image seemed to frighten her into silence.

"May I see the box and the pictures?"

"No you don't! This is my last chance to get a little capital together. Without capital you're nobody, you don't exist. You're not going to cheat me out of my last chance."

She seemed to be full of anger, but it was probably sorrow she was feeling. She'd stepped on a rotten place and fallen through the floor and knew she was trapped in poverty forever. The dream she was defending wasn't a dream for the future. It was a dreaming memory of the past, when she had lived in San Marino with a successful husband and a forty-foot pool.

I told her I would discuss the matter with Truttwell, and advised her to take good care of the box and the pictures. Then Moira and I said good night to George Trask, and went out to my car.

"Poor people."

"You were a help."

"I wish I could have been." Moira paused. "I know that certain questions are out of bounds. But I'm going to ask one anyway. You don't have to answer."

"Go ahead."

"When you found Nick today, was he in this neighborhood?"

I hesitated, but not for long. She was married to another man, and in a profession with different rules from mine. I gave her a flat no.

"Why?"

"Mr. Trask told me his wife was involved with Nick. He didn't know Nick's name, but his description was accurate. Apparently he saw them together in Pacific Point."

"They spent some time together," I said shortly.

"Were they lovers?"

"I have no reason to think so. The Trasks and Nick make a very unlikely triangle."

"I've seen unlikelier," she said.

"Are you trying to tell me Nick may have killed the woman?"

"No, I'm not. If I thought so I wouldn't be talking about it. Nick has been our patient for fifteen years."

"Since 1954?"

"Yes."

"What happened in 1954?"

"Nick became ill," she said levelly. "I can't discuss the nature of his illness. I've already said too much."

We were almost back where we started. Not quite. Driving back to the hospital I could feel her leaning close to me, tentatively, lightly.

XXII

Moira left me at the hospital entrance to fix her face, as she said. I took the elevator to the second floor and found Nick's parents in the visitors' room. Chalmers was snoring in an armchair with his head thrown back. His wife sat near him, dressed in elegant black.

"Mrs. Chalmers?"

She rose with her finger to her lips, moving toward the door. "This is the first rest Larry's had." She followed me into the corridor. "We're both deeply grateful to you, for finding Nick."

"I hope it wasn't too late."

"It wasn't." She managed a pale smile. "Dr. Smitheram and the other doctors are most encouraging. Apparently Nick regurg—" She stumbled over the word. "He vomited some of the pills before they could take effect."

"What about his concussion?"

"I don't think it's too serious. Do you have any idea how he got it?"

"He fell or was hit," I said.

"Who hit him?"

"I don't know."

"Where did you find him, Mr. Archer?"

"Here in San Diego."

"But where?"

"I'd rather report the details through Mr. Truttwell."

"But he's not here. He refused to come. He said he had other clients to attend to." Her feelings had risen close to the surface, and anger broke through. "If he thinks he can give us the brush-off, he'll be sorry."

"I'm sure he didn't mean that." I changed the subject. "Since Truttwell isn't available, I should probably tell you I've been talking to a Mrs. Swain. She's Jean Trask's mother and she has some family pictures that I'd like to have a look at. But Mrs. Swain wants money for them."

"How much money?"

"Quite a lot. I may be able to get them for a thousand or so."

"That's ridiculous! The woman must be crazy."

I didn't press the point. Nurses were coming and going in the corridor. They already knew Mrs. Chalmers, and they smiled and nodded and looked inquiringly at her hot black eyes. Breathing deeply, she got herself under some control.

"I insist that you tell me where you found Nick. If he was the victim of foul play—"

I cut her short: "I wouldn't get off on that kick, Mrs. Chalmers."

"What do you mean?"

"Let's take a little walk."

We turned a corner and loitered along a hallway past offices that had been closed for the night. I told her in detail where I had found her son, in the garage next to the kitchen where Jean Trask had been murdered. She leaned on the white wall, her head hanging sideways as if I had struck her violently in the face. Without her coloring, her foreshortened shadow looked like that of a hunched old woman.

"You think he killed her, don't you?"

"There are other possibilities. But I haven't reported any of this to the police, for obvious reasons."

"Am I the only one you've told?"

"So far."

She straightened up, using her hands to push herself away from the wall. "Let's keep it that way. Don't tell John Truttwell—he's turned against Nick on account of that girl of his. Don't even tell my husband. His nerves are exhausted as it is, and he can't take it."

"But you can?"

"I have to." She was quiet for a moment, getting her thoughts in order. "You said there were other possibilities."

"One is that your son was framed. Say the murderer found him drugged and put him in the Trask garage as a patsy. It would be hard to convince the police of that one."

"Do they have to be brought in?"

"They're in. The question is how much we have to tell them. We'll need legal advice on that. My neck is out a mile as it is."

She wasn't much interested in the state of my neck. "What are the other possibilities?"

"I can think of one other. We'll get to that in a minute." I took out my wallet and produced the suicide note which had fallen from Nick's pocket. "Is this Nick's writing?"

She held it up to the light. "Yes, it is. It means he's guilty, doesn't it?"

I took it back. "It means he feels guilty of something. He may have stumbled across Mrs. Trask's body and had an overwhelming guilt reaction. That's the other possibility that occurred to me. I'm no psychiatrist, and I'd like your permission to talk this over with Dr. Smitheram."

"No! Not even Dr. Smitheram."

"Don't you trust him?"

"He knows too much about my son already." She leaned toward me urgently. "You can't trust anybody, don't you know that?"

"No," I said, "I don't know that. I was hoping we'd reached a point where the people responsible for Nick could do some candid talking with each other. The hush-hush policy hasn't been working too well."

She looked at me with a kind of wary surprise. "Do you like Nick?"

106

"I've had no chance to like him, or get to know him. I feel responsible for him. I hope you do, too."

"I love him dearly."

"You may love him too damn dearly. I think you and your husband have been giving him a bad break in trying to overprotect him. If he actually killed anyone the facts are going to have to be brought out."

She shook her head resignedly. "You don't know the circumstances."

"Then tell me."

"I can't."

"You might save yourself a lot of time and money, Mrs. Chalmers. You might save your son's sanity, or his life."

"Dr. Smitheram says his life is not in danger."

"Dr. Smitheram hasn't been talking to the people I've been talking to. There have been three killings over a period of fifteen years—"

"Be quiet."

Her voice was low and frantic. She looked up and down the corridor, her gesture mocked and cartooned by her shadow on the wall. In spite of her sex and her elegance I was reminded of Randy Shepherd's furtive sidelong peerings.

"I won't be quiet," I said. "You've lived in fear so long you need a taste of reality. There have been three killings, as I said, and they all seem to be connected. I didn't say that Nick was guilty of all three. He may not have done any of them."

She shook her head despairingly.

I went on: "Even if he killed the man in the railroad yards, it was a far cry from murder. He was protecting himself against a kidnapper, a wanted man named Eldon Swain who was carrying a gun. As I reconstruct the shooting, he made a rough pass at your little boy. The boy got hold of his gun and shot him in the chest."

She looked up in surprise. "How do you know all this?"

"I don't know all of it. It's partly reconstruction from what Nick told me himself. And I had a chance to talk today with an old con named Randy Shepherd. If I can believe him at all, he went to Pacific Point with Eldon Swain but got cold feet when Swain started planning the kidnapping."

"Why did they pick on us?" she said intently.

"That didn't come out. I suspect Randy Shepherd was

107

more deeply involved than he admits. Shepherd seems to be connected with all three killings, at least as a catalyst. Sidney Harrow was a friend of Shepherd's, and Shepherd was the one who got Jean Trask interested in looking for her father."

"Her father?"

"Eldon Swain was her father."

"And you say that this Swain person was carrying a gun?"

"Yes. We know it was the same gun that killed him, and the same gun that killed Sidney Harrow. All of which makes me doubt that Nick killed Harrow. He couldn't very well have kept that gun hidden for the last fifteen years."

"No." Her eyes were wide and bright yet somehow abstract, like a hawk's, looking over the entire span of those years. "I'm sure he didn't," she said finally.

"Did he ever mention the gun to you?"

She nodded. "When he came home—he found his own way home. He said a man picked him up on our street and took him to the railroad yards. He said he grabbed a gun and shot the man. Larry and I didn't believe him—we thought it was little-boy talk—till we saw it in the paper next day, about the body being found in the yards."

"Why didn't you go to the police?"

"By that time it was too late."

"It's not too late even now."

"It is for me—for all of us."

"Why?"

"The police wouldn't understand."

"They'd understand very well if he killed in self-defense. Did he ever tell you why he shot the man?"

"He never did." She paused, and her eyes were suffused with feeling.

"And what happened to the gun?"

"He left it lying there, I guess. The police said in the paper the weapon couldn't be found, and Nicky certainly didn't bring it home with him. Some hobo must have picked it up."

My mind went back to Randy Shepherd. He had been on or near the spot, and he had been very eager to disconnect himself from the kidnapping. I shouldn't have let him go, I thought: a half million dollars was a critical mass of money, enough to convert any thief into a murderer.

XXIII

Mrs. Chalmers and I walked back to the visitors' room, where Dr. Smitheram and his wife were talking to Larry Chalmers.

The doctor greeted me with a smile that failed to touch his dubious, probing eyes. "Moira tells me you took her to dinner. Thanks very much."

"It was a pleasure. What are my chances of talking to your patient?"

"Minimal. Nonexistent, in fact."

"Even for a minute?"

"It wouldn't be a good idea, for both physical and psychiatric reasons."

"How is he?"

"He has a giant hangover, of course, and he's depressed both physically and emotionally. That's partly the overdose of reserpine. Also he has a bit of a concussion."

"What caused it?"

"I'd say he was hit on the back of the head with a blunt object. But forensic medicine is not my line. Anyway, he's doing surprisingly well. I owe you a vote of thanks for getting him here in time."

"We all do," Chalmers said, and shook hands with me formally. "You saved my son's life."

"We were lucky, both of us. It would be nice if the luck continued."

"What do you mean, exactly?"

"I think Nick's room should be guarded."

"You think he might get away again?" Chalmers said.

"That's a thought. It hadn't occurred to me. What I had in mind was protection for him."

"He has round-the-clock nurses," Dr. Smitheram said.

"He needs an armed guard. There have been several killings; we don't want another." I turned to Chalmers: "I can get you three shifts for about a hundred dollars a day."

"By all means," Chalmers said.

I went downstairs and made a couple of phone calls. The

first was to a Los Angeles guard service with a San Diego branch. They said they would have a man named Maclennan on duty in half an hour. Then I called Conchita's Cabins in Imperial Beach. Mrs. Williams answered in a hushed and worried voice.

"This is Archer. Has Randy Shepherd been back?"

"No, and he probably won't be." She lowered her voice even further. "You're not the only one looking for him. They have the place staked out."

I was glad to hear it, because it meant I wouldn't have to stake it out myself.

"Thanks, Mrs. Williams. Take it easy."

"That's easier said than done. Why didn't you tell me Sidney Harrow was dead?"

"It wouldn't have done you any good to know."

"You can say that again. I'm putting this place up for sale as soon as I get *them* out of my hair."

I wished her good luck, and went out the front door for some air. After a while Moira Smitheram came out and joined me.

She lit a cigarette from a fresh pack and smoked it as if she was being timed by a stop watch. "You don't smoke, do you?"

"I gave it up."

"So did I. But I still smoke when I'm angry."

"What are you angry about now?"

"Ralph again. He's going to sleep in the hospital tonight so he can be on call. I might as well be married to a Trappist."

Her anger sounded superficial, as if it was masking some deeper feeling. I waited for that feeling to show itself. She threw her cigarette away and said: "I hate motels. You wouldn't be driving back to the Point tonight?"

"West Los Angeles. I can drop you off on the way."

"You're very kind." Under the formal language I could sense an excitement echoing mine. "Why are you going to West Los Angeles?"

"I live there. I like to sleep in my own apartment. It's just about the only continuity in my life."

"I thought you abhorred continuity. You said at dinner you liked to move in and out of people's lives."

"That's true. Particularly the people I meet in my work."

"People like me?"

"I wasn't thinking of you."

"Oh? I thought you were stating a general policy," she said with some irony, "to which everyone was expected to conform."

A tall, wide young man with a crew cut and wearing a dark suit emerged from the shadows of the parking lot and headed for the hospital entrance. I called to him:

"Maclennan?"

"Yessir."

I told Moira I'd be right back, and took Maclennan up in the elevator. "Don't let anyone in," I told him, "except hospital personnel—doctors and nurses—and the immediate family."

"How do I know who *they* are?"

"I'll get you started with them. The main thing I want you to look for is men, wearing white coats or not. Don't let any man in unless he's vouched for by a nurse or a doctor you know."

"You expecting a murder attempt?"

"It could happen. You're armed?"

Maclennan pulled back his jacket and showed me the butt of the automatic in his armpit. "Who do I look out for?"

"I don't know, unfortunately. You have one other duty. Don't let the boy run away. But don't use a gun on him, or anything else. He's what it's all about."

"Sure, I understand that." He had a large man's calmness.

I took him to the door of Nick's room and asked the private nurse for Smitheram. The doctor opened the door wide as he came out. I caught a glimpse of Nick lying still with his eyes closed, his nose pointed at the ceiling, his parents sitting on either side of him. The three of them looked like something in a frieze, a ritual in which the raised hospital bed served as a kind of sacrificial altar.

The door closed on them silently. I introduced Maclennan to Dr. Smitheram, who gave us both a bored and weary look:

"Are all these alarms and excursions really necessary?"

"I think so."

"I don't. I'm certainly not going to let you plant this man in the room."

"He'd be more effective there."

111

"Effective against what?"

"A possible murder attempt."

"That's ridiculous. The boy's perfectly safe here. Who would want to murder him?"

"Ask him."

"I will not."

"Will you let me ask him?"

"No. He's in no condition—"

"When will he be?"

"Never, if you plan to bullyrag him."

" 'Bullyrag' is a loaded word. Are you trying to make me sore?"

Smitheram let out a clever little laugh. "If I were, I appear to have succeeded."

"What are you sitting on, doctor?"

His eyes narrowed and his mouth talked very rapidly: "I'm standing—standing on my right and duty to protect my patient. And no junior G-men are going to talk to him now or ever, if I can help it. Is that clear?"

"What about me?" Maclennan said. "Am I hired or fired?"

I turned to him, swallowing my anger. "You're hired. Dr. Smitheram wants you to stay outside in the corridor. If anyone questions your right to be here, tell them you're employed by Nick Chalmers's parents to protect him. Dr. Smitheram or one of the nurses will introduce you to the parents when it's convenient."

"I can hardly wait," Maclennan said under his breath.

XXIV

Moira wasn't waiting downstairs or in my car. I found her eventually in a parking lot reserved for doctors' cars. She was sitting behind the wheel of her husband's Cadillac convertible.

"I got tired of waiting," she said lightly. "I thought I'd test your investigative skills."

"This is a hell of a time to be playing hide-and-seek."

My voice must have been rough. She closed her eyes in reaction. Then she climbed out of the convertible. "I was only kidding. But not really. I wanted to see if you would look for me."

"I looked. Okay?"

She took my arm and shook it gently. "You're still angry."

"I'm not angry at you. It's your goddam husband."

"What did Ralph do now?"

"He pulled rank on me and called me a junior G-man. That's the personal part. The other part is more serious. He refused to let me talk to Nick, now or ever. If I could have just five minutes with Nick, I could clear up a lot of points."

"I hope you're not asking me to take it up with Ralph?"

"No."

"I don't want to be caught in the middle between you."

"If you don't want that," I said, "you better go and find a better place to hide."

She looked up at me slantwise. I caught a glint of her naked self, shy and mercurial and afraid of being hurt. "Did you mean that? You want me to get lost?"

I took hold of her and answered her without words. After a minute, she broke away.

"I'm ready to go home now. Are you?"

I said I was, but I wasn't quite. My feeling about Smitheram, anger deepened now by suspicion, got in the way of my feeling for his wife. And it started me thinking along less pleasant lines: the possibility that I might use her to get back at him, or get at him. I pushed these thoughts away but they crouched like unwanted children in the shadows, waiting for the lights to be turned out.

We headed north on the highway. Moira noticed my preoccupation. "If you're tired I can drive."

"It's not that kind of tired." I tapped my skull. "I have a few problems to work through, and my computer is a fairly early pre-binary model. It doesn't say yes and no. It says mainly maybe."

"About me?"

"About everything."

We rode in silence past San Onofre. The great sphere of the atomic reactor loomed in the darkness like a dead and fallen moon. The actual moon hung in the sky above it.

"Is this computer of yours programmed for questions?"

"Some questions. Others put it completely out of whack."

113

"Okay." Moira's voice became soft and serious. "I think I know what's on your mind, Lew. You gave it away when you said five minutes with Nick could clear up everything."

"Not everything. A lot."

"You think he killed all three of them, don't you? Harrow and poor Mrs. Trask and the man in the railroad yards?"

"Maybe."

"Tell me what you really think."

"What I really think is maybe. I'm reasonably sure he killed the man in the railroad yards. I'm not sure about the others, and I'm getting less sure all the time. Right now I'm going on the assumption that Nick was framed for the others and may know who framed him. Which means he may be next."

"Is that why you didn't want to come with me?"

"I didn't say that."

"I felt it, though. Look, if you feel you have to turn around and go back there, I'll understand." She added: "I can always leave my body to medical science. Or put in an application for equal time."

I laughed.

"It's not so funny," Moira said. "Things keep happening, and the world keeps moving so fast, it's hard for a woman to compete."

"Anyway," I said, "there's no point in going back. Nick is well guarded. He can't get out, and nobody can get in."

"Which takes care of both your maybes, doesn't it?"

We were silent for a long time. I would have liked to question her at length, about both Nick and her husband. But if I started to use the woman and the occasion, I'd be using a part of myself and my life that I tried to keep unused: the part that made the difference between me and a computer, or a spy.

The unasked questions simmered down after a while, and my mind hung loose in silence. The sense of living inside the case, which I sometimes used as a drug to keep me going, slowly left me.

The woman beside me had a sensitive antennae. As if I'd withdrawn a protective shield, she moved in close to me. I drove with her warmth all down my right side and spreading through my body.

She lived on the Montevista shore in a rectilinear cliff-top house made of steel and glass and money.

"Put your car in the carport if you like. You will come in for a drink?"

"A short one."

She couldn't unlock the front door.

"You're using your car key," I told her.

She paused to consider. "I wonder what that means?"

"That you probably need glasses."

"I do use glasses for reading."

She let me in and turned on a light in the hall. We went down some steps into an octagonal room which was mostly window. I could see the moon almost close enough to touch, and, far below, the scrawled white lines of the breakers.

"It's a nice place."

"Do you think so?" She seemed surprised. "God knows the place was beautiful before we built on it, and when we were planning it with the architect. But the house never seemed to capture it." She went on after a moment: "Building a house is like putting a bird in a cage. The bird being yourself, I guess."

"Is that what they tell you at the clinic?"

She turned to me with a quick smile. "Am I being terribly talky?"

"You did mention a drink."

She leaned toward me, silver-faced, dark-eyed, and dark-mouthed in the thin light from outside. "What will you have?"

"Scotch." Then her eyes moved and I caught that naked glint of her again, like a light hidden deep in a building. I said: "May I change my mind?"

She was willing to be taken. We shed our clothes, more or less, and lay down like wrestlers going to the mat under special rules, where pinning and being pinned were equally lucky and meritorious.

She said at one point, between falls, that I was a gentle lover.

"There are some advantages in getting older."

"It isn't that. You remind me of Sonny, and he was only twenty. You make me feel like Eve in the garden again."

"That's pretty fancy talk."

"I don't care." She rose on one elbow, and her silver breast lay heavy on me. "Does it upset you when I mention Sonny?"

"Oddly enough, it doesn't."

"It shouldn't, either. He was a poor little nothing boy. But we were happy together. We lived like silly angels doing things for each other. He'd never been with a girl before, and I'd only been with Ralph."

Her voice changed on her husband's name, and my feeling also changed. "Ralph was always so terribly technical and self-assured. He came on in bed like an army pacifying an undeveloped country. But with Sonny it was different. He was so gentle and nutty. Love was like a game, a fantasy that we lived in, playing house together. Sometimes he pretended to be Ralph. Sometimes I pretended to be his mother. Does that sound sick?" she said with a nervous little laugh.

"Ask Ralph."

"I'm boring you, aren't I?"

"On the contrary. How long did this affair go on?"

"Nearly two years."

"Then Ralph came home?"

"Eventually he did. But I'd already broken with Sonny. The fantasy was running out of control and so was he. Besides, I couldn't just leap from his bed into Ralph's. As it was the guilt nearly killed me."

I looked down along her body. "You don't strike me as the guilt-ridden type."

She answered after a moment. "You're right. It wasn't guilt. It was simple pain. I'd given up my one true love. For what? A hundred-thousand-dollar house and a four-hundred-thousand-dollar clinic. In neither of which I'd be caught dead if I could help it. I'd rather be back in one room at the Magnolia."

"It isn't there any more," I said. "Aren't you building up the past a little large?"

She answered thoughtfully. "Maybe I am exaggerating, especially the good parts. Women do tend to make up stories featuring ourselves."

"I'm glad men never do."

She laughed. "I bet Eve made up the story of the apple."

"And Adam made up the story of the garden."

She crawled close against me. "You're a nut. That's a diagnosis. I'm glad I told you all this. Are you?"

"I can stand it. Why did you?"

"Various reasons. Also you have the advantage of not being my husband."

"That's the finest thing any woman ever said to me."

"I mean it seriously. If I told Ralph what I've told you, it would be the end of me as a person. I'd become just another of his famous psychiatric trophies. He'd probably have me stuffed and hang me up on the office wall with his diplomas." She added: "In a way that's what he has done."

There were questions I wanted to ask her about her husband but the time and place were wrong, and I was still determined not to use them. "Forget about Ralph. Whatever happened to Sonny?"

"He found another girl and married her."

"And you're jealous?"

"No. I'm lonely. I have no one."

We merged our lonelinesses once again, in something less than love but sweeter than self. I didn't get home to West Los Angeles after all.

XXV

In the morning I left early without waking Moira. Fog had moved in from the sea, blanketing the cliff-top house and the whole Montevista shore. I drove up the road very slowly between lines of phantom trees.

I came to the end of the fog suddenly. The sky was cloudless except for a couple of smeared jet contrails. I drove downtown and checked in at the police station.

Lackland was in his office. The electric clock on the wall above his head said that it was exactly eight o'clock. It bothered me for a minute. It made me feel as if Lackland had brought me in again at this particular time by the exertion of some occult force.

"Glad you dropped by," he said. "Sit down. I was wondering where everybody was."

"I went to San Diego on a lead."

"And you took your clients with you?"

"Their son had an accident. They went to San Diego to look after him."

"I see." He waited for a while, twisting and biting his lips as if to punish his mouth for asking questions. "What kind of an accident did he have, or is it a family secret?"

"Barbiturate, mainly. He also has a head injury."

117

"Was it a suicide attempt?"

"Could be."

Lackland leaned forward abruptly, pushing his face toward mine. "After he knocked off Mrs. Trask?"

I wasn't ready for the question, and I avoided answering it directly. "The prime suspect in the Trask killing is Randy Shepherd."

"I know that," Lackland said, making it clear that I hadn't given him anything. "We have an APB on Shepherd from San Diego."

"Does it mention that Shepherd knew Eldon Swain from 'way back?"

Lackland gnawed at his upper lip. "Do you know that for a fact?"

"Yes. I talked to Shepherd yesterday, before he was regarded as a suspect. He told me that Swain ran off with his daughter Rita and half a million dollars. Apparently Shepherd has spent his life trying to latch onto a piece of that money. It's fairly clear, by the way, that Shepherd talked Mrs. Trask into hiring Sidney Harrow and coming here to the Point. He was using them as cat's-paws to find out what he could without the risk of coming here himself."

"So Shepherd had a motive to kill Swain after all." Lackland's voice was low, as if his fifteen years on the case had used up all his energy at last. "And he had a motive to burn off Swain's fingerprints. Where did you talk to him?"

"On the Mexican border near Imperial Beach. He wouldn't be there any more."

"No. As a matter of fact, Shepherd was seen in Hemet last night. He stopped for gas, heading north in a stolen car, a late-model Merc convertible, black."

"Better check Pasadena. Shepherd came from there, and so did Eldon Swain."

I filled Lackland in on the Pasadena end of the case, on Swain and Mrs. Swain and their murdered daughter, and Swain's embezzlement from Rawlinson's bank. "Once you know these facts," I concluded, "you can't seriously go on blaming Nick Chalmers for everything. He wasn't even born when Eldon Swain took the money from the bank. But that was the real beginning of the case."

Lackland was silent for a while. His face in repose was like an eroded landscape in a dry season. "I know some history, too. Rawlinson, the man who owned the bank, used to spend his summers here back in the twenties and thirties. I could tell you more."

"Please do."

Lackland produced one of his rare smiles. It wasn't very different from his mouth-gnawings, except that a shy light flickered in his eyes. "I hate to disappoint you, Archer. But no matter how far back you go, Nick Chalmers is in the picture. Sam Rawlinson had a girl friend here in town, and after her husband died they spent their summers together. You want to know who his girl friend was?"

"Nick's grandmother," I said. "Judge Chalmers's widow."

Lackland was disappointed. He lifted a typed sheet from his in-basket, read it carefully, crushed it up in a ball, and threw it at a trash can in the corner of his office. It missed. I scooped it up and dropped it in.

"How did you find that out?" he asked me finally.

"I've been doing some digging in Pasadena, as I told you. But I still don't see how Nick comes into this. He's not responsible for his grandmother."

For once Lackland failed to offer an argument. But I thought as I left the police station that perhaps the reverse was true, and Nick's dead grandmother was responsible for him. Certainly there had to be a meaning in the old connection between the Rawlinson family and the Chalmers family.

I passed the courthouse on my way downtown. In a cast stone bas-relief above the entrance, a big old Justice with bandaged eyes fumbled at her scales. She needed a seeing-eye man, I told her silently. I was feeling dangerously good.

After a breakfast of steak and eggs I went into a barber-shop and had a shave. By this time it was close to ten o'clock, and Truttwell should be in his office.

He wasn't, though. The receptionist told me that he had just left and hadn't said when he'd be back. She was wearing a black wig this morning, and took my troubled stare as a compliment.

"I like to change my personality. I get sick of having the same old personality."

"Me, too." I made a face at her. "Did Mr. Truttwell go home?"

"I don't know. He received a couple of long-distance calls and then he just took off. If he goes on this way, he'll end up losing his practice." The girl smiled intensely up at me, as if

119

she was already looking for a new opening. "Do you think black hair goes well with my complexion? Actually I'm a natural brownette. But I like to keep experimenting with myself."

"You look fine."

"I thought so, too," she said, overconfidently.

"Where did the distance calls come from?"

"The one call came from San Diego—that was Mrs. Chalmers. I don't know who the other one was, she wouldn't give her name. It sounded like an older woman."

"Calling from where?"

"She didn't say, and it was dialed direct."

I asked her to call Truttwell's house for me. He was there, but he wouldn't or couldn't come to the phone. I talked to Betty instead.

"Is your father all right?"

"I guess he is. I hope so." The young woman's voice was serious and subdued.

"Are you?"

"Yes." But she sounded doubtful.

"If I come right over, will he be willing to talk to me?"

"I don't know. You'd better hurry. He's going out of town."

"Where out of town?"

"I don't know," she repeated glumly. "If you do miss him, Mr. Archer, I'd still like to talk to you myself."

Truttwell's Cadillac was standing in front of his house when I got there. Betty opened the front door for me. Her eyes were rather dull and unresponsive. Even her bright hair looked a little tarnished.

"Have you seen Nick?" she said.

"I've seen him. The doctor gave him a fairly good report."

"But what did Nick say?"

"He wasn't talkable."

"He'd talk to me. I wanted so badly to go to San Diego." She raised her fists and pressed them against her breast. "Father wouldn't let me."

"Why not?"

"He's jealous of Nick. I know that's a disloyal thing to say. But Father made it very clear. He said when Mrs. Chalmers dismissed him this morning that I would have to choose between him and Nick."

120

"Why did Mrs. Chalmers dismiss him?"

"You'll have to ask Father. He and I are not communicating."

Truttwell appeared in the hallway behind her. Though he must have heard what she'd just said, he made no reference to it. But he gave her a hard impatient look that I saw and she didn't.

"What's this, Betty? We don't keep visitors standing in the doorway."

She turned away without speaking, moving into another room and shutting the door behind her. Truttwell spoke in a complaining way, with a thin note of malice running through his complaint:

"She's losing her mind over that sad sack. She wouldn't listen to me. Maybe she will now. But come in, Archer. I have news for you."

Truttwell took me into his study. He was even more carefully dressed and groomed than usual. He wore a fresh sharkskin suit, a button-down shirt with matching silk tie and handkerchief, and the odors of bay rum and masculine scent.

"Betty tells me you're parting company with the Chalmerses. You look as if you're celebrating."

"Betty shouldn't have told you. She's losing all sense of discretion."

His handsome pink face was fretful. He pressed and patted his white hair. Betty had hurt him in his vanity, I thought, and apparently he didn't have much else to fall back on.

I was more disturbed by the change in Truttwell than by the change in his daughter. She was young, and would change again before she settled on a final self.

"She's a good girl," I said.

Truttwell closed the study door and stood against it. "Don't sell her to me. I know what she is. She let that creep get to her and poison her mind against me."

"I don't think so."

"You're not her father," he said, as if paternity conferred the gift of second sight. "She's put herself down on his level. She's even using the same crude Freudian jargon." His face was red now and his voice was choked. "She actually accused me of taking an unhealthy interest in her."

I said to myself: This is a healthy interest?

Truttwell went on: "I know where she picked up those

121

ideas—from Dr. Smitheram via Nick. I also know," he said, "why Irene Chalmers terminated their association with me. She made it quite clear on the telephone that the great and good Dr. Smitheram insisted on it. He was probably standing at her elbow telling her what to say."

"What reason did she give?"

"I'm afraid you were one reason, Archer. I don't mean to be critical," though he did. "I gathered that you asked too many questions to suit Dr. Smitheram. He seems determined to mastermind the entire show, and that could be disastrous. No lawyer can defend Nick without knowing what he's done."

Truttwell gave me a careful look. As our talk moved back onto more familiar ground, he had regained some of his lawyer's poise. "You're better acquainted with the facts than I could possibly be."

It was a question. I didn't answer it right away. My attitude to Truttwell was undergoing an adjustment. It wasn't a radical one, since I had to admit to myself that from the beginning of the case I hadn't wholly understood or trusted his motivations.

It was becoming fairly evident now that Truttwell had been using me and intended to go on using me. In the same way as Harrow had served as Randy Shepherd's cat's-paw, I was Truttwell's. He was waiting now, handsome and quick-eyed and well-groomed as a cat, for me to spill the dirt on his daughter's friend. I said:

"Facts are hard to come by in this case. I don't even know who I'm working for. Or if I'm working."

"Of course you are," he said benevolently. "You'll be paid in full for everything you've done, and I'll guarantee payment through today at least."

"Who will be doing the paying?"

"The Chalmerses, naturally."

"But you don't represent them any more."

"Don't let that worry you. Just submit your bill through me, and they'll pay it. You're not exactly a migratory worker, and I won't let them treat you as one."

His good will was self-serving, I thought, and would probably last only as long as he could use me. I was embarrassed by it, and by the conflict that had risen. In cases like this, I was usually the expendable one.

"Shouldn't I report to the Chalmerses?"

"No. They've already dismissed you. They don't want the truth about Nick."

"How is he?"

Truttwell shrugged. "His mother didn't say."

"Who do I report to now?"

"Report to me. I've represented the Chalmers family for nearly thirty years, and they're going to find that I'm not so very readily dispensable." He made the prediction with a smile, but there was the hint of a threat in it.

"What if they don't?"

"They will, I guarantee it. But if you're concerned about your money, I'll undertake to pay you personally as of today."

"Thanks. I'll give it some thought."

"You'd better think in a hurry," he said smiling. "I'm on my way to Pasadena to meet Mrs. Swain. She phoned me this morning about investing in her family pictures—after Mrs. Chalmers dismissed me. I'd like to have you come along, Archer."

In my trade you don't often have your own way. If I refused to deal with John Truttwell, he could push me off the case and probably close the county to me. I said:

"I'll take my own car and meet you at Mrs. Swain's house. That's where you're going, isn't it?—Pasadena?"

"Yes, I can count on you to follow me then?"

I said he could, but I didn't follow him right away. There was something more to be said beween me and his daughter.

XXVI

Betty came to the front door, as if by prearrangement, and asked me in again. "I have the letters," she said quietly, "the letters that Nick took from his father's safe."

She led me upstairs to her workroom and brought a manila envelope out of a drawer. It was stuffed with airmail letters arranged for the most part in serial order. There must have been a couple of hundred of them.

"How do you know Nick took them from the safe?"

"He told me so himself the night before last. Dr. Smitheram left us alone for awhile. Nick told me where he'd hidden them in his apartment. I went and got them yesterday."

"Did Nick say why he took them?"

"No."

"Do you know why?"

She perched on a large multicolored hassock. "I've had a lot of different thoughts," she said. "It has to do with the whole father-son business, I suppose. In spite of all the trouble, Nick has always had a lot of respect for his father."

"Does that go for you and your father?"

"We aren't talking about me," she said in a stiff-mouthed way. "Anyway, girls are different—we're much more ambiguous. A boy either wants to be like his father or he doesn't. I think Nick does."

"It still doesn't explain why Nick stole the letters."

"I didn't say I could explain it. But maybe he was trying, you know, to steal his father's bravery and so on. The letters were important to him."

"Why?"

"Mr. Chalmers made them important. He used to read them aloud to Nick—parts of them, anyway."

"Recently?"

"No. When Nick was a little boy."

"Eight?"

"It started about that age. I think Mr. Chalmers was trying to indoctrinate him, make a man of him and all like that." Her tone was a little contemptuous, not so much of Nick or his father as of the indoctrination.

"When Nick was eight," I said, "he had a serious accident. Do you know about it, Betty?"

She nodded deeply. Her hair slid forward, covering most of her face. "He shot a man, he told me the other night. But I don't want to talk about it, okay?"

"Just one question. What was Nick's attitude toward that shooting?"

She hugged herself as if she was chilly. Encircled by her arms and masked by her hair, she huddled on the hassock like a gnome. "I don't want to talk about it."

She pulled up her knees and rested her face against them, almost as if she was imitating Nick in his posture of despair.

124

I carried the letters to a table by a front window. From where I sat I could see the façade of the Chalmerses' house glistening white under its red tile roof. It looked like a building with a history, and I read the first of the letters in the hope of filling in my knowledge of it.

Mrs. Harold Chalmers
2124 Pacific Street
Pacific Point, Calif.

Pearl Harbor
October 9, 1943

Dear Mother:
All I have time for is a short letter. But I wanted you to know as soon as possible that I have got my exact wish. This letter will be censored for military details, I am told, so I will simply mention the sea and the air, and you will understand what kind of duty I have been assigned to. I feel as if I had just been knighted, Mother. Please tell Mr. Rawlinson my good news.

The trip from the mainland was dull but rather pleasant. A number of my fellow pilots spent their time on the fantail shooting at flying fish. I finally told some of them that they were wasting their time and spoiling the beauty of the day. I thought for a while that I might have to fight four or five of them at once. But they recognized the moral superiority of my view, and retreated from the fantail.

I hope you are well and happy, dear Mother. I have never been happier in my life. Your affectionate son,

Larry

I suppose I had been expecting some further light on the case, and the letter was a disappointment to me. It had evidently been written by an idealistic and rather conceited boy who was unnaturally eager to get into the war. The only remarkable thing about it was the fact that the boy had since become a dry stick of a man like Chalmers.

The second letter from the top had been written about eighteen months after the first. It was longer and more interesting, the work of a more mature personality sobered by the war.

Lt. (j.g.) L. Chalmers
SS Sorel Bay (CVE 185)
March 15, 1945

Mrs. Harold Chalmers
2124 Pacific Street
Pacific Point, Calif.

Dearest Mother:
Here I am in the forward area again so my letter won't go off for a while. I find it hard to write a letter that I have to hold on to. It's like keeping a diary, which I detest, or carrying on a conversation with a dictaphone. But writing to you, my dearest, is another matter.

Apart from the things that wouldn't get past the censor, the news about me is very much the same. I fly, sleep, read, eat, dream of home. We all do. For a nation that has built up not only the most powerful but the most expert Navy in the world, we Americans are a bunch of awful landlubbers. All we want is to get back to Mother Earth.

This applies to regular Navy men, who constantly look forward to shore duty and retirement, all but the brass hats, who are having a career. It's even true of the British Navy, some of whose officers I met not long ago in a certain port. A rumor of Germany's collapse reached us that night, and it was touching to see the hopeful wishing of those Britishers. The rumor turned out to be premature, as you must know, but Germany may be finished by the time you get this letter. Give Japan one year after that.

I met a couple of fellow pilots who had been over Tokyo and they told me how it felt: pretty good, they said, because none of the planes in their group got hit. (My squadron has not been so lucky.) They were on their way back to the U.S. after completing their missions and they were happy about that. But they were tensed up, their faces were stiff and reacted quite violently to their emotions. There's something about pilots that reminds you of racehorses—developed almost to an unhealthy point. I hope I'm not that way to other eyes.

Our squadron leader Commander Wilson is, though. (He's no longer censoring mail so I can say this.) He's been in for over four years now, but he seems to be exactly the same gentlemanly Yale man he was when he came in. He has, however, a certain air of arrested development. He has given his best to the war, and will never become the man he was meant to be. (He plans to go into the consular service afterwards.)

Apart from one or two rain squalls the weather has been good: bright sun and shining blue sea, which helps with the flying. But there's a fairly strong swell, which doesn't. The old tub lurches and strains along, and every now and then she wiggles like a hula girl and things slide off onto the floor. The cradle of the deep, to coin a phrase. Well, I'm off to bed.

Affectionately,

Larry

It was a fairly impressive letter, with a certain sadness running gray through its perceptions. One sentence stayed in my mind—"He has given his best to the war, and will never become the man he was meant to be"—because it seemed to apply to Chalmers himself as well as his squadron commander. The third letter was dated 4 July 1945:

Dearest Mother:

We're fairly near the equator and the heat is pretty bad, though I don't mean to complain. If we're still anchored at this atoll tomorrow I'm going to try to get off the ship for a swim, which I haven't had since we left Pearl months ago. One of my big daily pleasures, though, is the shower I take every night before going to bed. The water isn't cold, because the sea at temperatures around 90 can't cool it, and you're not supposed to use much, because all the water we use on board has to be condensed from seawater. Still, I like my shower.

Other things I would like: fresh eggs for breakfast, a glass of cold milk, a sail off the Point, a chance to sit and chat with you, Mother, in our garden between the mountains and the sea. I'm terribly sorry to hear that you are ill and your sight has failed. Please thank Mrs. Truttwell on my behalf (hi, Mrs. Truttwell!) for reading aloud to you.

You have no cause to worry about me, Mother. After a not-unexciting period (in which our squadron lost Commander Wilson, and too many others) we are fighting a safe war. So safe I feel guilty, but not so guilty that I'm going to jump overboard and swim rapidly in the direction of Japan. Good news from there, eh?—I mean re the destruction of their cities. It's no secret by now that we're going to do to Japan what we've already done to that certain island (which shall be nameless) where I flew so many missions.

Affectionately,

Larry

I put the letters back in the envelope. They seemed to mark points on a curve. The boy or man who had written them had passed from the eager idealism of the first letter into the rather impressive quick maturity of the second, and declined in the third into a kind of tiredness. I wondered what Chalmers himself could see in his letters that made him want to read them aloud to his son.

I turned to the girl, who hadn't moved from her hassock: "Have you read these letters, Betty?"

She raised her head. The look in her eyes was very dark and far. "I beg your pardon? I was thinking."

"Have you read these letters?"

"Some of them. I wanted to see what all the shouting was about. *I* think they're boring. I *hated* the one about bombing Okinawa."

"May I keep the three I've read?"

"Keep them all, why don't you? If Father finds them here, I'll have to explain where I got them. And it will be just another nail in Nick's coffin."

"He isn't in his coffin. It doesn't help matters to talk as if he is."

"Don't fatherize, please, Mr. Archer."

"Why not? I don't believe people know everything at birth and forget it as they get older."

She reacted positively to my sharp tone. "That's the doctrine of Platonic reminiscence. I don't believe it, either." She slid off the hassock and out of her lethargy and came toward me. "Why don't you give the letters to Mr. Chalmers? You wouldn't have to tell him where you got them."

"Is he at home?"

"I'm afraid I have no idea. I don't really spend all my time at this window watching the Chalmers house." She added with a quick wan smile: "Not more than six or eight hours a day, anyway."

"Don't you think it's time you broke the habit?"

She gave me a disappointed look. "Are you against Nick, too?"

"Obviously I'm not. But I hardly know him. You're the one I know. And I hate to see you caught here, between two fairly dismal alternatives."

"You mean Nick and my father, don't you? I'm not caught."

"You are, though, like a maiden in a tower. This low-grade war of attrition with your father may feel like a battle for freedom, but it isn't. You just get more and more deeply engaged with him. Even if you do succeed in breaking away, it won't be into freedom. You've got it arranged so another demanding male will take you over. And I do mean Nick."

"You've got no right to attack him—"

"I'm attacking you," I said. "Or rather the situation you've put yourself in. Why don't you move out of the middle?"

"Where could I go?"

"You shouldn't have to ask me. You're twenty-five."

"But I'm afraid."

"What of?"

"I don't know. I'm just afraid." After a silence she said in a hushed voice: "You know what happened to my mother. I told you, didn't I? She looked out this very window—this used to be her sewing room—and she saw a light in the Chalmers house when there wasn't supposed to be one. She went over there and the burglars chased her out and ran over her and killed her.'"

"Why did they kill her?"

"I don't know. It may have been just an accident."

"What did the burglars want from the Chalmers house?"

"I don't know."

"When did it happen, Betty?"

"In the summer of 1945."

"You were too young to remember, weren't you?"

"Yes, but my father told me about it. I've been afraid ever since."

"I don't believe you. You didn't act afraid the other night, when Mrs. Trask and Harrow came to Chalmers house."

"I was afraid, though, terribly. And I should never have gone there. They're both dead."

I was beginning to understand the fear that held her. She believed or suspected that Nick had killed both Harrow and Mrs. Trask, and that she herself had acted as a catalyst. Perhaps in some dark place of her mind, back beyond memory and below the level of speech, was the false but guilty knowledge that her infant self had somehow killed her mother in the street.

XXVII

The movement of a car below the window drew my thoughts out of the past. It was Chalmers's black Rolls. He got out and moved rather uncertainly across the courtyard to his house. He unlocked the front door and went in.

"Now you've got me doing it," I said to Betty.

"Doing what?"

"Watching the Chalmers house. They're not all that interesting."

"Maybe not. But they're special people, the kind other people watch."

"Why don't they watch us?"

She entered into my mood. "Because they're more interested in themselves. They couldn't care less about us." She smiled not very cheerfully. "Okay, I get the message. I have to become more interested in myself."

"Or something. What *are* you interested in?"

"History. I've been offered a traveling fellowship. But I felt I was needed here."

"To pursue a career of house-watching."

"You've made your point, Mr. Archer. Don't spoil it now."

I left her and, after putting the letters in the trunk of my car, crossed the street to the Chalmers house. I was having a delayed reaction to the death of Betty's mother, which seemed now to be an integral part of the case. If Chalmers was willing, he might be able to help me understand it.

He came to the door himself. A worried look had lengthened his bony brown face. His tan looked rather sallow, and his eyes were reddish and tired.

"I wasn't expecting to see *you*, Mr. Archer." His tone was polite and neutral. "I understood my wife had severed diplomatic relations."

"We're still talking to each other, I hope. How is Nick doing?"

"Quite well." He went on in a careful voice: "My wife and I have reason to be grateful for your help. I want you to know that. Unfortunately, you were caught in the middle, between Truttwell and Dr. Smitheram. They can't cooperate, and under the circumstances we have to stay with Smitheram."

"The doctor's assuming a great deal of responsibility."

"I suppose he is. But that's not your affair." Chalmers was getting a little edgy. "And I hope you didn't come here to make an attack on Dr. Smitheram. In a situation like this, a man has to lean on someone. We're not islands, you know," he said surprisingly. "We can't bear the weight of these problems all alone."

His angry sorrow bothered me. "I agree with you, Mr. Chalmers. I'd still like to help if I can."

He looked at me suspiciously. "In what way?"

"I'm getting the feeling of the case. I think it started before Nick was born, and that his part in it is fairly innocent. I can't promise to get him off the hook entirely. But I hope to prove that he's a victim, a patsy."

"I'm not sure I understand you," Chalmers said. "But come inside."

He took me into the study where the case had begun. I felt slightly cramped and smothered, as if everything that had happened in the room was still going on, using up space and air. I was struck by the thought that Chalmers, with family history breathing down his neck, may have felt smothered and cramped most of the time.

"Will you have some sherry, old man?"

"No thanks."

"Then neither will I." He turned the swivel chair in front of the desk and sat facing me across the refectory table. "You were going to give me an overview of the situation, I think."

"I'll try, with your help, Mr. Chalmers."

"How can I help? Events have gone quite beyond me." He made a helpless gesture with his hands.

"With your forbearance, then. I've just been talking to Betty Truttwell about her mother's death."

"That was a tragic accident."

"I think it may have been more than an accident. I understood Mrs. Truttwell was your mother's closest friend."

"She was indeed. Mrs. Truttwell was wonderfully kind to my mother in her last days. If I have any criticism at all, it has to do with her failure to tell me how bad things were with Mother. I was still overseas that summer, and I had no

131

idea that Mother was close to death. You can imagine my feelings when my ship came back to the West Coast in mid-July, and I found that both of them were dead." His troubled blue gaze came up to mine. "Now you tell me Mrs. Truttwell's death may not have been an accident."

"I'm raising the question, anyway. The question of accident versus murder isn't crucial, really. When someone is killed in the course of a felony, it's murder under the law, in any case. But I'm beginning to suspect Mrs. Truttwell was intentionally killed. She was your mother's closest friend, she must have known all her secrets."

"My mother had no secrets. The whole community looked up to her."

Chalmers rose angrily, spinning the creaky swivel chair. He took up a stance with his back to me, which reminded me oddly of a stubborn boy. Facing him was the primitive picture that concealed the door of the safe: the sailing ship, the naked Indians, the Spanish soldiers marching in the sky.

"If the Truttwells have been maligning my mother," he said, "I'll sue them for slander."

"Nothing like that happened, Mr. Chalmers. Nothing's been said against your mother by anyone. I'm trying to get at who the people were that broke into the house in 1945."

He turned. "They certainly wouldn't have been known to my mother. Her friends were the best people in California."

"I don't doubt it. But your mother was probably known to the burglars, and they probably knew what was in the house that made it worth breaking into."

"I can answer that," Chalmers said. "My mother kept her money in the house. It was a habit she inherited from my father, along with the money itself. I repeatedly urged her to put it in the bank, but she wouldn't."

"Did the burglars get it?"

"No. The money was intact when I got home from overseas. But Mother was dead. And Mrs. Truttwell, too."

"Was there very much money involved?"

"Quite a sum, yes. Several hundred thousand."

"Where did it come from?"

"I told you: Mother inherited it from my father." He gave me a pale suspicious look, as if I was planning to insult her again. "Are you suggesting the money wasn't hers?"

"Certainly not. Couldn't we forget her for a bit?"

132

"I can't." He added in a kind of gloomy pride: "I live with the thought of my mother constantly."

I waited, and tried again: "What I'm trying to get at is this. Two burlgaries or at least two thefts occurred in this house, in this very room, over twenty-three years apart. I think they were connected."

"In what way?"

"Through the people involved."

Chalmers's eyes were puzzled. He sat down opposite me again. "I'm afraid you've lost me."

"I'm simply trying to say that some of the same people, with the same motives, may have been involved in both these burglaries. We know who did the recent one. It was your son Nick, acting under pressure from a couple of other people, Jean Trask and Sidney Harrow."

Chalmers leaned forward, resting his forehead on his hand. His bald spot gleamed, defenseless as a tonsure.

"Did he kill those people?"

"I doubt it, as you know, but I can't prove he didn't. Yet. Let's stick to the burglaries for now. Nick took a gold box which had your letters in it." I was being careful not to name his mother. "The letters were probably incidental. The gold box was the main thing: Mrs. Trask wanted it. Do you know why?"

"Presumably because she was a thief."

"She didn't think so, though. She was quite open about the box. Apparently, it had belonged to Mrs. Trask's grandmother, and after her grandmother's death it was given to your mother by her grandfather."

Chalmers's head sank lower. The fingers supporting it raked up through his hair. "You're talking about Mr. Rawlinson, aren't you?"

"I'm afraid I am."

"This is infinitely depressing to me," he said. "You're twisting a harmless relationship between an elderly man and a mature woman—"

"Let's forget about the relationship."

"I can't," he said. "I can't forget about it." His head had sunk closer to the table, guarded by his hands and arms.

"I'm not judging anyone, Mr. Chalmers, certainly not your mother. The point is simply that there was a connection between her and Samuel Rawlinson. Rawlinson ran a bank, the Pasadena Occidental, and it was ruined by embezzlement around the time of the burglary. His son-in-law, Eldon

133

Swain, was blamed for the embezzlement, perhaps correctly. But it's been suggested to me that Mr. Rawlinson may have looted his own bank."

Chalmers sat up rigidly. "Who suggested that, for heaven's sake?"

"Another figure in the case—a convicted burglar named Randy Shepherd."

"And you'd take the word of a man like that, and let him blacken my mother's name?"

"Who said anything about your mother?"

"Aren't you about to offer me the precious theory that my mother took stolen money from that whoremaster? Isn't that what you have on your rotten mind?"

Hot wet rage had flooded his eyes. He stood up blinking and swung an open hand at my face. It was a feeble attempt. I caught his arm by the wrist and handed it back to him.

"I'm afraid we can't talk, Mr. Chalmers. I'm sorry."

I went out to my car and turned downhill toward the freeway. Fog still lay in a grey drift across the foot of the town.

XXVIII

Inland in Pasadena the sun was hot. Children were playing in the road in front of Mrs. Swain's house. Truttwell's Cadillac, which stood at the curb, acted like a magnet on the children.

Truttwell was sitting in the front seat, engrossed in business papers. He glanced up impatiently at me.

"You took your time about getting here."

"Something came up. Also, I can't afford a Cadillac."

"I can't afford to waste hours waiting for people. The woman said she'd be here at twelve."

It was twelve thirty by my wristwatch. "Is Mrs. Swain driving from San Diego?"

"I presume so. I'll give her until one o'clock to get here."

"Maybe her car broke down, it's pretty old. I hope nothing's happened to her."

"I'm sure nothing has."

"I wish I could be sure. The leading suspect in her daughter's death was seen in Hemet last night. Apparently, he was heading this way in a stolen car."

"Who are you talking about?"

"Randy Shepherd. He's the ex-con who used to work for Mrs. Swain and her husband."

Truttwell didn't seem much interested. He turned to his papers, and rattled them at me. From what I could see of them, they were Xeroxed copies of the articles of incorporation of something called the Smitheram Foundation.

I asked Truttwell what it was. He didn't answer me, or even look up. Irritated by his bad manners, I went and got the envelope of letters out of the trunk of my car.

"Have I mentioned," I said in a casual voice, "that I recovered the letters?"

"Chalmers's letters? You know very well you haven't. Where did you get hold of them?"

"They were in Nick's apartment."

"I'm not surprised," he said. "Let's have a look at them."

I slid into the front seat beside him and handed him the envelope. He opened it and peered at its contents:

"God, but this brings back the past. Estelle Chalmers lived for these letters, you know. The early ones were nothing much, as I recall. But Larry's epistolary style improved with practice."

"You've read them?"

"Some of them. Estelle gave me no choice. She was so proud of her young hero." His tone was just faintly ironic. "Toward the end, when her sight failed completely, she asked us—my wife and me—to read them aloud to her as they came. We tried to persuade her to hire a nurse-companion, but she refused. Estelle had a very strong sense of privacy, and it got stronger as she got older. The main burden of looking after her fell on my wife." He added in quiet regret: "I shouldn't have let it happen to my young wife."

He fell into a silence, which I finally broke: "What was the matter with Mrs. Chalmers?"

"I believe she had glaucoma."

"She didn't die of glaucoma."

"No. I think she died of grief—grief for my wife. She gave up eating, she gave up everything. I took the liberty of calling a doctor, very much against her wishes. She lay in bed

135

with her face to the wall and wouldn't let the doctor examine her, or even look at her. And she wouldn't let me try to get Larry home from overseas."

"Why not?"

"She claimed to be perfectly well, though obviously she wasn't. She wanted to die alone and unseen, I think. Estelle had been a real beauty, and some of it lasted almost to the end. Also, as she grew older, she became a bit of a miser. You'd be surprised how many older women do. The idea of having a doctor come to the house, or hiring a nurse, seemed like a horrible extravagance to Estelle. Her poor-mouthing actually had me convinced. But of course she'd been quite wealthy all along.

"I'll never forget the day following her funeral. Larry was finally en route home after the usual snafu, and in fact he arrived a couple of days later. But the County Administrator didn't want to wait to check the house and its contents. As a member of the courthouse crowd he'd known Estelle all his life. I think he knew or suspected that she kept her money in the house, as Judge Chalmers had before her. And of course there had been the attempted burglary. If I had been in full possession of my faculties, I'd have checked the safe the morning after the break-in. But I had troubles of my own."

"You mean your wife's death?"

"The loss of my wife was the main disaster, of course. It left me with full responsibility for an infant girl." He looked at me with painful candor. "A responsibility I haven't handled too well."

"The point is that it's over. Betty's grown up. She has to make her own choices."

"But I can't let her marry Nick Chalmers."

"She will if you keep saying that."

Truttwell went into another of his silences. He seemed to be catching up at last with great stretches of lost time. When his eyes changed back to present time, I said:

"Do you have any idea who killed your wife?"

He shook his white head. "The police failed to come up with a single suspect."

"What was the date of her death?"

"July 3, 1945."

"Exactly how did it happen?"

"I'm afraid I don't really know. Estelle Chalmers was the only surviving witness, and she was blind and saw nothing.

136

Apparently my wife noticed something wrong at the Chalmers house and went over there to investigate. The thieves chased her out into the road and ran her down with their car. Actually it wasn't their car—it had been stolen. The police recovered it in the tules below San Diego. There were—physical evidences on the bumper that proved it had been used to murder my wife. The murderers probably escaped over the border."

Truttwell's forehead was shining with sweat. He wiped it with a silk handkerchief.

"I'm afraid I can't tell you anything more about the events of that night. I was in Los Angeles on business. I got home in the small hours and found my wife in the morgue and my little girl being cared for by a policewoman."

His voice broke, and for once I saw through Truttwell's surface into his hidden self. He lived with a grief so central and consuming that it drained the energy from his external life and made him seem a smaller man than he was, or had once been.

"I'm sorry, Mr. Truttwell. I had to ask you these questions."

"I don't quite see their relevance."

"Neither do I, yet. When I interrupted you, you were telling me about the County Administrator checking the house."

"So I was. As the representative of the Chalmers family I opened the house for him. I also turned over the combination of the safe, which Estelle had given me some time before. It turned out to be stuffed with money, of course."

"How much?"

"I don't recall the exact figure. Certainly it was up in the hundreds of thousands. It took the Administrator most of the day to count it, even though some of the notes were in large denominations, up to ten thousand."

"Where did it all come from, do you know?"

"Her husband probably left her some of it. But Estelle was widowed when she was still quite young, and it's not exactly a secret that there were other men in her life. One or two of them were very successful men. I suppose they gave her money, or told her how to make it."

"And how to avoid taxes on it?"

Truttwell shifted uneasily in the car seat. "It hardly seems necessary to raise that question. All this is far away and long ago."

"It seems here and now to me."

"If you must know," he said impatiently, "the tax issue is dead. I persuaded the government to settle for inheritance taxes on the full amount. They had no way of proving the source of the money."

"The source is what interests me. I understand the Pasadena banker Rawlinson was one of the men in Mrs. Chalmers's life."

"He was, for many years. But that was a long time before her death."

"Not so very," I said. "In one of these letters, written in the fall of 1943, Larry asked to be remembered to him. Which means that his mother was still seeing Rawlinson."

"Really? How did Larry feel about Rawlinson?"

"The letter was noncommittal."

I could have given Truttwell a fuller answer, but I had decided to suppress my interview with Chalmers, at least for the present. I knew that Truttwell wouldn't approve of it.

"What are you getting at, Archer? You're not suggesting that Rawlinson was the source of Mrs. Chalmers's money?"

As if he had pushed a significant button which closed a circuit, the phone began to ring in Mrs. Swain's front room. It rang ten times, and stopped.

"It was your idea," I said.

"But I was speaking generally about the men in Estelle's life. I didn't single out Samuel Rawlinson. As you perfectly well know, he was ruined by the embezzlement."

"His bank was."

Truttwell's face twisted in surprise. "You can't mean he embezzled the money himself."

"The idea has come up."

"Seriously?"

"I hardly know. I got it from Randy Shepherd. It originated with Eldon Swain. Which doesn't help to make it true."

"I should think not. We *know* that Swain ran off with the money."

"We know that he ran off. But the truth isn't always so obvious; in fact, it's usually just as complex as the people who make it. Consider the possibility that Swain took some of the bank's money and Rawlinson caught him at it and took a great deal more. He used Mrs. Chalmers's safe to cache the money, but she died before he could recover it."

Truttwell gave me a look of appalled interest. "You have a

138

tortuous imagination, Archer." But he added: "What was the date of the embezzlement?"

I consulted my black notebook. "July 1, 1945."

"That was just a couple of weeks before Estelle Chalmers died. It rules out the possibility you suggest."

"Does it? Rawlinson didn't know she was going to die. They may have been planning to use the money, go someplace and live together."

"An old man and a blind woman? It's ridiculous!"

"That still doesn't rule it out. People are always doing ridiculous things. Anyway, Rawlinson wasn't so very old in 1945. He was about the age that you are now."

Truttwell flushed. He was self-conscious about his age. "You'd better not mention this wild idea of yours to anyone else. He'd slap a libel suit on you." He turned and gave me another curious look. "You don't think much of bankers, do you?"

"They're no different from anyone else. But you can't help noticing that a high proportion of embezzlers are bankers."

"That's a simple matter of opportunity."

"Exactly."

The phone in Mrs. Swain's house began to ring again. I counted fourteen rings before it stopped. At the moment my sensibility was pretty highly keyed, and I felt as if the house had been trying to say something to me.

It was one o'clock. Truttwell climbed out of the car and began to pace the broken sidewalk. A clownish youngster walked behind him, aping his movements, until Truttwell shooed him away. I got the envelope of letters out of the front seat and locked them in a metal evidence case in the trunk of my car.

When I looked up, Mrs. Swain's old black Volkswagen had entered the little street. It turned onto the strips of concrete that formed her driveway. Some of the children lifted their hands to her and said: "Hi."

Mrs. Swain got out and walked toward us across the brown January grass. She moved awkwardly in her high heels and tight black dress. I introduced her to Truttwell and they shook hands stiffly.

"I'm awfully sorry to keep you waiting," she said. "A policeman came to my son-in-law's house just as I was about to leave. He asked me questions for over an hour."

"What about?" I asked her.

"Several matters. He wanted a full history of Randy Shepherd from the time he was our gardener in San Marino. He seemed to think that Randy might come after me next. But I'm not afraid of Randy, and I don't believe he killed Jean."

"Who do you suspect?" I said.

"My husband is capable of it, if he's alive."

"It's pretty definite that he's dead, Mrs. Swain."

"What happened to the money, if he's dead?" She leaned toward me, both hands out, like a starving beggar.

"Nobody knows."

She shook my arm. "We've got to find the money. I'll give you half if you find it for me."

There was a high shrieking in my head. I thought I was having a bad reaction to poor old Mrs. Swain. Then I realized that the shrieking wasn't in me.

It came from a siren whirling its whip of sound over the city. The sound grew louder but it was still far away and irrelevant.

On the boulevard there was another, nearer, sound of tires shuddering and squealing. An open black Mercury convertible turned into the little street. It skidded wide on the turn and scattered the children like confetti, nearly running some of them down.

The man at the wheel had a beardless face and bright red synthetic-looking hair. In spite of it I recognized Randy Shepherd. And he recognized me. He kept on going past us to the end of the block, and turned north out of sight. At the other end of the block a police car appeared for an instant. Without turning or pausing, it fled on up the boulevard.

I followed Shepherd, but it was a hopeless chase. He was on home territory, and his stolen convertible had more speed than my almost-paid-for car. Once I caught a glimpse of it crossing a bridge far ahead, with Shepherd's bright red hair like artificial fire in the front seat.

XXIX

I found myself in a blind street ending in a barricade. Beyond it a deep ravine opened. I turned off my engine and sat getting my bearings.

At just about my level, a red-tailed hawk was circling over the treetops in the ravine. There were scrub oak and sycamores along the hidden watercourse. I realized after a while that this was the same ravine that cut across Locust Street, where Rawlinson lived. But I was on the other side of it, facing west.

I drove the long way around to Locust Street. The first thing I saw when I entered it was an open black Mercury convertible standing at the curb half a block from Rawlinson's house. The keys were in the ignition. I put them in my pocket.

I left my own car in front of Rawlinson's house and mounted the veranda uneasily, tripping on the broken step. Mrs. Shepherd opened the door with her finger to her lips. Her eyes were deeply troubled.

"Be quiet," she whispered. "Mr. Rawlinson is taking his nap."

"Can I talk to you for a minute?"

"Not right now. I'm busy."

"I've come all the way from Pacific Point."

This information seemed to fascinate her. Without removing her gaze from my face, she closed the front door quietly behind her and stepped out onto the veranda.

"What's going on in Pacific Point?"

It sounded like a routine question, but it probably stood for questions she was afraid to ask in detail. She gave the impression that in her age she had stumbled back into all the desperate uncertainties of youth.

"More of the same," I said. "Trouble for everybody. I think it all started with this."

I showed her the copy of Nick's graduation picture that I'd taken from Sidney Harrow. She shook her head over it:

"I don't know who it would be."

"Are you sure?"

"I'm sure." She added solemnly: "I never saw that young man in my life."

I almost believed her. But she had neglected to ask me who he was.

"His name is Nick Chalmers. This was supposed to be his graduation picture. But Nick won't be graduating."

She didn't say, "Why not?" But her eyes said it.

"Nick's in the hospital recovering from a suicide attempt. The trouble started, as I said, when a man named Sidney Harrow came to town and began hounding Nick. He brought this picture with him."

"Where did he get it?"

"From Randy Shepherd," I said.

Her face had taken on an underlying pallor which made it almost gray. "Why are you telling me these things?"

"You're obviously interested." I went on in the same quiet tone: "Is Randy in the house now?"

Her uncontrolled upward glance probably meant that Shepherd was upstairs. She didn't speak.

"I'm pretty sure he's in there, Mrs. Shepherd. If I were you I wouldn't try to hide him. The police are after him, and they'll be arriving any time now."

"What do they want him for this time?"

"Murder. The murder of Jean Trask."

She moaned. "He didn't tell me."

"Is he armed?"

"He has a knife."

"No gun?"

"I didn't see one." She reached out and touched my chest. "Are you certain Randy gave that picture to the other man —the man who went to the Point?"

"I'm sure now, Mrs. Shepherd."

"Then he can burn in hell." She started down the steps.

"Where are you going?"

"The neighbors' to phone the police."

"I wouldn't do that, Mrs. Shepherd."

"Maybe you wouldn't. But I've suffered enough in my life on his account. I'm not going to jail for him."

"Let me go in and talk to him."

"No. It's *my* neck. And I'm calling the police." She turned away again.

"Don't be in such a hurry. We have to get Mr. Rawlinson out of there first. Where *is* Randy?"

"In the attic. Mr. Rawlinson's in the front parlor."

She went in and helped the old man to walk out. He was limping and yawning, and blinking against the sun. I put him in the front seat of my car and drove him to the barricade at the end of the street. The police used a lot of firepower nowadays.

The old man turned to me impatiently. "I'm afraid I don't understand what we're doing here."

"It would take a long time to explain. Briefly, we're wrapping up the case that started in July 1945."

"When Eldon Swain robbed me blind?"

"If it was Eldon."

Rawlinson turned his head to look at me, the flesh of his neck twisting in stringy folds. "Is there some doubt that Eldon was responsible?"

"The question has been raised."

"Nonsense. He was the cashier. Who else could have embezzled all that money?"

"You could have, Mr. Rawlinson."

His eyes grew small and bright in their nests of wrinkles. "You must be joking."

"No. I admit the question is partly hypothetical."

"And pretty damn insulting," he said without much real heat. "Do I look like the kind of man who would ruin his own bank?"

"Not unless you had a powerful reason."

"What possible reason could I have?"

"A woman."

"What woman?"

"Estelle Chalmers. She died rich."

He manufactured a quick small rage. "You're throwing dirt on the memory of a fine woman."

"I don't think so."

"I do. If you persist in following this line, I refuse to talk with you." He made a move to get out of my car.

"You better stay here, Mr. Rawlinson. Your house isn't safe. Randy Shepherd's in the attic, and the police will be here soon."

"Is this Mrs. Shepherd's doing? Did she let him in?"

"He probably didn't give her any choice." I brought out my picture of Nick again, and showed it to Rawlinson. "Do you know who this is?"

He took the picture in his swollen arthritic fingers. "I'm afraid I don't know his name. I could guess who the boy is, but you don't want that."

"Go ahead and guess."

"It's someone near and dear to Mrs. Shepherd. I saw this in her room early last week. Then it disappeared, and she blamed me for it."

"She should have blamed Randy Shepherd. He was the one who took it." I lifted the picture out of his hands and replaced it in the inside pocket of my jacket.

"That's what she gets for letting him into my house!" His eyes were moist, leaking away his old-man's anger. "The police are coming, you say. What's Randy been up to now?"

"He's wanted for murder, Mr. Rawlinson. The murder of your granddaughter Jean."

He made no response, except that he sank a little lower in the seat. I felt sorry for the man. He had had everything and bit by bit lost nearly all of it. Now he had outlived his own granddaughter.

I looked out over the ravine, hoping to lose my borrowed pain in its deep green spaces. The red-tailed hawk I had seen from the other side was visible from this side, too. He turned, and his ruddy wedge of tail flashed in the sun.

"You knew about Jean, Mr. Rawlinson?"

"Yes. My daughter Louise phoned me yesterday. But she didn't say that Shepherd was responsible."

"I don't think he is."

"Then what is this all about?"

"The police think he is."

Almost as if he could hear us talking about him, Randy Shepherd appeared at the side of Rawlinson's house and looked in our direction. He was wearing a wide-brimmed Panama hat with a striped band, and a moth-eaten tan polo coat.

"Hold on there, that's my hat!" Rawlinson cried. "By God, that's my coat, too!"

He started to get out of the car. I told him to stay where he was, in a tone which he obeyed.

Shepherd sauntered up the street like a gentleman out for a stroll. Then he scampered across to the black convertible, holding the loose hat on his head with one hand. He sat in the car for a frantic minute, looking for the keys, then got out and headed for the parkway.

By this time the sirens were rising in the distance, curdling the daylight at the edges. Shepherd stopped dead and stood perfectly still in a listening attitude. He turned and started back in our direction, pausing for an instant at the Rawlinson house as if he was thinking of going back in.

Mrs. Shepherd came out on the front porch. By this time two patrol cars were in the street and rolling toward Shepherd. He looked at them over his shoulder, and all around at the long Victorian faces of the houses. Then he ran in my direction. His Panama hat flew off. His coat billowed out behind.

I got out of the car to head him off. It was an unconsidered reflex. The patrol cars stopped abruptly, ejecting four policemen who began to fire their revolvers at Shepherd.

He went down flat on his face and slid a little. Then splashes on the back of his neck and down the back of his light coat were darker and realer than his slipping red wig.

A bullet ripped into my shoulder. I fell sideways against the open door of my car. Then I lay down and pretended to be as dead as Shepherd was.

XXX

I ended up high on pentothal in a Pasadena hospital room. A surgeon had had to dig for the slug, and my arm and shoulder would be immobilized for some time.

Fortunately, it was the left shoulder. This was pointed out more than once by the police and D.A.'s men who came to visit me late that afternoon. The police apologized for the incident, while managing to suggest at the same time that I had collided with the bullet, not it with me. They offered to do what they could for me, and agreed at my suggestion to have my car brought to the hospital parking lot.

Still, their visit made me angry and concerned. I felt as if my case had run away and left me lying. I had a bedside phone, and I used it to make a call to Truttwell's house. The housekeeper said he wasn't at home, and neither was Betty. I put in a call to Truttwell's office and left my name and number with his answering service.

Later, as night was coming on, I got out of bed and opened the door of the closet. I was feeling a little lightheaded but I was worried about my black notebook. My jacket was hanging in the closet with my other clothes and in spite

145

of the blood and the bullet hole the notebook was in the pocket where I'd put it. So was Nick's picture.

As I was on my way back to bed the floor tilted up and smacked me on the right side of the face. I blacked out for a while. Then I sat up with my back against a leg of the bed.

The night nurse looked in. She was pretty and dedicated and wore a Los Angeles General cap. Her name was Miss Cowan.

"What in the world are you doing?"

"Sitting on the floor."

"You can't do *that*." She helped me to get to my feet and into bed. "I hope you weren't trying to get out of here."

"No, but it's a good idea. When do you think I'll be sprung?"

"It's up to the doctor. He may be able to tell you in the morning. Now do you feel up to a visitor?"

"It depends on who it is."

"She's an elderly woman. Her name is Shepherd. Is that the same Shepherd—?" Delicately, she left the question unfinished.

"Same Shepherd." My pentothal high had changed to a pentothal low, but I told the nurse to send the woman in.

"You're not afraid she'll try to pull something on you?"

"No. She's not the type."

Miss Cowan went away. Shortly afterwards, Mrs. Shepherd came in. Gray pallor seemed to have become her permanent color. Her dark eyes were very large, as if they had been distended by the events they'd witnessed.

"I'm sorry you were injured, Mr. Archer."

"I'll survive. It's too bad about Randy."

"Shepherd was no loss to anybody," she said. "I just finished telling that to the police and now I'm telling you. He was a bad husband and a bad father, and he came to a bad end."

"That's a lot of badness."

"I know whereof I speak." Her voice was solemn. "Whether he killed Miss Jean or not, I know what Shepherd did to his own daughter. He ruined her life and drove her to her death."

"Is Rita dead?"

My use of the name stopped her. "How do you know my daughter's name?"

"Somebody mentioned it. Mrs. Swain, I think."

"Mrs. Swain was no friend of Rita's. She blamed my

146

daughter for everything that happened. It wasn't fair. Rita was beneath the age of consent when Mr. Swain got interested in her. And her own father pandered to Mr. Swain and took money from him for her."

The words came pouring out of her under pressure, as if Shepherd's death had opened a deep volcanic fissure in her life.

"Did Rita go to Mexico with Swain?"

"Yes."

"And died there?"

"Yes. She died there."

"How do you know that, Mrs. Shepherd?"

"Mr. Swain told me himself. Shepherd brought him to see me when he came back from Mexico. He said she died and was buried in Guadalajara."

"Did she leave any children?"

Her dark eyes wavered and then held firm, meeting mine. "No. I have no grandchildren of any kind."

"Who's the boy in the picture?"

"The picture?" she said with a show of puzzlement.

"If you want to refresh your memory, it's in my jacket in the closet."

She glanced at the closet door. I said:

"I mean the one Randy Shepherd stole from your room."

Her puzzlement became real. "How do you know that? How come you're digging so deep in my family affairs?"

"You know why, Mrs. Shepherd. I'm trying to wrap up a case that started nearly a quarter of a century ago. On July 1, 1945."

She blinked. Apart from this tiny movement of her eyelids, her face had recovered its immobility. "That was the date that Mr. Swain robbed Mr. Rawlinson's bank."

"Is that what really happened?"

"What other story did you hear?"

"I've found a few bits and pieces of evidence pointing another way. And I'm beginning to wonder if Eldon Swain ever got the money."

"Who else could have taken it?"

"Your daughter Rita, for one."

She reacted angrily, but not as angrily as she should have. "Rita was sixteen years old in 1945. Children don't plan bank robberies. You *know* it had to be somebody in the bank."

"Like Mr. Rawlinson?"

"That's just plain silly, and you know it."

"I thought I'd try it on you."

"You'll have to try harder than that. I don't know why you're straining so hard to make Mr. Swain into a whited sepulchre. I know he took that money, and I know Mr. Rawlinson didn't. Why, the poor man lost everything. He's lived from hand to mouth ever since."

"On what?"

She answered quietly: "He has a little pension, and I have my savings. For a long time I worked as a nurse's aide. That helped to keep him going."

What she said sounded like the truth. Anyway, I couldn't help believing her.

Mrs. Shepherd was looking at me more kindly, as if she sensed a change in our relations. Very gently, she touched my bandaged shoulder with her fingers. "Poor man, you need a rest. You oughtn't to be troubling your head with all these questions. Aren't you tired?"

I admitted that I was.

"Then why don't you get some sleep?" Her voice was soporific. She laid her palm on my forehead. "I'll stay in the room and watch for a while if you don't mind. I like the smell of hospitals. I used to work in this very hospital."

She sat down in the armchair between the closet and the window. The imitation-leather cushions creaked under her weight.

I closed my eyes and slowed down my breathing. But I was very far from going to sleep. I lay and listened to Mrs. Shepherd. She was completely still. Sounds drifted in through the window: the sounds of cars, a mockingbird tuning up for a night song. He kept postponing his song until the sense of something about to happen had screwed my nerves up tight.

The imitation-leather cushions of the chair emitted a tiny noise. There was the faintest possible sibilance from Mrs. Shepherd's feet sliding across the composition floor, the rattle of a doorknob, the paired whispers of a door opening and closing.

I opened my eyes. Mrs. Shepherd wasn't visible. Apparently she had shut herself up in the closet. Then its door began to open slowly again. She came out sideways, and held the picture of Nick up to the light. Her face was full of love and longing.

She glanced at me, and saw that my eyes were open. But

she thrust the picture under her coat and left the room quietly, without a word.

I didn't say anything to her, or do anything. After all, it was her picture.

I turned out the light and lay listening to the mockingbird. He was singing all-out now, and still singing when I went to sleep. I dreamed that I was Nick and that Mrs. Shepherd was my grandmother who used to live with birds in the garden in Contra Costa County.

XXXI

In the morning, as I was eating a poached egg on a damp piece of toast, the resident surgeon came in.

"How are you feeling?"

"Fine," I lied. "But I'll never build up my strength on this kind of rations. When can I get out of here?"

"Don't be in such a hurry. I'm going to have to ask you to take it easy for at least a week."

"I can't stay here for a week."

"I didn't say you had to. You're going to have to look after yourself, though. Regular hours, mild exercise followed by rest, no rough stuff."

"Sure," I said.

I rested very carefully all morning. Truttwell failed to return my call, and the waiting began to get in the way of the resting and finally displaced it.

Shortly before noon I called his office again. The switchboard girl informed me that he wasn't there.

"*Really* not there?"

"Really. I don't know where he is."

I did some more resting and waiting. A Pasadena motorcycle officer brought me the keys to my car and told me where to find it in the hospital parking lot. I took this as an omen.

After an early lunch I got out of bed and to a certain extent put on my clothes. By the time I had on underwear, trousers, and shoes I was wet and shaking. I sort of draped my bloody shirt over my chest and shoulders and covered it with my jacket.

In the corridor, the nurses and nurses' aides were still busy with lunch. I crossed the corridor to a gray metal door that opened on the fire stairs and walked down three stories to the ground floor.

A side exit let me out into the parking lot. I found my car and got in and sat for a while. Mild exercise followed by rest.

The freeway was crowded and slow. Even with all the concentration I was giving it, my driving wasn't too good. My attention kept slipping away from the traffic. I was moving in. Once I had to burn rubber to avoid running into the rear end of another car.

I'd originally intended to drive to Pacific Point. I barely made it to West Los Angeles. In the last block of the trip, on my home street, I caught a glimpse in the rear-view mirror of a bearded man carrying a bedroll. But when I turned to look at him directly he wasn't there.

I left my car at the curb and climbed the outside stairs to my apartment. The phone started to ring, like an aural booby-trap, just as I opened the door. I picked it up and carried it to my armchair.

"Mr. Archer? This is Helen at the answering service. You've had a couple of urgent calls, from a Mr. Truttwell and a Miss Truttwell. I've been ringing your office."

I looked at the electric clock. It was just two o'clock. Helen gave me the number of Truttwell's office, and the less familiar number his daughter had left.

"Anything else?"

"Yes, but there must be some mistake about this call, Mr. Archer. A hospital in Pasadena claims that you owe them a hundred and seventy dollars. That includes the cost of the operating room, they said."

"It's no mistake. If they call again, tell them I'm putting a check in the mail."

"Yessir."

I got out my checkbook and looked at the balance and decided to call Truttwell first. Before I did, I went out to the kitchen and put a frozen steak in the gas broiler. I tasted the milk in the refrigerator, found that it was still sweet, and drank half of the remaining quart. I wanted a shot of whisky as a chaser, but it was exactly what I didn't need.

My call to Truttwell's office was taken by a junior member of the firm named Eddie Sutherland. Truttwell wasn't in at the moment, he said, but he had set up an appointment for

150

me at four thirty. It was very important that I should be there, though Sutherland didn't seem to know why.

I remembered as I was dialing the number Betty had left that it belonged to the phone in Nick's apartment.

Betty answered. "Hello?"

"This is Archer speaking."

She drew in her breath. "I've been trying to get you all day."

"Is Nick with you?"

"No. I only wish he were. I'm very concerned about him. I went to San Diego yesterday afternoon to try and see him. They wouldn't let me into his room."

"Who wouldn't?"

"The guard on the door, backed up by Dr. Smitheram. They seemed to think I was spying for my father. I did manage to get a glimpse of Nick, and let him see me. He asked me to get him out. He said they were holding him against his will."

" 'They'? "

"I think he meant Dr. Smitheram. Anyway, it was Dr. Smitheram who ordered him to be moved last night."

"Moved where?"

"I don't know for certain, Mr. Archer. I think they're holding him prisoner in the Smitheram Clinic. That's where the ambulance took him."

"And you seriously believe that he's a prisoner?"

"I don't know what I believe. But I'm afraid. Will you help me?"

I said that she would have to help me first, since I wasn't up to driving. She agreed to pick me up in an hour.

I went out to the kitchen and turned my steak. It was hot and sizzling on one side, frozen solid on the other, like schizophrenic people I had known. I wondered just how crazy Nick Chalmers was.

The immediate problem was clothes. My not very extensive wardrobe included a stretchable nylon shirt that I managed to get into without putting the left arm in the armhole. I completed my costume with a soft cardigan jacket.

By this time my schizoid steak was brown on both sides and red in the center. It bled on the plate when I stabbed it. I let it cool and ate it with my fingers.

I finished the quart of milk. Then I went back to the armchair in the front room and rested. For just about the first time in my life I knew how it must feel to get old. My

151

body was demanding special privileges and offering not much in return.

The yelp of Betty's horn brought me out of a half-sleep. She gave me a hard look as I climbed rather awkwardly into her car.

"Are you sick, Mr. Archer?"

"Not exactly. I took a slug in the shoulder."

"Why didn't you tell me?"

"You mightn't have come. I want to be in at the end of this thing."

"Even if it kills you?"

"It won't."

If I was looking worse, she was looking better. She had decided after all not to be a gnome who lived in the gray underground.

"Who on earth shot you?"

"A Pasadena cop. He was aiming at another man. I got in the way. Didn't your father tell you any of this?"

"I haven't seen my father since yesterday." She spoke these words rather formally, as if they constituted an announcement.

"Are you leaving home?"

"Yes, I am. Father said I had to choose between him and Nick."

"I'm sure he didn't mean it."

"Yes, he did."

She made her engine roar. At the last moment I remembered that Chalmers's war letters were still in the trunk of my car. I went back to get them, and looked over the top ones again as Betty drove me to the freeway.

The heading of the second letter stopped me:

Lt. (j.g.) L. Chalmers
USS Sorrel Bay (CVE 185)
March 15, 1945

I turned to Betty. "You mentioned Nick's birthday the other day. Didn't you say it was in December?"

"December 14," she said.

"And what year was he born?"

"Nineteen forty-five. He was twenty-three last month. Is it important?"

"It could be. Did Nick rearrange these letters, with certain ones up front and out of chronological order?"

152

"He may have. I think he had been reading them. Why?"

"Mr. Chalmers wrote a letter at sea in the forward area, dated March 15, 1945."

"I'm not too good at arithmetic, especially when I'm driving. Is it nine months from March 15 to December 14?"

"Exactly."

"Isn't that strange? Nick always suspected that his fa—that Mr. Chalmers wasn't his real father. He used to think he was adopted."

"Maybe he was."

I put the three top letters in my wallet. The girl turned up the on-ramp to the freeway. She drove with angry speed under a brown firmament of smog.

XXXII

Southward along the coast it was a bright, windy day. From the mesa above Pacific Point I could see occasional whitecaps on the water, and a few sails leaning far over.

Betty took me directly to the Smitheram Clinic. The well-groomed, rather formal young woman who presided over the reception desk said that Dr. Smitheram was with a patient and couldn't possibly see us. He would be with patients all the rest of the day, including the evening.

"What about a week from Tuesday at midnight?"

The young woman looked me over disapprovingly. "Are you sure you don't want the emergency ward at the hospital?"

"I'm sure. Is Nicholas Chalmers a patient here?"

"I'm not authorized to answer questions like that."

"Can I see Mrs. Smitheram?"

The young woman didn't answer for a while. She pretended to be busy with her papers. Finally she said:

"I'll see. What did you say your name was, again?"

I told her. She opened an inner door. Before she closed it behind her, I heard a flash of noise that made the back of my neck bristle. It was a high yell; someone crying out wordlessly in pain and desolation.

Betty and I looked at each other. "That may be Nick," she said. "What are they doing to him?"

"Nothing. You shouldn't be here."

"Where should I be?"

"At home reading a book."

"Dostoevsky?" she said sharply.

"Something lighter than that."

"Like *Little Women*? I'm afraid you don't understand me, Mr. Archer. You're fatherizing again."

"You're daughterizing."

Moira and the receptionist opened the inner door and came out unaccompanied by any sound. Moira gave me a look of surprise and Betty a more complex look which seemed to combine both envy and contempt. Betty was younger, Moira's look seemed to say, but she herself had survived longer.

She moved toward me. "What on earth's been happening, Mr. Archer?"

"I was accidentally shot, if you mean this." I touched my left arm. "Is Nick Chalmers here?"

"Yes. He is."

"Was that him yelling?"

"Yelling? I don't believe so." She was flustered. "We have several patients in the closed wing. Nick isn't one of the more disturbed ones."

"Then you won't object if we see him. Miss Truttwell is his fiancée—"

"I know that."

"—and she's quite concerned about him."

"There's no need to feel that way." But she herself seemed deeply concerned. "I'm sorry I can't let you see him. Dr. Smitheram makes these decisions. He evidently thinks that Nick needs seclusion."

Her mouth twisted sideways. The strain of keeping up her public face and voice was telling on Moira.

"Could we discuss this in private, Mrs. Smitheram?"

"Yes. Come into my office, please."

The invitation excluded Betty. I followed Moira into an office which was partly sitting room and partly file room. The room was windowless but hung with abstract paintings, like inward windows replacing the outward ones. Moira closed the door and locked it and stood against it.

"Am I your prisoner?" I said.

She answered without trying to be light: "I'm the prisoner. I wish I could get out of this." A slight upward movement of

154

her hands and shoulders suggested the almost insupportable weight of the building. "But I can't."

"Won't your husband let you?"

"It's a little more complicated than that. I'm the prisoner of all my past mistakes—I'm feeling sententious today—and Ralph is one of them. You're a more recent one."

"What did I do wrong?"

"Nothing. I thought you liked me, is all." She had dropped her public face and voice entirely. "I acted on that assumption the other night."

"So did I. It was a true assumption."

"Then why are you giving me a bad time?"

"I didn't mean to. But we seem to be ending up on different sides."

She shook her head. "I don't believe it. All I want is a decent life, a possible life, for the people concerned." She added: "Including me."

"What does your husband want?"

"The same thing, according to his lights. We don't agree about everything, of course. And I made the mistake of going along with all his large ideas." Once again the movement of her arms referred to the entire building. "As if we could save our marriage by giving birth to a clinic." She added wryly: "We should have rented one."

She was a complex woman, spinning off ambiguities, talking too much. I moved solidly against her, held her not very masterfully with one arm, and silenced her mouth.

The wound in my shoulder was beating like an auxiliary heart.

As if she could sense the pain directly, Moira said:

"I'm sorry you're hurt."

"I'm sorry *you're* hurt, Moira."

"Don't waste your sympathy on me." Her tone reminded me that she was or had been a kind of nurse. "I'll survive. But it isn't going to be much fun, I'm afraid."

"You're losing me again. What are we talking about?"

"Disaster. I can feel it in my bones. I'm partly Irish, you know."

"Disaster for Nick Chalmers?"

"For all of us. He's part of it, of course."

"Why don't you let me take him out of here?"

"I can't."

"Is his life in danger?"

"Not as long as he stays here."

"Will you let me see him?"

"I can't. My husband won't allow it."

"Are you afraid of him?"

"No. But he's a doctor and I'm just a technician. I simply can't second-guess him."

"How long is he proposing to keep Nick here?"

"Until the danger is over."

"Who's the source of the danger?"

"I can't tell you that. Please don't ask any more questions, Lew. The questions spoil everything."

We stood and held each other for a while, leaning against the locked door. The warmth of her body and her mouth revived me, even though our minds were at odds and part of my mind was keeping track of the time.

She said in a low voice, "I wish we could walk out of here this minute, you and I, and never come back."

"You have a marriage."

"It isn't going to last."

"On account of me?"

"Of course not. Will you promise me one thing, though?"

"After I know what it is."

"Don't tell anyone about Sonny. You know, my little La Jolla postal clerk. I made a mistake in talking about him to you."

"Has Sonny cropped up again?"

She nodded. Her eyes were somber. "You won't tell anyone, will you?"

"I have no reason to."

I was hedging a little, and she sensed this. "Lew? I know you're a powerful man, and a very one-way man. Promise me you won't do anything to us. Give Ralph and me a chance to work this thing out."

I stepped away from her. "I can't make a blind commitment. And you're not being clear, as you bloody well know."

She made an anguished monkey-face which wiped out her good looks. "I can't be clear. This is a problem that won't be solved by talking. There are too many people involved, and too many years of life."

"Who are the people involved?"

"Ralph and I and the Chalmerses and the Truttwells—"

"And Sonny?"

"Yes. He's in it." The focus of her eyes shifted to some-

156

thing beyond my knowledge. "That's why you mustn't tell anyone what I told you."

"Why did you tell me?"

"I thought you might be able to advise me, that we might become better friends than we have."

"Give it more time."

"That's what I'm asking you for."

XXXIII

Betty was waiting impatiently in the parking lot. Her gaze narrowed on the lower part of my face.

"There's lipstick on you. Wait." She got a piece of tissue out of her bag and dabbed at me quite hard. "There. That looks better."

In her car, she spoke to me in a neutral voice: "Are you having an affair with Mrs. Smitheram?"

"We're friends."

She said in the same neutral tone: "No wonder I can't trust anybody, or do anything for Nick." She turned to me: "If you're such a good friend of Mrs. Smitheram's, why won't she let me see Nick?"

"Her husband is the doctor. She's only a technician, she says."

"Why won't her husband let him go?"

"They're holding Nick for his protection. Against what or who isn't clear, but I agree he needs protection. It shouldn't be handled entirely by his doctor, though. He needs legal counsel."

"If you're trying to bring my father into this—" Her knuckles struck the wheel of her car in a sharp blow that must have hurt her.

"He is in it, Betty. There's not much use arguing about it. And you're not really helping Nick by turning against your father."

"He's the one who turned against *us*—against Nick and me."

"Maybe so. But we need his help."

"*I* don't," she said loudly and indecisively.

"Anyway, I need yours. Will you drive me to his office?"

"All right. But I'm not going in."

She took me to the parking lot behind her father's building. A polished black Rolls was standing in one of the Reserved slots.

"That's the Chalmerses' car," Betty said. "I thought they'd had a falling-out with Father."

"Maybe they're falling back in. What time is it?"

She looked at her wristwatch. "Four thirty-five. I'll wait out here for you."

I was interested in the Rolls. I went and looked it over, admiring its deep leather upholstery and walnut trim. The whole car was immaculate, except for a yellow spillage on a plaid traveling rug in the back seat. It looked like a dried froth of vomit.

I scraped some of it up with the edge of a plastic credit card. When I looked up a thin man in a dark suit and a chauffeur's cap was coming toward me across the parking lot. It was the Chalmerses' houseman, Emilio.

"Get away from that car," he said.

"All right."

I slammed the rear door of the Rolls and stepped away from it. Emilio's black eyes focused on the card in my hand. He made a grab for it. I pulled it out of his reach.

"Give me that."

"The hell I will. Who's been sick in the car, Emilio?"

The question worried him. I asked it again. His anger evaporated suddenly. He turned away from me and climbed in behind the wheel of the Rolls, raising the automatic window on my side.

"What was all that about?" Betty said as we walked away.

"I'm not sure. What kind of a character is he?"

"Emilio? He's pretty dour."

"Is he honest?"

"He must be. He's been with the Chalmerses for over twenty years."

"What sort of life does he lead?"

"A very quiet bachelor life, I believe. But I'm no great authority on Emilio. What's that yellow stuff on the card?"

"That's a good question. Do you have an envelope?"

"No. But I'll get one."

She entered the building through the back door and came out right away with one of her father's business envelopes. I put my findings in it, with her help, sealed and initialed it.

"What laboratory does your father use?"

"Barnard's. It's between here and the courthouse."

I handed her the envelope. "I want this tested for chloral hydrate and Nembutal. They're fairly simple tests, I believe, and they can be done right now if you tell them your father says it's urgent. And tell them to take good care of the sample, will you?"

"Yes sir."

"Will you bring me the results? I'll probably still be in your father's office. You can wear a disguise or something."

She refused to smile. But she trotted dutifully away on the errand. I could feel new adrenalin in my own veins, making me feel stronger and more aggressive. If my hunch was good, the froth of vomit in the envelope could break the case.

I went into Truttwell's building and started along the corridor to the waiting room at the front. I was stopped at an open door by Truttwell's voice:

"Archer? I'd just about given up on you."

He drew me into his law library, which was completely lined with shelves of reference books. A young man in an Ivy League suit was working over a film projector. A screen had already been set up at the far end of the room.

Truttwell surveyed me with not very sympathetic eyes. "Where have you been?"

I told him, and dropped the subject. "I gather you bought Mrs. Swain's home movies."

"No money changed hands," he said with satisfaction. "I persuaded Mrs. Swain it was her duty to serve the truth. Also I let her keep the Florentine box, which was her mother's. In return she gave me some film. Unfortunately, the reel I'm about to show you is nearly twenty-six years old and in rather poor condition. It broke as I was running it through just now." He turned to the young man at the projector. "How are you doing, Eddie?"

"I'm splicing it. It should be ready in a minute."

Truttwell said to me: "Do me a favor, Archer. Irene Chalmers is in the waiting room."

"Is she back in the fold?"

"She will be," he said with a glint of teeth. "At the moment she's here rather against her will. Just go and make sure she doesn't run away."

"What are you planning to spring on her?"

"You'll see."

"That her maiden name was really Rita Shepherd?"

159

Truttwell's satisfied look fell apart. A kind of rivalry had been growing between us, perhaps rising from the fact that Betty had trusted me.

"How long have you known that?" he said in a prosecutor's voice.

"About five seconds. I've suspected it since last night." It wouldn't have been a good idea to tell him that the idea had come to me in a dream about my grandmother.

As I moved along the corridor, the dream came back into my mind and blunted my aggression. Mrs. Shepherd merged with the memories of my grandmother long since buried in Martinez. The passion with which Mrs. Shepherd had guarded her daughter's secret gave it some value.

Irene Chalmers lifted her face to me as I entered the waiting room. She didn't seem to know me right away. The switchboard girl spoke to me in a whisper, like someone speaking in the presence of illness or mental retardation:

"I didn't think you were going to make it. Mr. Truttwell is in the library. He said to send you right in."

"I've just been talking to him."

"I see."

I sat next to Irene Chalmers. She turned and looked at me with slow recognition, almost like a woman coming awake from a dream. As if the dream had been frightening, her mood was apologetic and subdued:

"I'm sorry, my mind's been wandering. You're Mr. Archer. But I thought you weren't with us any more."

"I'm still on the case, Mrs. Chalmers. By the way, I've recovered your husband's letters."

She said without much interest: "Do you have them with you?"

"Just a few of them. I'll return them through Mr. Truttwell."

"But he isn't our lawyer any longer."

"I'm sure you can trust him to give you the letters, anyway."

"I don't know." She looked around the little room with a kind of primitive suspicion. "We all used to be the best of friends. But we aren't any more."

"On account of Nick and Betty?"

"I guess that was the last straw," she said. "But we had our real trouble some time ago, over money. It always seems to be over money, doesn't it? Sometimes I almost wish I was poor again."

"You say you had trouble over money?"

"Yes, when Larry and I set up the Smitheram Foundation. John Truttwell refused to draw the papers for us. He said we were being taken by Dr. Smitheram, setting him up in a free clinic. But Larry wanted to do it, and I thought it was a nice idea myself. I don't know where we'd be without Dr. Smitheram."

"He's done a lot for you, has he?"

"You know he has. He saved Nick from—you know what. I think John Truttwell is jealous of Dr. Smitheram. Anyway, he isn't our friend any more. I only came here this afternoon because he threatened me."

I wanted to ask her what she meant, but the girl at the switchboard was listening openly. I said to the girl:

"Go and ask Mr. Truttwell if he's ready for us, please."

Unwillingly, she went. I turned back to Mrs. Chalmers.

"What did he threaten you with?"

She didn't respond defensively. She was acting as if a numbing blow had knocked all discretion out of her:

"It was Nick again. Truttwell went to San Diego today and dug up some new dirt. I don't think I should tell you what it was."

"Did it have to do with Nick's birth?"

"He told you, then."

"No, but I read some of your husband's letters. Apparently he was overseas when Nick was conceived. Is that true, Mrs. Chalmers?"

She looked at me in confusion and then with hard disdain. "You have no right to ask me that. You're trying to strip me naked, aren't you?"

Even in her anger there was an ambiguous erotic underplay, which seemed to ask for my complicity. I offered her a smile which felt strange from inside.

The switchboard girl came back and said that Mr. Truttwell was waiting for us. We found him alone in the library, standing behind the projector.

Irene Chalmers reacted to the machine as if it was a complex weapon pointed at her. Her fearful gaze moved from Truttwell to me, standing between her and the door. I closed the door. Her face and body froze.

"You didn't say anything about movies," she complained to Truttwell. "You said you wanted to review the case with me."

He answered smoothly, very much in command of the

situation. "This film is a part of the case. It was taken at a swimming party in San Marino in the summer of 1943. Eldon Swain, who gave the party, shot most of it himself. The bit at the end, where he appears, was taken by Mrs. Swain."

"Have you talked to Mrs. Swain?"

"Somewhat. Frankly, I'm much more interested in your reaction." He tapped the back of an armchair near the projector. "Come and sit down and be comfortable, Irene."

She remained stubbornly unmoving. Truttwell approached her smiling and took her arm. She moved slowly and heavily like a statue thawing reluctantly into flesh.

He settled her in the armchair, leaning over her from behind, withdrawing his hands lingeringly from her upper arms.

"Turn off the lights, will you, Archer?"

I flicked the switch and sat down beside Irene Chalmers. The projector whirred. Its quiet shotgun blast of light filled the screen with images. A large rectangular pool with a diving board and a slide reflected a blue old-fashioned sky.

A young blonde girl with a mature figure and an immature face climbed onto the diving board. She waved at the camera, bounced excessively, and did a comic dive with her legs apart and kicking like a frog's. She came up with a mouthful of water and spurted it at the camera. Jean Trask, young.

Irene Chalmers, née Rita Shepherd, was next on the diving board. She walked to the end of it gravely, as if the eye of the camera was judging her. The black rubber helmet in which her hair was hidden made her look oddly archaic.

She stood for quite a while with the camera on her, not once returning its stare. Then she bounced and did a swan dive, cutting the water without much splash. It wasn't until she disappeared from sight that I realized how beautiful she had been.

The camera caught her coming up, and she smiled and turned onto her back directly under it. Jean came up behind and ducked her, shouting or laughing, splashing water at the camera with her hands.

A third young person, a boy of eighteen or so whom I didn't immediately recognize, climbed up onto the board. Slowly, he walked to the forward end, with many backward looks, as if there were pirates behind him. There was one. Jean rushed him and shoved him into the water, laughing or

162

shouting. He came up floundering, his eyes closed. A woman wearing a wide-brimmed hat held out a padded hook to him at the end of a long pole. She used it to tow him to the shallow end. He stood there, in water up to his waist, with his narrow back turned to the camera. His rescuer took off her floppy hat and bowed toward unseen spectators.

The woman was Mrs. Swain, but Swain's camera failed to linger on her. It shifted to the spectators, a handsome older couple who were sitting together on a shaded swing. In spite of the shadow falling across him, I recognized Samuel Rawlinson and guessed that the woman beside him was Estelle Chalmers. The camera moved again before I had a chance to study her thin, passionate face.

Rita and Jean went down the slide, singly and together. They raced the length of the pool, with Jean coming out ahead. She splashed the hydrophobic boy still standing as if rooted in waist-deep water. Then she splashed Rita.

I caught a fuzzy background glimpse of Randy Shepherd, red-headed and red-bearded in gardener's dungarees, looking over a hedge at his daughter taking her place in the sun. I glanced sideways at Irene Chalmers's face, which was fitfully lit by the flickering inexact colors reflected from the screen. She looked as if she were dying under the soft bombardment of the past.

When my eyes returned to the screen, Eldon Swain was on the diving board. He was a man of middle size with a large handsome head. He bounced and did a swan dive. The camera met him coming up and followed him back onto the diving board. He performed flips, front and back.

Next came a double dive with Jean on his shoulders, and finally a double dive with Rita. As if controlled by a documentary interest, the camera followed the pair as Rita stood spraddled on the diving board, and Eldon Swain inserted his head between her legs and lifted her. Tottering slightly, he carried her out to the end of the board and stood for a long moment with his head projecting from between her thighs like the head of a giant smiling baby being born again.

The two fell off the board together and stayed underwater for what seemed a long time. The eye of the camera looked for them but caught only sparkling surfaces netted with light and underlaid by colored shadows dissolving in the water.

XXXIV

After the reel ended, none of us spoke for a while. I turned on the lights. Irene Chalmers stirred and roused herself. I could sense her fear, so powerful it seemed to make her drowsy.

She said in an effort to throw it off: "I was pretty in those days, wasn't I?"

"More than pretty," Truttwell said. "The word is beautiful."

"A lot of good it ever did me." Her voice and language were changing, as if she was falling back on her earlier self. "Where did you get this movie—from Mrs. Swain?"

"Yes. She gave me others."

"She would. She's always hated me."

"Because you took up with her husband?" I said.

"She hated me long before that. It was almost as if she knew it was going to happen. Or maybe she *made* it happen, I don't know. She sat around and watched Eldon, waiting for him to jump. If you do that to a man, sooner or later he's going to jump."

"What made you jump?" I said.

"We won't talk about me." She looked at me and then at Truttwell and then at nothing. "I'm taking the fifth."

Truttwell moved closer to her, gentle and suave as a lover. "Don't be foolish, Irene. You're among friends here."

"I bet."

"It's true," he said. "I went to enormous trouble, and so did Mr. Archer, to get hold of this evidence, get it out of the hands of potential enemies. In my hands it can't be used against you. I think I can guarantee it never will be."

She sat up straight, meeting him eye to eye. "What is this? Blackmail?"

Truttwell smiled. "You're getting me confused with Dr. Smitheram, I'm afraid. I don't want anything from you at all, Irene. I do think we should have a free and frank discussion."

She looked in my direction. "What about him?"

164

"Mr. Archer knows this case better than I do. I rely completely on his discretion."

Truttwell's praise made me uneasy: I wasn't prepared to say the same things about him.

"I don't trust his discretion," the woman said. "Why should I? I hardly know him."

"You know me, Irene. As your attorney—"

"So you're our lawyer again?"

"I never ceased to be, really. It must be clear to you by now that you need my help, and Mr. Archer's help. Everything we've learned about the past is strictly in confidence among the three of us."

"That is," she said, "if I go along. What if I don't?"

"I'm ethically bound to keep your secrets."

"But they'd slip out anyway, is that the idea?"

"Not through me or Archer. Perhaps through Dr. Smitheram. Obviously I can't protect your interests unless you let me."

She considered Truttwell's proposition. "I didn't want to break with you myself. Especially not at this time. But I can't speak for my husband."

"Where is he?"

"I left him at home. These last few days have been awfully hard on Larry. He doesn't look it, but he's the nervous type."

Her words touched a closed place in my mind. "Was that your husband in the film? The boy who got pushed into the water?"

"Yes it was. It was the first day I met Larry. And his last free weekend before he went into the Navy. I could tell that he was interested in me, but I didn't get to know him that day, not really. I wish I had."

"When did you get to know him?"

"A couple of years later. He grew up in the meantime."

"What happened to you in the meantime?"

She turned away from me abruptly, her white neck ridged with strain. "I'm not going to answer that," she said to Truttwell. "I didn't hire a lawyer and a detective to dig up all the dirt in my own life. What kind of sense would that make?"

He answered her in a quiet careful voice: "It makes more sense than trying to keep it secret. It's time the dirt, as you call it, was laid out on the table, among the three of us. I needn't remind you there have been several murders."

"*I* didn't kill anybody."

"Your son did," I reminded her. "We've already discussed that death in the hobo jungle."

She turned back to me. "It was a kidnapping. He killed in self-defense. You said yourself the police would understand."

"I may have to take that back, now that I know more about it. You held back part of the story—all the really important parts. For example, when I told you that Randy Shepherd was involved in the kidnapping you didn't mention that Randy was your father."

"A woman doesn't have to tell on her husband," she said. "Isn't it the same for a girl and her father?"

"No, but it doesn't matter now. Your father was shot dead in Pasadena yesterday afternoon."

Her head came up. "Who shot him?"

"The police. Your mother called them."

"My mother did?" She was silent for a while. "That doesn't really surprise me. The first thing I remember in my life is the two of them fighting like animals. I had to get away from that kind of life, even if it meant—" Our eyes met, and the sentence died under the impact.

I continued it for her: "Even if it meant running off to Mexico with an embezzler."

She shook her head. Her black hair fluffed out a little, and made her look both younger and cheaper.

"I never did."

"You never ran off with Eldon Swain?"

She was silent.

"What did happen, Mrs. Chalmers?"

"I can't tell you—not even at this late date. There are other people involved."

"Eldon Swain?"

"He's the most important one."

"You don't have to worry about protecting him, as you very well know. He's as safe as your father, and for the same reason."

She gave me a lost look, as if her game with time had failed for a moment and she was caught in the limbo between her two lives. "Is Eldon really dead?"

"You know he is, Mrs. Chalmers. He was the dead man in the railroad yards. You must have known or suspected it at the time."

Her eyes darkened. "I swear to God I didn't."

"You had to know. The body was left with its hands in the

166

fire so that the fingerprints would be erased. No eight-year-old boy did that."

"That doesn't mean it was me."

"You were the one with the motivation," I said. "If the dead man was identified as Swain, your whole life would collapse. You'd lose your house and your husband and your social standing. You'd be Rita Shepherd again, back on your uppers."

She was silent, her face working with thought. "You said my father was involved with Eldon. It must have been my father who burned the body—did you say he burned the body?"

"The fingers."

She nodded. "It must have been my father. He was always talking about getting rid of his own fingerprints. He was a nut on the subject."

Her voice was unreflective, almost casual. It stopped suddenly. Perhaps she had heard herself as Rita Shepherd, daughter of an ex-con, trapped again in that identity without any possible escape.

The knowledge of her predicament seemed to be striking down into her body and penetrating her mind through layers of indifference, years of forgetfulness. It struck a vital place and crumpled her in the chair, her face in her hands. Her hair fell forward from her nape and sifted over her fingers like black water.

Truttwell stood over her looking down with an intensity that didn't seem to include any kind of love. Perhaps it was pity he felt, laced with possession. She had passed through several hands and been slightly scorched by felony, but she was still very beautiful.

Forgetful of me, and of himself, Truttwell put his hands on her. He stroked her head very gently, and then her long tapering back. His caresses weren't sexual in any ordinary sense. Perhaps, I thought, his main feeling was an abstract legal passion which satisfied itself by having her as a client. Or a widower's underground desire held in check by the undead past.

Mrs. Chalmers recovered after a while, and asked for water. Truttwell went to another room to fetch it. She spoke to me in an urgent whisper:

"Why did my mother call the police on Randy? She must have had a reason."

"She had. He stole her picture of Nick."

"The graduation picture I sent her?"

"Yes."

"I shouldn't have sent it. But I thought for once in my life I could act like a normal human being."

"You couldn't, though. Your father took it to Jean Trask and talked her into hiring Sidney Harrow. That's how the whole thing started."

"What did the old man want?"

"Your husband's money, just like everyone else."

"But not you, eh?" Her voice was sardonic.

"Not me," I said. "Money costs too much."

Truttwell brought her a paper cup of water and watched her drink it. "Are you feeling up to a little drive?"

Her body jerked in alarm. "Where to?"

"The Smitheram Clinic. It's time we had a chat with Nick."

She looked profoundly unwilling. "Dr. Smitheram won't let you in."

"I think he will. You're Nick's mother. I'm his attorney. If Dr. Smitheram won't cooperate, I'll slap a writ of *habeas corpus* on him."

Truttwell wasn't entirely serious, but her mood of alarm persisted. "No. Please, don't do anything like that. I'll talk to Dr. Smitheram."

On the way out I asked the switchboard girl if Betty had come back with the lab report. She hadn't. I left word for her that I'd be at the clinic.

XXXV

Irene Chalmers dismissed Emilio. She rode between Truttwell and me in the front seat of his Cadillac. When she got out of the car in the parking lot of the clinic she moved like a drugged woman. Truttwell gave her his arm and guided her into the reception room.

Moira Smitheram was behind the desk, as she had been the day I met her. It seemed like a long time ago. Her face had aged and deepened, or maybe I could see more deeply into her. She looked from Truttwell to me.

"You didn't give me much time."

"We're running out of time."

Truttwell said: "It's very important that we talk to Nick Chalmers. Mrs. Chalmers agrees."

"You'll have to take that up with Dr. Smitheram."

Moira went and got her husband. He came through the inner door, striding angrily in his white smock.

"You don't give up easily, do you?" he said to Truttwell.

"I don't give up at all, old man. We're here to see Nick, and I'm very much afraid that you can't stop us."

Smitheram turned his back on Truttwell and said to Mrs. Chalmers: "How do you feel about this?"

"You better let us in, doctor," she said without raising her eyes.

"Have you re-engaged Mr. Truttwell as your attorney?"

"Yes I have."

"And has Mr. Chalmers concurred?"

"He will."

Dr. Smitheram gave her a probing look. "What sort of pressure are you under, anyway?"

Truttwell said: "You're wasting time, doctor. We're here to talk to your patient, not to you."

Smitheram swallowed his anger. "Very well."

He and his wife conducted us through the inner door, along a corridor to a second door which had to be unlocked and relocked. The wing beyond it contained eight or ten rooms beginning with a suicide room in which a woman sat on the padded floor looking out at us through thick glass.

Nick had a bed-sitting room with an open door. He sat in an armchair holding an open textbook. In his light wool robe he looked almost like any other young man interrupted at his studies. He stood up when he saw his mother, his black eyes large and bright in his pale face. His dark glasses were on the desk beside him.

"Hello, Mother, Mr. Truttwell." His glance traveled across our faces without pausing. "Where's Dad? Where's Betty?"

"This isn't a social occasion," Truttwell said, "though it's good to see you. We have some questions to ask you."

"Keep them as brief as possible," Smitheram said. "Sit down, Nick."

Moira took his book and put a marker in it; then stood beside her husband in the doorway. Irene Chalmers sat in the other chair, Truttwell and I on the single bed facing Nick.

"I'm not going to beat around the bush," Truttwell said. "About fifteen years ago, when you were a small boy, you shot a man in the railroad yards."

Nick raised his eyes to Smitheram's and said in a flat disappointed tone: "You told him."

"No, I did not," Smitheram said.

Truttwell said to the doctor: "You took on quite a responsibility when you kept that shooting quiet."

"I know that. I acted in the best interests of an eight-year-old who was threatened with autism. The law isn't the only guide to the conduct of human affairs. Even if it were, the homicide was justifiable or accidental."

Truttwell said wearily: "I didn't come here to argue law or ethics with you, doctor."

"Then don't attack my motives."

"Which are, of course, as pure as the driven snow."

The doctor's large body made a small threatening move in Truttwell's direction. It was inhibited by Moira's hand on his elbow.

Truttwell turned back to Nick. "Tell me about that shooting down by the tracks. Was it an accident?"

"I don't know."

"Then just tell me how it happened. How did you get to the railroad yards in the first place?"

Nick answered haltingly as if his memory operated by fits and starts like a teletype ticker. "I was on my way home from school when the man picked me up in his car. I know I shouldn't have got in. But he seemed terribly serious. And I felt sorry for him. He was sick and old.

"He asked me a lot of questions about who my mother was, and who my father was, and when and where I was born. Then he said that he was my father. I didn't exactly believe him, but I was interested enough to go along to the hobo jungle with him.

"He took me to a place behind the old roundhouse. Someone had left a fire burning and we added some wood and sat beside it. He got out a pint of whisky and took a pull and gave me a taste of it. It burned my mouth. But he drank it down like water, and finished the bottle.

"It made him foolish. He sang some old songs, and then he got sentimental. He said I was his darling boy and when he came into his rights he'd assume his true position and look after me. He started to paw me and kiss me, and that was

170

when I shot him. He had a gun in the waistband of his trousers. I pulled it out and shit him, and he died."

Nick's pale face was still composed. But I could hear his rapid breathing.

"What did you do with the gun?" I said.

"I didn't do anything with it. I left it lying there and walked home. Later I told my parents what I'd done. They didn't believe me at first. Then it came out in the paper, about the dead man, and they believed me. They brought me to Dr. Smitheram. And," he added with wry bitterness, "I've been with him ever since. I wish I'd gone to the police in the first place." His eyes were on his mother's half-averted face.

"It wasn't your decision," I said. "Now let's get on to the Sidney Harrow killing."

"Good Lord, do you think I killed him, too?"

"You thought so, remember?"

His gaze turned inward. "I was pretty confused, wasn't I? The trouble was I really felt like killing Harrow. I went to his motel room that night to have a showdown with him. Jean told me where he was staying. He wasn't there, but I found him in his car on the beach."

"Alive or dead?"

"He was dead. The gun that killed him was lying beside his car. I picked it up to look at it and something clicked in my head. And the ground literally shifted under my feet. I thought at first it was an earthquake. Then I realized it was in me. I was confused for a long time, and suicidal." He added: "The gun seemed to want me to do something with it."

"You already had done something with it," I said. "It was the same gun that you left in the railroad yards."

"How could that be?"

"I don't know how it could be. But it was the same gun. The police have ballistic records that prove it. Are you sure you left the gun beside the body?"

Nick was confused again. His eyes looked at our faces in naked helplessness. He reached for his dark glasses and put them on. "Harrow's body?"

"Eldon Swain's body. The man in the railroad yards who said he was your father. Did you leave the gun there beside him, Nick?"

"Yes. I know I didn't take it home with me."

"Then someone else picked it up and kept it for fifteen years and used it on Harrow. Who would that be?"

"I don't know." The young man shook his head slowly from side to side.

Smitheram stepped forward. "He's had enough. And you're not learning anything." His eyes were full of anxiety, but whether it was for Nick I couldn't tell.

"I'm learning a good deal, doctor. So is Nick."

"Yes." The young man looked up. "Was the man in the railroad yards really my father as he said?"

"You'll have to ask your mother."

"Was he, Mother?"

Irene Chalmers looked around the room as if another trap had closed on her. The pressure of our silence forced words out of her:

"I don't have to answer that and I'm not going to."

"That means he was my father."

She didn't answer Nick or look at him. She sat with her head bowed. Truttwell stood up and put a hand on her shoulder. She inclined her head sideways so that her cheek rested against his knuckles. In contrast with her flawless skin, his hand was spotted with age.

Nick said insistently: "I knew that Lawrence Chalmers couldn't be my father."

"How did you know that?" I asked him.

"The letters he wrote from overseas—I don't remember the dates exactly, but the timing wasn't right."

"Is that why you took the letters out of the safe?"

"Not really. I stumbled onto that aspect of it. Sidney Harrow and Jean Trask came to me with a wild story that my father—that Lawrence Chalmers had committed a crime. I took the letters to prove to them that they were mistaken. He was overseas at the time the theft occurred."

"What theft?"

"Jean said he stole some money from her family—from her father—actually an enormous amount of money, half a million or so. But his letters proved that Jean and Harrow were wrong. On the day of the alleged theft—I think it was July 1, 1945—my fa—Mr. Chalmers was at sea aboard his carrier." He added with a look of sad irony: "In proving that I also proved that he couldn't be my father. I was born on December 14, 1945, and nine months before, when I must have been—" He looked at his mother, and couldn't find the word.

172

"Conceived?" I said.

"When I must have been conceived, he was aboard his ship in the forward area. Do you hear that, Mother?"

"I hear you."

"Haven't you any other comment?"

"You don't have to turn against me," she said in a low tone. "I'm your mother. What does it matter who your father was?"

"It matters to me."

"Forget it. Why don't you forget it?"

"I have some of the letters here." I brought out my wallet and showed Nick the three letters. "I think these are the ones you were particularly interested in."

"Yes. Where did you get them?"

"From your apartment," I said.

"May I have them for a minute?"

I handed him the letters. He went through them quickly.

"This is the one he wrote on March 15, 1945: 'Dearest Mother: Here I am in the forward area again, so my letter won't go off for a while.' That would seem to prove conclusively that whoever my father was, he wasn't and isn't Lieutenant (j.g.) L. Chalmers." He looked at his mother again in murky speculation: "Was it the man in the railroad yards, Mother? The man I killed?"

"You don't want an answer," she said.

"That means the answer is yes," he said in bleak satisfaction. "At least I know that much for certain. What did you say his name was? My father's name?"

She didn't answer.

"Eldon Swain," I said. "He was Jean Trask's father."

"She *said* we were brother and sister. You mean it's really true?"

"I don't have the answers. You're the one who seems to have them." I paused, and went on: "There's one very important answer I have to ask you for, Nick. What took you to Jean Trask's house in San Diego?"

He shook his head. "I don't recall. The whole thing is a blank. I don't even remember *going* to San Diego."

Dr. Smitheram came forward again. "I have to call a halt now. I'm not going to let you undo what we've done for Nick in the last couple of days."

"Let's finish it off," Truttwell said. "After all, it's been dragging on now for most of Nick's young life."

"I want to finish it, too," Nick said, "if I can."

"And so do I." It was Moira coming out of a long silence.

The doctor turned on her coldly. "I don't remember asking for your opinion."

"You have it, anyway. Let's get it over with."

Moira's voice had overtones of weary guilt. The two of them confronted each other for a moment as if they were the only ones in the room.

I said to Nick: "When did you start remembering in San Diego?"

"When I woke up in the hospital that night. I was missing the whole day."

"And what was the last you remembered before that?"

"When I got up that morning. I'd been awake all night, with one thing and another, and I was feeling awfully depressed. That horrible scene in the railroad yards kept coming back. I could smell the fire and the whisky.

"I decided to turn off my mind with a sleeping pill or two, and I got up and went into the bathroom where they kept them. When I saw the red and yellow capsules in the bottles I changed my mind. I decided to take a lot of them and turn off my mind for good."

"Was that when you wrote your suicide note?"

He considered my question. "I wrote it just before I took the pills. Yes."

"How many did you take?"

"I didn't count them. A couple of handfuls, I guess, enough to kill me. But I couldn't just sit in the bathroom and wait. I was afraid they'd find me and not let me die. I climbed out the bathroom window and dropped to the ground. I must have fallen and hit my head on something." He balanced the letters on his knee and touched the side of his head tenderly. "Next thing I knew I was in the San Diego hospital. I've already told Dr. Smitheram all this."

I glanced at Smitheram. He wasn't listening. He was talking in intense, low tones to his wife.

"Dr. Smitheram?"

He turned abruptly, but not in response to me. He reached for the letters in Nick's lap. "Let's have a look at these, eh?"

Smitheram riffled through the flimsy pages and began to read aloud to his wife: " 'There's something about pilots that reminds you of racehorses—developed almost to an unhealthy point. I hope I'm not that way to other eyes.

174

" 'Commander Wilson is, though. (He's no longer censoring mail so I can say this.) He's been in for over four years now, but he seems to be exactly the same gentlemanly Yale man he was when he came in. He has, however, a certain air of arrested development. He has given his best to the war—' "

Truttwell said dryly: "You read beautifully, doctor, but this is hardly the occasion."

Smitheram acted as if he hadn't heard Truttwell. He said to his wife: "What was the name of my squadron leader on the Sorrel Bay?"

"Wilson," she said in a small voice.

"Do you remember I made this comment about him in a letter I wrote you in March 1945?"

"Vaguely. I'll take your word for it."

Smitheram wasn't satisfied. He went through the pages again, his furious fingers almost tearing them. "Listen to this, Moira: 'We're very near the equator and the heat is pretty bad, though I don't mean to complain. If we're still anchored at this atoll tomorrow I'm going to try to get off the ship for a swim, which I haven't had since we left Pearl months ago. One of my big daily pleasures, though, is the shower I take every night before going to bed.' And so on. Later, the letter mentions that Wilson was shot down over Okinawa. Now I distinctly remember writing this to you in the summer of 1945. How do you account for that, Moira?"

"I don't," she said with her eyes down. "I won't attempt to account for it."

Truttwell stood up and looked past Smitheram's shoulder at the letter. "I take it this isn't your writing. No, I see it's not." He added after a pause: "It's Lawrence Chalmers' writing, isn't it?" And after a further pause: "Does this mean his war letters to his mother were all a fake?"

"They certainly were." Smitheram shook the documents in his fist. His eyes were on his wife's downcast face. "I still don't understand how these letters got written."

"Was Chalmers ever a Navy pilot?" Truttwell said.

"No. He did make an attempt to get into the pilot training program. But he was hopelessly unqualified. In fact, he was given a general discharge by the Navy a few months after he enlisted."

"Why was he discharged?" I said.

"For reasons of mental health. He broke down in boot camp. It happened to quite a few schizoid boys when they tried to assume a military role. Particularly those whose mothers were the dominant parent, as in Larry's case."

"How do you know so much about his case, doctor?"

"I was assigned to it, in the Navy Hospital in San Diego. Before we turned him loose on the world, we gave him a few weeks of treatment. He's been my patient ever since—except for my two years' sea duty."

"Was he the reason you settled here in the Point?"

"One of the reasons. He was grateful to me and he offered to help set me up in practice. His mother had died and left him a good deal of money."

"One thing I don't understand," Truttwell said, "is how he could fool us with these phony letters. He must have had to fake Fleet Post Office envelopes and markings. And how could he receive answers if he wasn't in the Navy?"

"He had a job in the Post Office," Smitheram said. "I got him that job myself before I shipped out. I suppose he set up a special box for his own mail." As if his head was being wrenched around by an external force, Smitheram looked at his wife again. "What *I* don't understand, Moira, is how he got a chance—repeated chances—to copy my letters to you."

"He must have taken them," she said.

"Did you know he was taking them?"

She nodded glumly. "Actually, he borrowed them to read, or so he said. But I can understand why he copied them. He hero-worshipped you. He wanted to be like you."

"How did he feel about you?"

"He was fond of me. He made no secret of it, even before you left."

"After I left, did you see him regularly?"

"I could hardly help it. He lived next door."

"Next door in the Magnolia Hotel? You mean you lived in adjoining rooms?"

"You asked me to keep an eye on him," she said.

"I didn't tell you to live with him. Did you live with him?" He was speaking in the hectoring voice of a man who was hurting himself and knew it but kept on doing it.

"I lived with him," his wife said. "I'm not ashamed of it. He needed someone. I may have had just as much to do with saving his mind as you had."

"So it was therapy, was it? That's why you wanted to come here after the war. That's why he's—"

176

She cut him short: "You're off the track, Ralph. You usually are where I'm concerned. I quit with him before you ever came home."

Irene Chalmers lifted her head. "That's true. He married me in July—"

Truttwell leaned toward her and touched her mouth with his finger. "Don't volunteer any information, Irene."

She lapsed into silence, and I could hear Moira's intense low voice.

"You knew about my relationship with him," she was saying to her husband. "You can't treat a patient for twenty-five years without knowing that much about him. But you chose to act as if you hadn't known."

"If I did," he said—"I'm not admitting anything but if I did, I was acting in my patient's interest, not my own."

"You really believe that, don't you, Ralph?"

"It's true."

"You're fooling yourself. But you're not fooling anyone else. You knew Larry Chalmers was a fake, just as I did. We conspired with his fantasy and went on taking his money."

"I'm afraid you're fantasying, Moira."

"You know I'm not."

He looked around at our faces to see if we were judging him. His wife brushed past him and left the room. I followed her down the corridor.

XXXVI

I caught Moira at the locked door beside the suicide room. For the second time in our acquaintance she was having trouble unlocking a door. I mentioned this.

She turned on me with hard bright eyes. "We won't talk about the other night. It's all in the past—so long ago I hardly remember your name."

"I thought we were friends."

"So did I. But you broke that."

She flung one arm out toward Nick's room. The woman in the suicide room began to moan and cry.

Moira unlocked the door which let us out of the wing and

took me to her office. The first thing she did there was to take her handbag out of a drawer and set it on top of the desk, ready to go.

"I'm leaving Ralph. And don't say anything, please, about me going with you. You don't like me well enough."

"Do you always think people's thoughts for them?"

"All right—I don't like *myself* well enough." She paused and looked around her office. The glowing paintings on the walls seemed to reflect her anger with herself, like subtle mirrors. "I don't like making money from other people's suffering. Do you know what I mean?"

"I ought to. It's how I live."

"But you don't do it for the money, do you?"

"I try not to," I said. "When your income passes a certain point you lose touch. All of a sudden the other people look like geeks or gooks, expendables."

"That happened to Ralph. I won't let it happen to me." She sounded like a woman in flight, but more hopeful than afraid. "I'm going back to social work. It's what I really love. I was never happier than when I lived in La Jolla in one room."

"Next door to Sonny."

"Yes."

"Sonny was Lawrence Chalmers, of course."

She nodded.

"And the other girl he took up with was Irene Chalmers?"

"Yes. She called herself Rita Shepherd in those days."

"How do you know?"

"Sonny told me about her. He'd met her at a swimming party in San Marino a couple of years before. Then one day she walked into the post office where he worked. He was terribly upset by the meeting at first, and now I can understand why. He was afraid his secret would leak out, and his mother would learn he was just a postal clerk instead of a Navy pilot."

"Did you know about the deception?"

"Naturally I knew he was living a fantasy life. He used to dress up in officers' clothes and walk the streets at night. But I didn't know about his mother—there were some things he didn't talk about, even to me."

"How much did he tell you about Rita Shepherd?"

"Enough. She was living with an older man who kept her stashed in Imperial Beach."

178

"Eldon Swain."

"Was that his name?" She added after a thinking pause: "It all comes together, doesn't it? I didn't realize how much life, and death, I was involved with. I guess we never do until afterwards. Anyway, Rita shifted to Sonny and I moved to the sidelines. By then I didn't much care. It was pretty wearing, looking after Sonny, and I was willing to pass him on to the next girl."

"What I don't understand is how you could stay interested in him for over two years. Or why a woman like his wife would fall for him."

"Women don't always go for the solid virtues," she said. "Sonny had a wild psychotic streak. He would try almost anything once."

"I'll have to cultivate my wild psychotic streak. But I must say Chalmers keeps his pretty well hidden."

"He's older now, and under tranquilizers all the time."

"Tranquilizers like Nembu-Serpin?"

"I see you've been boning up."

"Just how sick is he?"

"Without supportive therapy, and drugs, he'd probably have to be hospitalized. But with these things he manages to lead a fairly well-adjusted life." She sounded like a salesman who didn't quite believe in her product.

"Is he dangerous, Moira?"

"He *could* be dangerous, under certain circumstances."

"If somebody found out that he was a fake, for example?"

"Perhaps."

"You're very perhapsy all of a sudden. He's been your husband's patient for twenty-five years, as you pointed out. You must know something about him."

"We know a good deal. But the doctor-patient relationship involves a right to privacy."

"Don't lean too heavily on that. It doesn't apply to a patient's crimes, or potential crimes. I want to know if you and Dr. Smitheram considered him a threat to Nick."

She sidestepped the question. "What kind of a threat?"

"A mortal threat," I said. "You and your husband knew that he was dangerous to Nick, didn't you?"

Moira didn't answer me in words. She moved around her office and began to take the pictures down from the walls and pile them on the desk. In a token way she seemed to be trying to dismantle the clinic and her place in it.

A knock on the door interrupted her work. It was the young receptionist. "Miss Truttwell wants to speak to Mr. Archer. Shall I send her in?"

"I'll go out," I said.

The receptionist looked around in dismay at the empty walls. "What happened to all your pictures?"

"I'm moving out. You could help me."

"I'll be glad to, Mrs. Smitheram," the young woman said brightly.

Betty was standing in the middle of the outer room. She looked windblown and excited.

"The lab said there was quite a lot of Nembutal in the sample. Also some chloral hydrate, but they couldn't tell how much without further testing."

"I'm not surprised."

"What does it mean, Mr. Archer?"

"It means that Nick was in the back of the family Rolls some time after he took his overdose of pills. He vomited some of them up, and that may have saved his life."

"How is he?"

"Doing quite well. I had a talk with him just now."

"Can I see him?"

"That isn't up to me. His mother, and your father, are with him right now."

"I'll wait."

I waited with her, each of us thinking his own thoughts. I needed quiet. The case was coming together in my mind, constructing itself in inner space like a movie of a falling building reversed.

The inner door opened, and Irene Chalmers came through on Truttwell's arm, leaning on him heavily, like a survivor. She had shifted her weight from Chalmers to Truttwell, I thought, as she had once shifted it from Eldon Swain to Chalmers.

Truttwell became aware of his daughter. His eyes moved nervously, but he didn't try to disengage himself from Irene Chalmers. Betty gave them a so-that's-how-it-is look.

"Hello, Dad. Hello, Mrs. Chalmers. I hear Nick is much better."

"Yes, he is," her father said.

"Can I talk with him for a minute?"

He hesitated for a thoughtful moment. His gaze flicked across my face, and back to his daughter's. He answered her

180

in a careful, gentle voice: "We'll take it up with Dr. Smitheram."

He led Betty through the inner door and closed it carefully behind them.

I was alone in the reception room with Irene Chalmers. As she knew. She looked at me with a kind of dull formality, in the hope that nothing real would be said between us.

"I'd like to ask you a few questions, Mrs. Chalmers."

"That doesn't mean I have to answer them."

"Once and for all, now, was Eldon Swain Nick's father?"

She faced me in passive stubbornness. "Probably. Anyway he thought he was. But you can't expect me to tell Nick he killed his own natural father—"

"He knows it now," I said. "And you can't go on using Nick to hide behind."

"I don't understand what you mean."

"You suppressed the facts about Eldon Swain and his death for your own sake, not for Nick's. You let him carry the burden of the guilt, and take the rap for you."

"There isn't any rap. We kept everything quiet."

"And let Nick live in mental torment for fifteen years. It was a lousy trick to pull on your own son, or anybody's son."

She bowed her head as if in shame. But what she said was: "I'm not admitting anything."

"You don't have to. I've got enough physical evidence, and enough witnesses, to make a case against you. I've talked to your father and your mother, and Mr. Rawlinson, and Mrs. Swain. I've talked to Florence Williams."

"Who in hell is she?"

"She owns Conchita's Cabins, in Imperial Beach."

Mrs. Chalmers raised her head and swept her fingers across her face, as if there was dust or cobwebs in her eyes. "I'm sorry I ever set foot in that dump, I can tell you. But you can't make anything out of it, not at this late date. I was just a juvenile at the time. And anything I did away back then—the statute of limitations ran out on it long ago."

"What did you do away back then?"

"I'm not going to testify against myself. I said before that I was taking the fifth." She added in a stronger voice: "John Truttwell will be back in a minute, and this is his department. If you want to get rough, he can get rougher."

I knew I was on uncertain ground. But this might be the

181

only chance I would have to reach Mrs. Chalmers. And both her responses to my accusations, and her failures to respond, had tended to confirm my picture of her. I said:

"If John Truttwell knew what I know about you, he wouldn't touch you with a sterilized stick."

She had no answer this time. She moved to a chair near the inner door and sat down inexactly and abruptly. I followed and stood over her.

"What happened to the money?"

She twisted sideways away from me. "Which money do you mean?"

"The money Eldon Swain embezzled from the bank."

"He took it across the Mexican border with him. I stayed behind in Dago. He said he'd send for me but he never did. So I married Larry Chalmers. That's the whole story."

"What did Eldon do with the money in Mexico?"

"I heard he lost it. He ran into a couple of bandits in Baja and they took it off him and that was that."

"What were the bandits' names, Rita?"

"How should I know? It was just a rumor I heard."

"I'll tell you a better rumor. The bandits' names were Larry and Rita, and they didn't steal the money in Mexico. Eldon Swain never got it across the border. You set him up for a highjacking, and fingered him for Larry. And the two bandits lived happily ever after. Until now."

"You'll never prove that! You can't!"

She was almost shouting, as if she hoped to drown out the sound of my voice and the rumors of the past. Truttwell opened the inner door.

"What's going on?" He gave me a stern look. "What are you trying to prove?"

"We were discussing what happened to Swain's half million. Mrs. Chalmers claims that Mexican bandits got it. But I'm fairly certain she and Chalmers highjacked it from Swain. It must have happened a day or two after Swain embezzled the money and brought it to San Diego, where she was waiting for him."

Mrs. Chalmers glanced up, as if my freewheeling reconstruction had touched on a factual detail. Truttwell noticed the giveaway movement of her eyes. His whole face opened and closed like a grasping hand.

"They stole a car," I went on, "and brought the money here to Pacific Point, to his mother's house. This was July 3, 1945. Larry and Rita staged a burglary in reverse. It wasn't

182

hard, since Larry's mother was blind and Larry must have had keys to the house, as well as the combination of the safe. They put the money in the safe and left it."

Mrs. Chalmers got to her feet and went to Truttwell and took hold of his arm. "Don't believe him. I wasn't within fifty miles of here that night."

"Was Larry?" Truttwell said.

"Yes! It was all Larry's doing. His mother never used the safe after she lost her sight and he figured it was a perfect place to stash—I mean—"

Truttwell took her by the shoulders with both hands and held her at arm's length.

"You were here with Larry that night. Weren't you?"

"He forced me to come along. He held a gun on me."

"That means you were driving," Truttwell said. "You killed my wife."

The woman hung her head. "It was Larry's fault. She recognized him, see. He twisted the wheel and stomped on my foot and speeded up the car. I couldn't stop it. It went right over her. He wouldn't let me stop till we got back to Dago."

Truttwell shook her. "I don't want to hear that. Where is your husband now?"

"At home. I already told you he isn't feeling well. He's just sitting around in a daze."

"He's still dangerous," I said to Truttwell. "Don't you think we better call Lackland?"

"Not until I've had a chance to talk to Chalmers. You come along with me, eh? You too, Mrs. Chalmers."

Once again she sat between us in the front seat of Truttwell's car. She peered far ahead along the freeway like an accident-prone subject living in dread of still further disasters.

"The other morning," I said, "when Nick took all those sleeping pills and tranquilizers, where were you?"

"In bed asleep. I took a couple of chloral hydrates myself the night before."

"Was your husband in bed asleep?"

"I wouldn't know. We have separate rooms."

"When did he take off to look for Nick?"

"Right after you left that morning."

"Driving the Rolls?"

"That's right."

"Where did he go?"

"All over the place, I guess. When he gets excited he runs around like a maniac. Then he sits around like a dummy for a week."

"He went to San Diego, Mrs. Chalmers. And there's evidence that Nick rode along with him, lying unconscious under a rug in the back seat."

"That doesn't make sense."

"I'm afraid it did to your husband. When Nick climbed out the bathroom window, your husband intercepted him in the garden. He knocked him out with a spade or some other tool and hid him in the Rolls until he was ready to leave for San Diego."

"Why would he do a thing like that to his own son?"

"Nick wasn't his son. He was Eldon Swain's son, and your husband knew it. You're forgetting your own life history, Mrs. Chalmers."

She gave me a quick sideways look. "Yeah, I wish I could."

"Nick knew or suspected whose son he was," I said. "In any case, he was trying to get at the truth about Eldon Swain's death. And he was getting closer all the time."

"Nick shot Eldon himself."

"We all know that now. But Nick didn't drag the dead man into the fire to burn off his fingerprints. That took adult strength, and adult motives. Nick didn't keep Swain's gun, to use it on Sidney Harrow fifteen years later. Nick didn't kill Jean Trask, though your husband did his best to frame him for it. That was why he took Nick to San Diego."

The woman said in a kind of awe: "Did Larry kill all those people?"

"I'm afraid he did."

"But why?"

"They knew too much about him. He was a sick man protecting his fantasy."

"Fantasy?"

"The pretend world he lived in."

"Yeah, I see what you mean."

We left the freeway at Pacific Street and drove up the long slope. Behind us at the foot of the town the low red sun was glaring on the water. In the queer, late light the Chalmers mansion looked insubstantial and dreamlike, a castle in Spain referring to a past that had never existed.

The front door was unlocked, and we went in. Mrs. Chalmers called her husband—"Larry!"—and got no answer.

Emilio appeared laggingly in the corridor that led to the back of the house. Mrs. Chalmers rushed toward him.

"Where is he?"

"I don't know, ma'am. He ordered me to stay in the kitchen."

"Did you tell him I searched the Rolls?" I said.

Emilio's black eyes slid away from mine. He didn't answer me.

The woman had climbed the short flight of stairs to the study. She pounded with her fist on the carved oak door, sucked her bleeding knuckles, and pounded again.

"He's in there!" she cried. "You've got to get him out. He'll do away with himself."

I pushed her to one side and tried the door. It was locked. The room beyond it was terribly still.

Emilio went back to the kitchen for a screwdriver and a hammer. He used them to unhinge the door of the study.

Chalmers was sitting in the judge's swivel chair, his head inclined rather oddly to one side. He had on a blue naval uniform with a full commander's three gold stripes. Blood from his cut throat had run down over his row of battle ribbons, making them all one color. An old straight razor lay open beside his dangling hand.

His wife stood back from his body as if it gave off mortal laser rays.

"I knew he was going to do it. He wanted to do it the day they came to the front door."

"Who came to the front door?" I said.

"Jean Trask and that muscle boy she traveled with. Sidney Harrow. I slammed the door in their faces, but I knew they'd be coming back. So did Larry. He got out Eldon's gun that he'd kept in the safe all those years. What he had in mind was a suicide pact. He wanted to shoot me and then himself. Dr. Smitheram and I talked him into a trip to Palm Springs instead."

"You should have let him shoot himself," Truttwell said.

"And me too? Not on your life. I wasn't ready to die. I'm still not ready."

She still had passion, if only for herself. Truttwell and I were silent. She said to him:

"Look, are you still my lawyer? You said you were."

He shook his head. His eyes seemed to be looking through and beyond her, into a sad past or a cold future.

"You can't go back on me now," she said. "You think I

haven't suffered enough? I'm *sorry* about your wife. I still wake up in the middle of the night and see her in the road, poor woman, laying there like a bundle of old clothes."

Truttwell struck her face with the back of his hand. A little blood spilled from her mouth, drawing a line across her chin like a crack in marble.

I stepped between them so that he couldn't hit her again. It wasn't the sort of thing that Truttwell should be doing.

She took some courage from my gesture. "You don't have to hurt me, John. I feel bad enough without that. My whole time here, it's been like living in a haunted house. I mean it. The very first night we came, when we were here in the study, putting the packages of money in the safe—Larry's blind old mother came down in the dark. She said: 'Is that you, Sonny?' I don't know how she knew who it was. It was creepy."

"What happened then?" I said.

"He took her back to her room and talked to her. He wouldn't tell me what he said to her, but she didn't bother us after that."

"Estelle never mentioned it," Truttwell said to me. "She died without mentioning it to anyone."

"Now we know what she died of," I said. "She found out what had become of her son."

As though he had overheard me, the dead man seemed to have cocked his head in an attitude of stiff embarrassment. His widow moved toward him like a sleepwalker and stood beside him. She touched his hair.

I stayed with her while Truttwell phoned the police.

———